Choices

The Guardian Trilogy
Book Two

Liz Schulte

4 Corners Press

No Boundaries

4 Corners Press
-Arizona-

Published in the United States by 4 Corners Press.
www.4cornerspress.com

4 Corners Press design is a registered trademark of 4 Corners
Press

Printed in the United States of America

Cover Design by Donna Dull of 4CP
Cover Formatting by Donna Dull of 4CP

Library of Congress Cataloging-in-Publication Data

ISBN-13: 978-1475099645
ISBN-10: 1475099649
LCCN: 2012936149

Praise for Liz Schulte's Secrets

Olivia and Holden are the couple that you love to see fight and make up. The fire between the two of them makes the book a page turner alone. Throw in the obstacles (I don't want to give anything away!) that they're up against, and the book consumes you. I CANNOT wait to see what Choices (Book #2) brings for our beloved couple, and to find out what their fates will hold.

This book is a page turner. The story is vivid and the characters and story are brought to life off the page.

This was an emotional and mysterious story that got me hooked early on and as the story progressed it just got better and better. I felt like it was different from other paranormal books I've read but in a positive sense.

Schulte did a fab job of keeping the story moving, I fell completely in love/lust? with Holden (who wouldn't?) and Olivia is a strong female character who I think women can relate to -- so much coming at her that's confusing and scary, yet she seems to figure out much of it and still stay strong...eventually.

The ending -- oooh, Liz. You leave us wanting so much more. The mark of an excellent author.

I immediately fell in love with the characters in this book. The author does an amazing job of making the reader empathize and even root for the most terrible people.

Liz Schulte is quickly becoming my favorite author. She will soon be sharing shelf space with Anne Rice and Kim Harrison and I have very limited shelf space. Forget Twilight, forget the Hunger Games; this is the new series to follow and fall in love with.

This was one of those books that I couldn't put down and read deep into the night. We get to hear both Liv's and Holden's versions of what is going on and OH HOLDEN! Ultimate bad boy but he has incredible depth to him.

Acknowledgments

I would like to thank my family, friends, and fans for supporting me and reading my work—there would literally be no reason for me to do this if you didn't.

A special thanks to my mom who has enough enthusiasm for ten publicists. My best friend Kim who always lets me bounce ideas off of her and asks me the right questions at the right time.

Mandie Stevens, who has taught me about promotions and whose love of my characters keeps me giddy.

Cait Lavender, who might be my soul mate.

Kristin Beaird, who threatened to drive to my house and stand over me until I finished the series after she read *Choices*.

And lastly to M.d. Christie and all of my partners at 4 Corners Press for being a constant source of inspiration.

Liz Schulte

ONE

"Olivia," I gasped, sitting up in bed.

I felt her for just a moment, could have sworn I felt her caress against my mind. My eyes darted around my new apartment cautiously; she wasn't here.

Of course I didn't see her, she's dead. *She's dead, get a grip.*

I collapsed back onto my new bed. I'd been doing well. It took three years to go from thinking about her every second of everyday to only thinking of her when I was trying to fall asleep. Progress. Bedtime, early mornings—those were the only time I allowed myself the luxury of Olivia. She wasn't coming back. I accepted it. She was gone for good and by my own hands no less.

My brain knew I needed to let her go. It was completely on board with operation elimination. My heart—who would've thought I had one— would give the rest of my life just to feel her light up my mind for one more minute. I closed my eyes against the newest regret. My traitorous heart wouldn't leave me alone. What did I have to do to make it shut up? I sure as hell couldn't bring her back. All I had left was the job. I took a deep breath and filed the pain away to use later.

I got out of bed, unable to stay still any longer. One of the two girls in my bed moved around as if she was waking up. "Shhhh" I touched her forehead until she settled down. I was in no mood to speak with Tweedle Dee or Tweedle Dumb, I had a meeting. I kicked their garments closer to the bed as I made my way to the bathroom. The lamp was knocked over and the covers lay in a twisted heap on the floor. I didn't even look at them. *This used to be fun.*

"I will beat this," I said to myself as I got in the shower, but memories were already scratching at the surface. It was easier to forget her and what I'd done in Chicago. Nothing reminded me of her here; the only place she could haunt me was in my head. And the more I embraced the jinni, the less Olivia could torture me there. Soon I could be rid of her completely and back to my empty pain free existence. Slightly more twisted and dead to the world around, but at least my mind would be back in the game.

I finished my shower, pulled on a pair of jeans and a black shirt, and grabbed my keys slamming the apartment door shut behind me.

"Be a machine," I muttered. "A machine." It was a good reminder—and an effective one. I *was* a machine where work was concerned. Recruiting more new members than ever before, causing a wake of chaos and destruction in the lives of all of those who crossed my path, and I felt wonderfully disconnected every single time. With every new sucker a little piece of Olivia slipped through the cracks and away from me— or so I kept trying to convince myself anyway.

Shaking off the doubts trying to fog from my mind, I cleared my head for the more immediate issue at hand: my meeting with Danica, the regional commander of my territory. I had no idea what she wanted. We'd never met in all the years I was a jinni, but then again, we'd never been in the same city 'til now. Ultimately, I wasn't overly concerned. If they had any idea of all the things I'd done when Olivia was alive, they'd have killed me long ago. I was an exemplary jinni now. *Hell,* I thought, *maybe they're going to give me an award.*

Danica set up the meeting on the south side of Chicago in one of the seedier neighborhoods past Hyde Park. The smell of sweat and bodily fluids assaulted me as I walked into some dank strip club—nothing but class here. I found Danica in a back room with a private dancer and a couple other jinn. She was slender and petite with long glossy black hair, small dark eyes, and plump lips smothered in cherry red lipstick. Her corset and skin tight leather pants were black and her four inch spiked heels were red; she looked like a tiny Dr. Frank-N-Furter. Rocky #1 glanced at me when I walked through the door, obviously unconcerned with my presence. Danica continued stroking Rocky #2's leg as I stood to the side watching the freak show unfold. The stripper danced in a complete daze. The room filled with a heady stupor that seemed to affect nearly everyone in this den of iniquity, including the two lesser jinn companions Danica kept.

My annoyance grew as she made me wait through more nonsense. She began making out with the two Rockys and the stripper looked like she was about to fall over from exhaustion, but continued her increasingly less than provocative dance. I had better things to do than watch the lame spectacle Danica was putting on as a demonstration of her power. I tried to be cool, knowing this was a test of some sort. I eyed the foul sofa, but didn't care to sit on it. I stepped out of the room and snatched a flimsy wooden chair from a nearby table. Plopping it down in what had become my spot in the room, I sat and waited for her to grow bored with her tedious games. However, she continued wasting my time showing no signs of giving up on the horizon, so I pulled out my cell phone and began my own game. Got to love the 21st century.

As I was about to reach the 30th level of Tetris, her sultry voice broke into my concentration. "You're welcome to sit on the couch, Holden dear."

"I'm fine here. Whenever you're ready, let me know," I said barely glancing in her direction. I could see her pouting, but I pretended I only saw my game. I hated women like that.

"You're completely unaffected by my powers?" she rasped and waved her hand. The stripper and the two Rockys scurried out of the room.

The bright colored shapes I was so carefully organizing fell too fast and piled up beyond my control. Game over. I put the phone back in my pocket. "You've given me a bit of a headache."

"You seem to have come out of nowhere. How old are you? 150? 200? Why is it that you've only now drawn my attention? Your power should have enticed notice much sooner than this."

"I don't make a spectacle of myself," I told her flatly, making no effort to hide my disgust at the squalor she surrounded herself with.

Her laughter filled the air. "I do."

"That's evident."

The laughter disappeared as quickly as it started. "You do not approve?"

"I don't care what you do. Just don't waste my time." She was a typical oversexed, power hungry jinni who couldn't see the big picture. The inability to put off short-term pleasure for long-term gain was the downfall of our entire race, or at least why we could never gain any real ground.

"I'm *so* sorry I wasted your *precious* time," Danica mocked as she strutted toward me, then stroked the back of her fingernails against my cheek until they came to my neck where she used them to draw blood. Before she could pull her hand away, I caught it and raised it to my mouth. I sucked my blood from her fingers. More games. With my blood she could possibly make her powers work on me, or, at the very least, track me a whole lot easier. I tossed her hand to the side when I was sure all of my blood had been removed. The scratch on my neck had already healed.

She smiled lazily. "That was fun," she purred, pressing her body against mine.

"What do you want?"

"So much, Holden, so much."

"Great, let's get started."

"Are you always business first?"

I stared at her, letting the full extent of my boredom register on my face until she looked away. Nothing about being around her was pleasure.

"An uptight jinni. Never thought I'd see the day," she muttered.

I stood up and moved my chair back to the wall. "Give me a call when you're in the mood to have this meeting. I have other business to attend."

"Wait," she said when I reached the doorway. Her voice was normal now, no longer purring or raspy. I looked back at her. "We'll have the meeting now."

I gave her a single nod and waited for her to begin.

"How would you feel about becoming the commander of the North American region?"

"That's your job."

"Well, apparently it's yours now. Management, in light of recent events and recent *deaths*, has chosen *you* to take over this region. Imagine my surprise when a little nobody undercut me and took my position."

Killing Augustus, my jinn superior up until a few years ago, must have bumped me to next in line. I had no idea I was so close in seniority, but probably still wouldn't have done it, had he not threatened Olivia.

"Is this going to be a problem?" I asked her. It wasn't like I wanted or asked for the damn promotion, but it wasn't a gig one could turn down. You do as you are told— she knew that. . Why me anyway? I wasn't a leader. I could barely tolerate people, let alone jinn, and I didn't even know where to begin with running an entire territory. Basically, the promotion meant one thing for me: I was screwed.

"Oh, you're going to have plenty of problems, the least of which is me. I know how this game works, Holden. It's only a matter of time before I get my territory back. They're testing you, throwing you into the big leagues. How long do you think you can survive before you're eaten alive?"

"Perhaps I should just kill you now while I have the opportunity."

"Aw, Holden, my pet, I'm just trying to help."

"I'll manage on my own."

"I'd hate for anything to happen to this pretty, pretty face."

I brushed her annoying hands away once more. "When do I start?"

She looked away and frowned. "You already have. I fly out tomorrow." She tossed a set of keys to me. "These are the keys to this building and offices. I'll leave the combination for the safe somewhere special."

I rolled my eyes and turned to leave.

"Don't be a stranger," she called out behind me with a cackle.

Figures they'd punish me for being too good of an employee. I checked my watch. I was late. I thought I had plenty of time to meet Danica and make my meeting with Philip Pemberton, but I hadn't anticipated this meeting lasting over four hours. I grabbed a cab and headed north. A full hour after I should've met my soon to be newest recruit, I walked into the bar to get tonight's episode of Let's Make A Deal underway. Immediately I sensed the change in Philip; I could practically smell it on him. Pain in the ass guardians had been there.

"Phil, are you ready?" I said, taking a seat next to him at the bar.

"I don't know if it's a good idea." Christ, we'd been through this part already.

"It's not a good idea to avenge and bring justice to your family? Or did they mean so little to you?"

"Maybe I should forgive—"

"Forgive the man who ran a stop light and destroyed your life?"

"Well... I don't know."

"If it were me, Phil, I'd do everything in my power to make him pay. I'd see to it that he took his last breath knowing what he did to me. He would die knowing he deserved it."

"But I'll destroy *my* life."

"Oh, so you're worried about yourself? I see."

"No, but..."

I clenched my fists. This wasn't working. The guardian's ideas had started to take root. I needed to dig deeper, hit Phil with something a bit more personal.

"But what? Think of Annie, so bright and cheerful. The way she lit up your life and made you glad each and every day that she chose you. When she loved you above all others, you were the luckiest man in the world."

"How … how do you know that? You've never met Annie."

"I know, Phil, because I too have loved and lost. The only light in my life was ripped away from me."

Phil let out a shuddery sigh, and I was regaining lost ground. I let a sad smile soften my face. "Our time with the ones we love is always too short, but for someone to make that time even shorter, to steal what little time we do have…" I let my sentence trail off.

"Did you make the person who took her away pay?"

"I make him pay. Every. Single. Day." I felt disgusted with myself. This was a new low even for me, using what Olivia and I had to hook a mark, but the words I spoke were the truth. I did make myself pay for what I had done—probably why I couldn't let her memory go. If I didn't hold onto it, how could I properly punish myself?

"Do you feel better?"

Better, what's better? "I feel justified."

Philip pressed his head into his hands as I indicated for the bartender to pour him another drink. I could see doubt in the path the guardian had led him to trickle into his mind. He was nearly mine again.

"What about little Colin and Megan? Their lives cut so short; they barely had a chance to live. Don't you owe it to them? Hell, Phil, don't you owe it to yourself?"

"Please, stop." Tears streamed down Phil's weak face.

"I'll stop anytime you want, Phil. I'm just trying to help you obtain the means to right this incredible wrong."

"But murder?"

I leaned in close and whispered in his ear. "It's no more than he took from you." I saw anger once again solidify behind his eyes and his weepy forgiveness take the backseat to the more tangible emotion.

"How do we do this?"

"Come with me, I have someone for you to meet."

He nodded and satisfaction filled me, even as a little piece of my heart slipped away.

TWO

I strolled around the grounds of the Villa Borghese amongst the statues and fountains I loved. The gentle buzz of the city just outside vibrated in my ears. It was good to be home, but the peace was short lived. My former trainee, Ruth, stopped by to discuss her most recent assignment with me. She prattled on, but my mind was far away from her.

Why was it so hard to lose Olivia? The Jinni was devastated, but he was in love with her. I wasn't! I wanted him to kill her—I asked for it—because I knew it was the best way—the only way—for her to get to us. However, when I came into her apartment and saw how the cards fell, I no longer felt sure. Maybe I was wrong.

"Quintus, are you listening to me?"

"Of course I am," I lied. My mind was consumed, as it was so often these days, with whether or not Olivia would come back and just how far my mistakes would reverberate through the universe. Every action had a reaction, and I hadn't seen the last of this. The only thing I knew for certain was the jinni needed to be kept as far away from her as possible because she had no self-control around him.

"So what do you think?"

"I think—you know what's best in your heart."

"You've been telling me that for three hundred years, Quintus. Just once, I'd love for you to say, 'Yes, that's the right thing to do,' or 'No, of course not, what were you thinking?'"

I smiled at her. She was an excellent student. She didn't exactly excel in any one discipline and still doubted her instincts, but she never caused me any trouble. Ruth was exactly what a guardian should be: eager, faithful, kind, happy, and accepting. "If I tell you what to do, you'll never learn to make the hard decisions for yourself. They're your assignments to guide. I cannot know them as you know them. Your instincts are the best suited for them, which is why you were assigned to them."

"I know, I know—but the intervention I inspired his family to have didn't work. Neither did the support group I nudged him into joining or the affirmations I whispered in his ear at night. Can you think of anything else? What if I can't make a difference in Peter's life?"

"The high school teacher?"

She nodded.

"Don't give up on him. The slightest altering of his path can save him, just find the right one. His life touches many. It's imperative you succeed. Maybe try to get him into a rehabilitation facility."

Her steady brown eyes studied my face as she tugged on her lip. Then she rolled her shoulders back and straightened. "I'll do my best. Thanks, Quintus. Oh, by the way, have you seen Jeremiah?"

"Not for a week or so. Why, do you need him?"

"No, we were supposed to have coffee yesterday."

I shook my head. "Haven't laid eyes on him lately, but if I do, I'll tell him you're looking for him."

"Great, thanks again." Ruth dissolved into light leaving me with a rare peaceful moment.

Over three years passed, and Olivia still wasn't back. I didn't know if she was ever returning. No one else had taken this long to be reborn. With each passing day the chances of her emergence became less and less, and I couldn't shake the feeling I had done something incorrect. Actually, it was hard to think of anything I might have done right where Olivia was concerned. The way she perceived the world, the way she chose to understand it was different than other people. You couldn't tell her anything, she had to come to terms with it in her own way, yet there seemed to be nothing she couldn't eventually accept. I swore to myself I would do better *if she just came back.* So far, Olivia Martin had done nothing I expected of her. A familiar tug at my navel brought me back to the reality—back to work. The elders wanted to see me.

There was a high council of four elders who established our laws and made all necessary communication with the angels and a low council of seven elders who ran all earthly guardian affairs. Elders were born into their positions, chosen by God to lead our race. I didn't know what distinguished high elders from low elders, perhaps it was their abilities or lineage. The elders were human once, as we all were, then upon their death took the role as management. They had a variety of talents lesser guardians didn't possess. Some were capable of receiving heavenly messages—making them the prophets—and they all could summons any guardian anywhere in the world. It was even rumored they could travel through time.

Usually when I was summoned I ended up in a room filled with a blinding light and their booming voices sent down directives that were never to be questioned. This time I was brought to a small space filled with books stacked floor to ceiling along every wall. No door or window in sight—just books and a small writing desk littered with old curling paper and quills. I looked around, not exactly sure what to make of my surroundings. The call felt like the elders, but—

"Quintus, I presume." A deep, authoritative voice bounced off the walls making it sound like the speaker was everywhere. Sitting at the writing desk not three feet from me a slight man with eyes I had seen before, a curious blue green with a ring of gold, appeared.

"Yes."

"I am your elder, Ezra." He extended a hand, his eyes dissecting me. "You watched Olivia Martin before she was sent to us?"

My mouth fell open. Ezra was on the high council; they never met with regular guardians like me. He must've known what happened with Olivia, and I could only imagine where this line of questioning was going and in person too. My stomach twisted and I fought the urge to confess everything. "Yes, I did."

"Why *you*? Why not assign an underling to do so? Surely, you had more important matters to attend."

I had no choice, but to be honest. "She was unique. She saw me."

Erza nodded his head without an ounce of surprise. "She was also in grave danger."

"I was not immediately aware of that."

He nodded again. "She would not talk about her final weeks on earth. I assume she suffered much?"

"Yes. A demon was sent to prevent her change."

Ezra blinked, but made no comment. "After much deliberation Olivia has made her decision. She will be joining you. Are you aware of her destiny as elder?"

"I am."

"I would like you to personally take care of her training—and safety. I don't know how Hell found out what she was before she changed, but I am very interested in seeing her progress. She is unique—unexpected even. We must keep her focused and on target with our mission. Our world has become increasingly dangerous—she is proof of that—so discuss her with no one besides for me. She needs to know none of this, Quintus. We have the opportunity to help Olivia understand our goals. She can be a great asset to our race so long as she is part of the team. I need her to be a company man. Do you understand?"

A barrage of questions hit me. How was she unexpected? How much did he know about what happened before she changed? But elders' orders were never questioned, only obeyed. I was glad Olivia was coming back, but I had my doubts whether or not she would tow the company line. I thought of a way out of taking this new assignment. "I'm honored, but can I train an elder? I wouldn't know where to begin."

"Olivia does not need to be trained as an elder. She does not need to know of those powers until the high council deems it so. We have decided she should be trained first as a guardian; she will be advanced in time. You already have a relationship; it will be an easier transition. She trusts you."

"I'll try my best."

Ezra smiled. "I have the distinct impression Olivia will be a challenge."

"I had a similar notion."

"Good, you see her as she is. The less you tell her of her future position, the better. Let her believe she is just like the rest of you. Report her progress and any problems or strange behavior directly to me."

I didn't really know how to respond to this request. What exactly did they expect from her and me?

Ezra looked off to the side as if listening to something I couldn't hear. "It's time now, good luck, Quintus." He placed his finger tips on my forehead.

I opened my eyes in a forest. In any direction, I was surrounded by old gnarled trees. At my feet lay Olivia, as lovely as she was before, with mahogany hair cascading around her in soft waves, pale skin that glowed with the light of the moon, and not a stitch of clothing to her name. She opened those deep pools of swirling blue and green with a tinge of yellow and looked up at me solemnly. Then her mouth twitched into a frown and she shut her eyes again, pulling her eyebrows together.

Her voice was hoarse and sounded like she'd hoped for someone else. "Quintus."

"I've been waiting for you."

She shifted away from me still frowning, but nodded. "I'm back."

"I'm glad you are."

She stood up and brushed dirt and leaves off of her body, unconcerned by its current state of undress. "Everything looks different." She gazed around, reaching out to touch the air and make patterns with her own light like a sparkler. I watched her childlike wonderment and felt the same sensation growing in me. I was used to seeing the world through the film of the Abyss, so it was easy to forget how lovely it was. Olivia studied her surroundings as if they were part of a strange and glorious painting. The beauty suddenly washed over me, and I experienced the world with new eyes.

"Tell me what you see." I wanted to prolong the experience for as long as possible.

"Everything looks—different. Brighter, more alive. My hand leaves a trail of light. You look like you're inside a light bulb. Look at that tree—amazing."

The tree in question was a large oak with twisted branches that looked black against the setting sun. The leaves glowed with the fiery colors of fall like they were lit with an eternal flame.

"It's very nice," I agreed.

"No, look at it."

I looked at the tree again, still not understanding what she wanted me to see.

"It's alive. Can't you see it, the ancient life radiating from its branches? It's practically buzzing with energy."

I looked closer, failing to see what she was talking about. It was a beautiful tree, but I couldn't see its life force. Was this part of her elder ability? Or were her senses overly stressed from coming back? I smiled reassuringly, not committing to an opinion one way or another. Olivia continued inspecting the woods, darting from one place to the next like a firefly, looking at everything that caught her eyes.

She gasped as she crouched next to a bush. "What are these?"

I joined her and peered into the shrub. "Wood nymphs."

"Wood nymphs?"

"Faeries," I whispered, "but they don't like to be called that."

"They're real?"

"Of course. They reside in the Abyss."

"The *Abyss*?"

"Yes—what you're seeing, the space between the other side and the human world.   As a human you resided firmly on earth, you saw the physical world in black and white. A tree was a tree, green only had so many variations in the color, and life forces were invisible. Here there are an infinite variety of colors, textures, smells, and sensations. You see through guardian eyes now, which are open to the Abyss." I paused letting her take in what I said. She nodded after a moment. "Wood nymphs, for example, live in the Abyss. Occasionally a human catches a glance of something from this world and it becomes a mythical creature in the stories they tell. Our existence is not shared with mankind."

"Are they friendly?"

"The nymphs? Yes, quite. They don't much care about us though. It's easier to get them to speak with you if you have something to bribe them with. "

"How strange."

"You have much to learn, firefly."

Olivia blinked, but didn't comment on the nickname. Her eyes glazed over for a moment, and she pressed her lips together, the wonderment gone from her face. "So why are you here?"

The sudden switch in mood caught me off guard. "I've been assigned to mentor you, since we have a relationship."

She laughed without humor and paced away, shaking her head and muttering to herself. Finally, she shook off whatever was bothering her and looked back. "So teach me."

I smiled, trying to understand what just happened. "In time."

Olivia sighed loudly. "What do we do now?"

"First, I believe you need clothing," I said.

"I forgot to pack a suitcase." Her cheeks colored in sudden awareness.

"I can help." I touched her shoulder, and she tensed. My light engulfed her while I envisioned her in a dress. When I pulled back she looked ethereal in a white gauzy gown with a golden sash wrapped just above her waist. She could have been straight out of Botticelli's imagination.

Olivia looked down at herself, then back to me. "*This* is how you choose to dress me?" She crossed her arms over her chest and glared. "In the forest?   Really?"

I grinned despite her foul mood. I hardly knew her, but I think I had missed her.

THREE

I don't know what I expected—certainly not the pain that tore through me when I opened my eyes. Feeling Holden immediately saturate my mind nearly shattered me and made me want to scream—or go back. I struggled and finally managed to shove him into a closet deep in my subconscious, where hopefully he'd stay until he disappeared forever—forgotten which was still better than he deserved.

Why did I agree to this?

Better yet, why didn't my heart understand what my brain so clearly explained? Holden didn't want us. He ... No, I wouldn't let myself do that. I would not think about Holden. He was dead to me. It was the only way it could be, the only way I could do this.

Quintus was waiting for me, all dimples and kindness—the traitorous bastard. Where was he when I needed him? Why didn't he save me? The accusations running through my mind fell aside, as I noticed how weird things were.

Everything looked different making me sad that my camera would never be able to capture what I now saw—not that I had a camera anymore. Lights and colors shimmered through the air and the trees, like I was inside a snow globe that someone was relentlessly shaking. How had I not seen all of this around me? It was incredible.

The more Quintus spoke, the more I realized I had a lot to learn and plenty to distract me from the person I wasn't thinking about. I was also not thinking about the fact that I'd been running around the forest stark naked giving Quintus quite a show until he made a crack about what we needed to do first.

I didn't think it could get worse until Quintus made some god awful dress appear on me.

"So what now?   Do we walk?" I squished my bare toes into the soft leaves beneath my feet. All I wanted was to not think about the past. The past was where he was and where I was angry at Quintus. I could only look forward now, because hindsight offered no solace, no future.

"Do you know where we are?"

"I assumed you knew. I mean you came here. I just appeared." I frowned at him.

"I was sent the same as you."

"So we're lost? Great! What kind of operation is this?"

"Guardians are never lost." Quintus flashed me his ridiculously deep dimples, but I felt no appreciation for them. There was only one smile I wanted to see—

Needing to keep moving, I trudged through the woods in the direction I was facing. I heard Quintus walking behind me. How could he come to get me without a better plan than this? How did I get stuck with the person who'd abandoned me to a demon? My afterlife sucked.

"Where exactly are you going?" he asked after a few minutes.

"East." I picked up pace as the memories became more demanding.

After another few yards, he asked, "Why east?"

I shrugged. "It's as good of a direction as any—feels right. Which way would you prefer?"

"East is fine."

I pushed through the forest, Quintus trailing behind silently. The stillness made the memories float too close to the surface, so I went faster. Branches tugged at my dress, and the past stabbed my heart. By the time I broke free from the trees, my walk verged on a run.

"What are you doing?" Quintus studied me like I was a specimen, and I didn't like it.

"Escaping," I mumbled.

"What?"

"Trying to find a road."

"What will you do once you find a road?"

"I don't know, Quintus. Honestly, I would've thought being a guardian and all, you'd have had a plan for how to get me to wherever it is I need to be. I'm not exactly impressed with your people's preparedness."

"*Our people*. And exactly where do you need to be?" He quirked a questioning eyebrow.

"Well, I—uh…" I hadn't thought that far ahead. I was more concerned with keeping myself busy, not with what I was doing or where I was going. "Surely there's something we need to do. We aren't going to hang out in the woods all night, are we?" I crossed my fingers and toes that the answer would be no. I couldn't imagine sitting around with only trees and Quintus to keep me company.

"Your first lesson, Firefly: Rushing is for humans, not us. We have all the time in the world, so you should use it. How can you guide someone if you're too busy rushing from this place to that to think about their problem. You are eternal now. You need to train yourself to slow down and see the world around you. Follow the action through the reactions so you know the best path."

"How does that help us get back to civilization?"

"Had you not raced off, had you asked me, I would have told you how guardians travel."

I looked at him and tried to keep my patience and focus, while combating images of Holden pointing a gun at me. "Okay. How do you travel?"

"*We* travel by light."

His finger pulling the trigger, cold resolve in his eyes. Death in the form of the man I loved stood before me. I wanted to shut my eyes, but I blinked until Holden faded away and Quintus came back. My throat burned from the tears I wouldn't cry.

Quintus's words barely registered. "Light?"

"Yes. It allows us to move from one location to another in a breath."

"Show me." I took his hand, hoping this was the distraction I needed as the scene in my head started to replay.

Quintus's warm whiskey colored eyes met mine and reflected the beam of the moon—or maybe it was my own glow reflected. "This will feel strange."

Everything around me disappeared into an intense light.

FOUR

Philip Pemberton come on down, you're the next contestant on *Sorry I Destroyed Your Life*.

Damn it all to hell, I felt bad for old Phil. He made his deal with the demon and was well on his way to avenging his family and becoming cursed to this cruel and Godforsaken existence. All because of yours truly. *What did she ever see in me?*

I walked away from the warehouse where I'd taken Phil to meet his destiny. All hope was gone for him now. I glanced at my watch, not even 11:00 p.m.—the night was just getting started. What else could I do this fine evening? Anything that could possibly squash this surge of humanity, I was up for trying.

It hit me like a tidal wave. One moment I was walking down the street, planning on having a little fun and the next moment I was nearly knocked over by a crushing light that washed over my mind and blinded me to anything in front of me. I staggered, fought to gain some sort of control, then I heard her voice. She said my name—I tried to reply, but she was gone as quickly as she came. It was like I'd been struck by lightning. Her voice rang in my ears.

I'd warred to forget the sound and timber of her voice. I'd battled to obliterate the memories of the smell of her skin and the taste of her lips. This one word from her and all that I tried to forget flooded back.

Could Olivia be alive? Was it a fluke, a coincidence? Did I finally reach her on the other side? Had I lost all grip with reality? Instead of going out, I caught a cab home. I walked into my empty apartment and stripped the sheets from my bed before collapsing onto it. I searched my mind for any change, any clue that she was really there, and I wasn't just losing my sanity.

Please don't let this be a hallucination, I begged the universe.

But I found nothing. There was no sign of her at all. *As if she's dead, you stupid fool.* I always knew insanity was possible and frankly it would have been a damn miracle if this didn't drive me to it, but I wasn't going to go easy. *Maybe it was just my subconscious punishing me for trying to get rid of her completely.* Whatever it was though, it didn't matter because it wasn't her. It couldn't possibly have been her.

I rolled over and looked at the clock, 3:13 a.m. I was bored. I didn't want to go out, but I didn't want to stay in. Yet something needed to keep me busy so I wouldn't obsess—I only had an eternity to fill. I rolled out of bed and hit the sidewalk. Walking around the city at night was one of my favorite things to do. Most of the innocents were off the street, everyone out here was guilt-free game. I strolled down the darkest streets and alleys heading towards an increasingly bad part of the city. A man stepped out from behind a dumpster.

"Hey, you lost or somethin'?" His arms spread wide to make himself as threatening as possible.

I popped my neck and rolled my shoulders back, a smile tugged at the corners of my mouth.

"I'm talking to you," he said, pushing me.

The mind clearing adrenaline that filled me when my fist connected with a perfect stranger's face was so good it was almost addictive. I didn't have to use my fist. I could have had him writhing with pain by a mere touch like Vetis did to Olivia, but this physical smashing and giving felt so much better. I beat the thug bloody, relishing in each punch. It felt so good, it was hard to stop. It quieted the impulse to let loose inside and allowed me the freedom I craved but rarely indulged. I looked at his half-dead, huddled body on the ground. I could finish him so easily. One well-placed blow and it'd be goodbye street living criminal.

I could walk away. Maybe he'd live. Maybe he'd die. Either way, it would be out of my control. His life would rest solely in the hands of that impossible to predict bitch, Fate. If it were me, would I rather die or take my chances with her? I decided to let her have a go at him. There was no need to kill him, the moment had passed.

I continued walking until I found myself nearing the strip club where I'd met Danica. Standing across the street I observed the plain, windowless exterior, and the abandoned buildings for sale on either side. The dimly lit sign flashed in a tired pulse and the door looked like it had been spray painted black. So this was the new office, yippee.

The smell is the first thing I'm going to work on, I thought as I walked into the slowly dying building. The lights were dim, the girls bordered on revolting, and the few slobbering drunks speckled throughout the room didn't inspire profit. Was I supposed to run this club or did I just work out of it? A waitress with stringy hair, yellow crusted teeth, and saggy breasts came up to me.

"Table or a room?"

"Neither," I brushed passed her heading back to the offices Danica had pointed out, keys in hand.

"Oh, you must be the new owner," she said, following me. "I'm Kourtni. If you need anything just let me know."

Owner, great. I unlocked the office and flipped the switch. It looked like it had been ransacked. Paper sat in piles everywhere I looked, including the floor. The furniture lay tipped over, draws half open. The trashcan overflowed. Tacky velvet paintings hung askew—even the couch leaned at an unnatural angle. "What the fuck?"

Kourtni stuck her head into the room. "Yeah, Danica wasn't too into keeping things straight. She had all of her meetings in the private rooms."

"How did she find anything?"

Kourtni shrugged as if to say "I only work here."

"What time is your shift over, Kourtni?"

"Six."

"I'm going to start cleaning up. Come back at 5:30 and get me—I'd like a tour of the rest of the club."

"You're the boss."

The door clicked behind her, and I surveyed the room. I had half a notion to get a trash bag and start throwing everything away. Who could work like this? I needed to figure out if Danica kept the club like this to keep it low profile or if she was just a poor manager. I also needed to figure out what in the hell I was supposed to be doing as a regional commander. As a grunt who officially worked under her, I wasn't exactly privy to the inner workings. As far as I could tell, they did nothing and judging by this office I could see why.

I sat, legs crossed in the center of the floor, and started four piles of paper: trash, financial documents, club related, and jinn related. The trash pile was the most overwhelming, but after a short excursion I came back with trash bags and began making a real dent in the sty.

At 5:30 sharp Kourtni swung open the door and stood in the frame with a hand on her hip. "Wow, I don't think I have ever seen the office this clean."

I stood up and looked around the room. There was still a lot to do, but at least most of the floor had been cleared.

"Where do you want to go?" she asked.

"Everywhere."

"Didn't you tour this place before you bought it?" I looked at her, but said nothing. "You aren't much of a talker are you?"

Top to bottom, rafters to employees, the club was grimy, sticky, cheap, and decaying. I couldn't imagine staying here another hour, let alone indefinitely. The filth gnawed at me, it all had to go.

"Who's in charge of the employees and scheduling?" I asked.

She looked at me blankly. "The manager," she said as if it were the most obvious answer in the world.

"And who might that be?"

"Julie Jones."

"And which one is she?" I asked, scanning the employees half-heartedly cleaning the bar with dingy washcloths.

"She isn't here."

"When will she be in?"

She shrugged. Kourtni was obviously not the sharpest tack, but I could tell why Danica had her around. She didn't run off at the mouth which is an invaluable trait. "When's your next shift?"

"I come in at ten tonight."

"If you see Julie before I do, tell her I'm looking for her. Do you have a piece of paper?"

She handed me a paper and pen, and I scratched down my cell number. "If I'm not in, have her call me." I spoke slowly to be sure she understood.

"Sure thing, boss."

"My name is Holden."

I headed back into the office and resumed my crusade. Hours rolled by. The desk was inhabitable, the piles were shrinking, and the filing cabinets were in the process of being alphabetized when there was a sharp knock upon my door.

"Come in," I said, reading last year's club tax return.

"Holden Smith?"

I looked up to face a demon in a nicely tailored suit with a pretty female jinni at his side. "How may I help you?" I asked, standing.

"Do you know who I am?"

"I do not."

"Do you know what I am?"

"I do."

He nodded. "Good. Call me Malphas." He handed me a business card with only a phone number printed on it. "You will be reporting to me directly."

"Are you responsible for my promotion?"

His inhuman eyes locked on mine and held on for a bit longer than necessary. "Yes."

"May I ask you why?"

"You have shown the most promise and self-control in the region. I have been watching you for a while. Danica's enthusiasm is unrivalled, but she doesn't have a head for business. The losses we suffered with her at the helm have become too great."

"What exactly am I supposed to do?"

"Lead."

I began to ask another question, but he cut me off impatiently. "No one cares how you do it, just get results and don't break the rules."

Malphas walked to the door.

"One more question."

Malphas turned back to me clearly annoyed.

"Is there any reason this club should continue to lose money?"

"As I said, run your businesses anyway you want. Just get me results."

The pretty jinni shut the door behind them, and I sat back in the chair, which would have to be replaced, mulling over options. Diamonds operated in the red for as many years as I had tax returns. I couldn't tell if Danica had embezzled or if business really was that bad. I cleared the old financial reports from the desk and begin working on my expansion plan.

I was on the phone with a realtor about the properties on either side of the club when my office door opened. Without looking up, I held up a hand to tell them just a minute and turned my back to finish my conversation. When the details were worked out and the realtor agreed to fax me the paperwork, I swiveled around to face the latest interruption. The sight of the person standing in front of me with her arms crossed over her chest made me freeze for just a moment.

"Juliet," I said as coolly as possible.

"Holden," she said just as solemnly.

FIVE

Olivia didn't yet have living accommodations, so I resigned myself to having a roommate. I figured I'd transport the two of us from the outskirts of the woods back to Rome. I'd get her settled in, then we'd have dinner and discuss a training schedule, and I'd introduce her to my fair city. Well, that was my plan anyway.

But I made another rookie mistake and forgot to explain transporting to Olivia at all. It was difficult process for a fledgling, even worse at great distances. We arrived safely in Rome, but her recovery was slow. Instead of dinner and settling in, I deposited her in the guest room where she fell in and out of consciousness and human form.

Guardians don't have a physical body in the same way a human or even a jinni does. We have the appearance of a body. Our bodies feel human to the touch, they appear human in their actions, but are comprised almost entirely of light. We travel by releasing our own light from bonds that hold it in human form and direct our thoughts to where we would like to be. Once at our destination we have to pull ourselves back into the bonds that make us look human again. Not a particularly hard task once you get the hang of it, but also not an easy one, especially if it hasn't been explained. With rest Olivia would naturally become whole again, so no real harm done, though it could take a week or two.

One thing was abundantly clear. I needed to find a way to focus around her. Firefly had a way of distracting me without my realizing I was distracted—well, until I did something stupid that made it painfully clear. I sat in her room watching her struggle to become whole. The room filled with her light, then faded, then relight, again and again in a pattern almost like breathing. It was the softest, most pure white light I had ever seen, and it made my skin tingle with static electricity. Most guardians were like me. A bold yellow light akin to sunshine. Hers was nothing like the sun; it was unobtrusive and alluring. I told myself I should use this time to devise a syllabus, but I stayed in the room, leaned back against the wall, and basked in the strange sensations coursing through me.

"Please…"

Her voice snapped me back to reality. Her light no longer filled the room. Everything seemed back to normal. She was once again whole. I had fallen asleep, sure, but only a few hours had passed. *Impressive.* Her sleep wasn't peaceful; she tossed and turned and whimpered. I moved closer, putting a hand on her arm to calm her.

"Holden!" She bolted upright and looked around the room frantically, but didn't seem to see anything.

"Firefly, you're okay, it's safe." My words didn't register with her. Her eyes continued darting. Her muscles were flexed and tight. "Olivia. Olivia, look at me. Look into my eyes," I coaxed. I put my hands on her shoulders and turned her towards me. "Breathe. Just breathe. You're okay. You're safe." Her eyes made their way to mine. It took a few moments, but recognition finally registered in them. The tension dissolved from her, and her eyes filled with tears, but didn't spill over.

"Quintus." Sadness pooled in each syllable as she spoke. "Are you okay?"

She closed her liquid eyes and took a few deep breaths. "I'm fine." She didn't look fine. "Just tired." She pulled away from me.

"I'll let you get some rest." I glanced back once before leaving; she curled herself into a ball. She didn't look like she'd be resting anytime soon.

I sighed heavily as I prepared her training schedule. Apparently her change hadn't eliminated Holden from her mind. Was there anyway the jinni wouldn't become a problem again? I liked Olivia a lot, but he couldn't come back into the picture, or I'd have to report it. I didn't have a choice.

Olivia came out of the room at sunrise, still wearing the dress I created. I smiled at the sight. She looked more like a statue of Athena than the comfortable young woman I knew before. There was the slightest possibility that my choice in her clothing was more reflective of the way I saw her than practical. It would have to be changed.

"Would you like something else to wear?"

Olivia looked down as if she'd completely forgotten what she was wearing and shrugged. "Whatever."

I searched my memory for an outfit I had seen her in. When I had a strong mental image, I once again focused my thoughts and touched her shoulder. This time when I stepped back she was the picture of casual. She sported a pair of worn jeans and a men's styled black button down shirt, just as she had been when I found her in Holden's apartment. Olivia became very still. I couldn't quite place the expression on her face.

"Those are the last thing I could remember you in. I can change it."

"It's—are these— are these the actual clothes I was wearing?" Her voice sounded strained as she lifted the collar to smell. "They're not the same clothes," she confirmed, shaking her head, blinking rapidly.

"We can do something different. Just describe what you want."

"This is fine. I was just startled. Maybe you should teach me how to do this."

"Light manipulation can be challenging. We'll get to it, but not for a while."

A begrudging smile twitching on her lips. "So there's an order to how I learn to be a guardian?"

"Well, no—"

"I'm incapable of putting on my own clothes at this point?"

"No, but—"

"But it's not first on *your* schedule."

"It's not the first lesson I had planned to teach you."

"Don't you think it would be beneficial to both of us if I could dress myself?"

"I didn't consider it."

"You think, maybe, we could bump it up to first priority?" Her small smile held, but her jaw was tight.

"Yes, of course. The schedule is more to keep me on track than you. You're perfectly right."

"I'm so glad."

It was then I realized she was mocking me, or more accurately, my attempt to assign her a routine.

"Sit down." I nodded towards a pair of overstuffed wingback chair. She sat in one of them cross-legged and looked at me expectantly. I took my seat in the other one and pointed to her feet. "Socks."

She stared at her feet, furrowing her brow, but nothing happened. "Okay, how do I do it?"

"First, close your eyes. Feel and visualize the light inside of you gathering into a ball. Can you feel it?"

"I don't know, I guess."

"Push that ball to your feet, once your feet are shrouded, visualize what you want on them, the more detailed the better."

She was still for several moments, but no light formed around her feet, no socks appeared. She opened one eye and peeked at her toes, then squeezed her eyes closed again. I let her carry on until she huffed out a frustrated sigh.

"What are you doing wrong?"

"I don't know. I'm doing everything you said."

"Are you?"

"Yes." Her eyes narrowed. "What am I not doing?"

"You haven't manifested the light."

"I'm visualizing it."

"But you aren't feeling it, are you?"

"Of course not. I don't believe in this stupid new age crap."

I laughed. "This isn't new age. It's been around for thousands upon thousands of years. The only way you can manipulate your life force is if you can call on it at will. Try again."

"Do you have any idea how stupid that sounds?"

"Stop thinking like a human."

"I'll get right on that." She rolled her eyes.

We spent the rest of the day working on her ability to collect and control her inner light. We had a couple slight glows, but nothing substantial enough to manifest socks from it. Around sunset, she threw her head back against the chair. "I'm done! I give up. I can't do it."

"Yes, you can. You have to get past whatever barrier it is in your mind that's keeping you from being able to do this."

"What makes you think I can do it at all?"

"First, you're a guardian and all guardians can manipulate light. Second, you did the very same thing last night, only on a much larger scale, when you pulled yourself back together after transporting—extremely fast too."

She sighed. "Well, I can't do anymore today."

"We'll rest."

She closed her eyes, shimmering like the moon reflecting on a lake.

"What was your dream about?" I asked casually. I watched the light seep back inside her and close itself off from the outside world completely. She could have passed for a genuine human. "How'd you do that?"

"Do what?"

"You're not glowing."

She cracked her knuckles, uninterested, "I don't know."

I took her hand and inspected it, not one trace of a beam shone anywhere. "Release it." I told her, wanting to see if she could.

She exhaled and her skin took on the same glow it had moments ago.

"Hide it."

She sighed, but somehow managed to make it disappear again. *Outstanding.*

"Wonderful, Olivia. That's wonderful." She gave me a half smile then looked away. "Back to your dream."

She frowned and didn't say anything. Instead she stared at her own hand.

"Was it about Holden?" She flinched at his name, but still said nothing. "You can talk about anything with me, Firefly— even Holden. It might help to discuss it."

"There's nothing to discuss." Her voice came out in barely a whisper.

"Olivia—"

"Let me rephrase." She glared and the light around her built in intensity. "*He*'s not a topic open for discussion. Period." She stood and stalked back to the guest bedroom.

Before I could decide what, if anything, I should do about this outburst, I felt a pull just under my navel. Two meetings with elders in as many days? Unprecedented. I transported to where they were calling me and once again I was in Ezra's office.

"How is she doing?" Ezra asked, hunched over papers on his writing desk.

"It's only been a day, sir."

"And…" He rolled his hand at me impatiently.

"She's fine. Not unmanageable."

"How is she adjusting?"

"Great."

"Has she asked to go home?"

"No."

"Has she asked about us?"

"No." I really didn't understand any of this. If he didn't want to train her himself then why was he micromanaging me? "She hasn't said anything about home or guardians. She has been eager to learn. We worked on light manipulation today."

"How did she do?"

"About the same as other trainees."

"Has she excelled at anything?"

"Well, we haven't done much. I'm not sure if this qualifies as excelling, but she can completely withdraw her light and release it at will. Is that normal for an elder?"

Ezra looked up. "Interesting. What else?"

"We transported out of the woods yesterday, and she was able to pull herself back together in a matter of hours with no knowledge of how to do it."

"Anything else?"

"Not yet." I decided not to mention Holden. She was obviously trying to deal with whatever emotions she retained on her own, no need to put more pressure on her. When—*if*—Holden became a problem, I would let Ezra know. "I've noticed a couple of the guardians haven't been around for a few weeks. Are they on assignment?"

Ezra stacked the papers on his desk before looking up at me. "This is not something that can be shared with anyone. Do you understand?"

I nodded, curiosity needling me.

"A steady stream of guardians have been disappearing. We are looking into it. I don't want you worried about them; stay focused on Olivia and keep a close eye on her. She is your only priority. But if any other guardians ask you about the missing people, do your best to diffuse their worries." He stood up. "I wasn't going to mention this, but as I've said, Olivia's *unexpected*. She could upset the balance of the elders—perhaps even bring an end to our way of life. There are authorities higher than our own, and we were left with no choice but to take her. Until we know where she stands we need to be careful. I don't know what her purpose is or what she is capable of. If she mentions anything," he searched for the right word, "out of the ordinary, let me know."

"Olivia wouldn't intentionally hurt anyone."

"I have no doubt you are correct, but nevertheless, can I trust you to keep an eye on her?"

I nodded. At least it made sense what he was worried about now. Ezra dismissed me and I transported back to my apartment thinking about my missing friends. Olivia was still shut in the guest bedroom. It had been a long, long time since I had a beautiful, angry woman locking herself in a room refusing to talk to me. I rather liked it.

SIX

Slamming the door behind me was a welcome release of some of the anger that had been building since I opened my eyes to this world. I wanted to scream, throw things, run away, but I kept it together. Quintus had no idea what he was stirring with his questioning and these clothes. *Christ, these clothes.*

I couldn't breathe. The room closed in on me. *Maybe it isn't too late to change my mind. Maybe I could just stay dead.* I sat cross-legged on the bed folding over to press my forehead into the mattress.

"You can do this, Liv. Just let him go." Fury erupted inside of me. It felt like it was just yesterday I was in the apartment. One instant, I was fighting for two more months with Holden, the next I was here, alone. I didn't even have a cell phone to call him if I wanted to hear his voice—*no, no thinking like that. You don't want to hear his voice or his lies.*

I didn't even know who I was angry with. Quintus for bringing up the dream? Myself for having it in the first place? Or Holden for, well, everything. The smart money was probably on number three. The pain and heartbreak of when I first woke up was nothing compared to the rage that was slowly taking over. Liar! Traitor! He'd betrayed me at his first opportunity. How could I have been so stupid? How did I not see him for who he was?

The worst of it was that despite everything, I still wanted to be near him. My heart almost stopped when I saw the shirt. The thought that this shirt might smell like Holden was almost too much. The dream, true to form, hadn't been a dream at all. For one shocking, glorious instant, the wonderful tidal wave of Holden drenched me, and God help me all I wanted to do was stay in it. Ripping myself away cracked the dam I erected against him and started the steady, slow stream of anger. I was still weak where he was involved. That would be the first thing I worked on conquering. Holden wasn't going to be my Achilles' heel, no matter what I had to do.

When my breathing calmed and I once again had a firm grasp on my emotions, I sat back up. I could do this stupid light thing. I just needed to focus and push the anger and Holden as far away from the surface as possible. I took some deep meditative breaths and focused inward as Quintus said. The light still didn't appear.

This is impossible.

I lay back in the bed with my eyes still closed and worked on clearing my mind completely. No thought whatsoever was the safest bet for me. That was when the light started to manifest. First it was hazy beneath my eye lids as if the light bulb in the room had gotten brighter. Then I started to feel it all around me. I slowly and calmly tried to collect it all together as Quintus said to do. I envisioned the light on my feet, then pictured socks.

The feel of something hard against my foot made my eyes fly open. Leaning against my sole was a hard flat sock without an opening, as if I'd photographed a sock and cut out the picture. I picked up the worthless image and drummed my fingers against the bed. More details seemed to be needed in my mental image.

I did it again, finding it easier to gather the energy now that I knew what it felt like. This time I pictured warm, soft, comfy socks—with proper openings. The socks I envisioned appeared on the bed, only they were five sizes too large. I tossed them to the side and tried again. It took several more tries before I mastered the sock creation. A joyous cry escaped my lips. I'd done it. I could do it! I was stronger than the emotions threatening to engulf me.

My fingers drifted over my new socks and felt the material. They felt like socks—nothing like what I associated with *light*. They were so real. . . . My eyes trailed back to my shirt. It wasn't quite right, not exactly like Holden's shirt. There was, of course, the lack of his scent, but also the material should have been soft like his touch and the shoulders wider. Fingering the hem, I imagined what the real shirt was like. Moments later the garment felt like I had just slipped it off his body and over mine—

Warmth washed over me, but I still kept him pushed far back into my mind. Having his shirt was one thing, having him in my head was another. The longer Holden didn't know I was back, the better. In fact, if he never knew, that would suit me just fine—not that he would come to find me or anything. He'd had his fun, what could he possibly want with me now?

I sniffed the shirt. It still didn't smell like him. It needed traces of his cologne, the clean scent of his soap, and the warm spiciness of his skin. Just imagining it sent lust spiking through my body. My cheeks flushed. I couldn't create fragrances, could I?

I chewed on my fingernail as I contemplated whether I was doing myself more harm than good. Perhaps the shirt would act as a fix—a patch—so I didn't obsess about the real thing. If I could just keep part of that time with him for a little while, could that really hurt?

I tried one of the layers of the smell first. Just his cologne. I thought about it clinging to the fabric and the way it occasionally drifted to my nose. A masculine, but not overpowering, scent. I pressed my face into the shirt, inhaling deeply. *Oh my God it worked.* I bit my lip, trying to decide if I should continue or if I should erase this lapse in judgment. My stomach twisted like a teenager sneaking out of the house for the first time.

I just need to smell him once—then I'll get rid of it. My concentration gathered even as my heart thumped wildly, knowing full well I was toying with something that should be left alone.

Liz Schulte

SEVEN

The pretty blonde in a turtleneck sweater looked as surprised to see me as I was her. She definitely wasn't the type for this sort of club. Her arms were crossed over her chest, and she took a step back at the sight of me.

"I thought you were dead," I told Juliet bluntly, watching her response to gage where we stood and how much she knew.

She quirked an odd smile, seeming to regain some confidence. "I am."

"You know what I mean."

"I do—just like you know what happened."

Obviously she'd made a deal. No matter where I went or how hard I tried, I couldn't get away from St. Louis. It found me wherever I ran. "Not the particulars. I didn't have a part in your transformation."

She tilted her head to one side. "But you played a large part in my transformation. You stole my best friend and set off the chain of events."

"Stole? That's going a bit far." What on earth was she talking about? Did she honestly believe all of that was about her? "And how did I set off the chain of events?"

"Semantics. One day Olivia and I were as close as can be and the next, well, there was you."

I couldn't help but to smile at the annoyance it still caused her.

"You killed Christopher which set off the chain of events that lead to my deal."

Christ, him again. My eyes rolled involuntarily at the thought of that douchebag. "What makes you think that?" I asked, still not giving her anything.

"I put the pieces together. Mark explained a few things and in retrospect, it was easy to see that a jinni was in the mix— once I knew a jinni didn't live in a lamp and grant wishes."

"Easy to see, is it?"

She flipped her hair back. "Well, yes, and obviously I was correct."

"Please, amaze me with your powers of deduction." I hoped I wouldn't have to kill her, but she was the only living person besides Olivia's mom who could link me to Olivia.

"One day Olivia was rational and normal, then she sees some stranger from across the room and suddenly becomes obsessed. Things like that don't really happen without a little push, especially not to people like her. Olivia started disappearing and keeping secrets. She didn't react as she should have to Christopher's death. . . . Hell, Christopher's death in general should have been suspicious. He was a self-absorbed asshole, but wasn't the type to kill himself." Anger radiated from her. "She stopped caring about me or what I felt. She was only worried about you. Joe breaking up with me for no reason just before all of that started—it was like dominos. Knowing Olivia like I did, I can't believe I bought all of that while it was happening."

"Check your emotions," I snapped. "I'm running a business here." She still harbored some resentment, but most of her ramble was poorly strung together accusations about Olivia. She didn't seem to know much, and if she told that story to anyone else, I would simply appear to have been doing my job. Juliet could live—for now.

She smirked. "You weren't as sneaky as you thought. My question is why didn't Mark tell me everything?"

I shrugged. "How was it any of your concern? They keep us on a need to know. It was probably easier to get you to agree to your deal not telling you. What did *Vetis* say?"

"Who's Vetis?"

I rolled my eyes. "The demon you knew as Mark."

She furrowed her brows and looked put out. "That he came for me. To help me. He was the only one who cared."

Either being a jinni was starting to break her down or she had absolutely no sense of self-worth and only saw herself reflected through other people. No wonder she liked Olivia, everyone's reflection through Olivia's eyes was far superior to their reality. "You believe that?"

Bitterness colored her expression. "What happened to Olivia?"

"She's dead."

"How do you know?" Her eyes narrowed.

"I watched her die." It was common for new jinn to be removed from their original territory. The only rule we had to follow in the Abyss was not exposing its existence, so she would've been sent far away. It was curious that she already managed to make it back this close to St. Louis.

"Good," she said with a self-satisfied smile that surprised me.

I understood she had a lot of misplaced anger towards Olivia, but I expected some deeper emotional connection to remain. The way Olivia reacted to Juliet's death and the way Juliet seemed pleased about Olivia's didn't add up. "I thought you were friends," I said, looking back at my papers in an effort to appear only half interested.

"I'm glad little Ms. Perfect is gone. I told him she would never agree to any deal, and he wouldn't want her if she did. She was always above such things. Olivia would have tried to hold me back. She would've recognized what he was, and she would've never understood what he could offer."

"Demons can be tricky."

"Olivia would've known." Juliet's face twisted in what I hoped was confusion. "How did she not recognize you for what you were?"

Because she had my heart, I thought and struggled not to moan. "Maybe she wasn't as good at judging people as you thought."

"Maybe." Her doubt was obvious. "Or maybe she was blinded by lust. She was really hung up on you, you know? I've never seen her like that with anyone. She would've followed you anywhere. You had her completely wrapped around your finger; you were the right person for the job. Fear would've never motivated her."

I smiled, but didn't comment. I wished Olivia had just been a job then I wouldn't be in this mess. Juliet's words nagged at me. Was all of what Olivia felt for me a product of my powers? Maybe I hadn't done as good a job holding them back as I thought. Maybe Olivia didn't love me at all, and that's why she didn't come back.

No. Our feelings were real. They were. Even time couldn't convince me otherwise. However, I was beginning to get the impression there was something else involved in all of this. I could only take so much coincidence. Something was moving all of us around like pieces on a chess board, and I didn't like it.

"Besides if she became a jinni, I'd have to kill her." Juliet's hiss brought me back to her still standing in my office.

"Really?" Like hell she would. She'd be dead on the ground before she even finished thinking the threat if Olivia were standing next to me.

"Absolutely."

"Even though she was your friend?"

"You know as well as I do, in the end, no one has friends."

Interesting. The change in her seemed extreme. I didn't know her well when she was alive, but Olivia couldn't have been best friends with someone like *this*, could she? It was getting to be ridiculous. First there was Christopher, then me, now Juliet. Did she purposefully surround herself with evil? "What did the demon offer you?"

She frowned. "Let's just say I found *Vetis'* terms agreeable."

"You don't want to tell me your agreement?"

"Do I have to?"

"You don't have to do anything, Juliet. What brings you here? How did you find me?" As much as I enjoyed having someone to talk about Olivia with, this conversation was only annoying me. I was bored with trying to get information out of her, and her bitter rambles told me little more than I already knew. Juliet may have been Olivia's best friend, but I was beginning to doubt she knew her at all.

"I work here. I take it you're the new boss." She smiled again. "I told Livi not to trust you."

"Ah, then you must be Julie Jones?"

"At your service." She did a mock curtsy.

I stared at her. Could I really allow her to work near me? Then again could I afford to send her away and not keep an eye on her?

"Have a seat." Juliet sat across the desk and waited for me to start. "Are we going to have a problem?"

"Whatever do you mean?" she asked, feigning innocence and batting her eyelashes.

"I mean I'm aware you've never liked me, and I could really care less. Do I have to kill you, or can you get past your hang ups and be professional?"

She laughed. "I don't dislike you, Holden. I thought you were wrong for Livi. And I was right, wasn't I?"

"So we can work together?"

"You bet."

"Great. I need you to let all the employees know that we're no longer in need of their services."

She arched a perfectly shaped eyebrow. "You're firing everyone?"

"After tonight, yes."

"What will be our front?"

"Something that makes money. I'm having the building renovated and we're expanding. That's all you need to know."

"Won't we need employees?"

"Surely we can do better than them," I said, picturing the filthy, toothless abominations we had working here. "We have the strength of hell backing us and yet we can't find one seductive woman? I find that highly doubtful."

"Will I still have a job?"

"You'll have some function here. How much or what type depends on you and how useful you can be."

"Oh, I can be very useful," she purred, leaning forward.

"Not what I meant." Juliet sat back in her chair and waited for me to continue. "Danica and I will have very different approaches as to how all of this should work. I was brought in to take over because she wasn't getting the results management expects. There'll be changes across the board. The jinn will be better streamlined with better reporting and checks will be initiated. And there's no reason the club should be losing money hand over fist. Both industries can be turned around."

"You want to organize agents of chaos? Lofty." She seemed a bit more normal, less irrational and embittered. Olivia was a button for her. Vetis must have really pushed their relationship through the grinder.

"I don't intend to saddle them with a lot of rules or paperwork, but the current system's ineffective. No one's checking on anyone else unless they have some sort of personal gain. You have no idea what jinn can and probably are getting away with right now." Just look at what I got away with.

She nodded. "Well, if that's your plan then you definitely need me."

"Why's that?"

"Public relations was my specialty. To get the jinn on board, and you'll need to, I'm your girl."

"I'm in the market for a good personal assistant."

"Oh, I can be *very* personable."

"I'm sure you can." I returned her smile, but ignored her overt flirting. It was annoying habit of ours. Jinn can't help but try to sexualize everything. It was settled, Juliet could be my personal assistant, and I could keep tabs on her.

"Don't tell the employees until after their shift. I want at least one productive night out of them. Call the ones who aren't here and let them know. I'll have the locks on the building changed in the morning and post a sign on the door in case someone doesn't get the message. I'll be meeting with contractors this week and will email a copy of my schedule to you. Be here for each of the appointments."

"Why?"

"I'm assuming the contractors will mostly be men. A pretty female jinni will have an easier time getting them to lower their bid then I would."

"You're much better at this than Danica."

"That's all." I waved her towards the door. "Wait, one more thing. Find me some boxes. We'll need to pack up this office. And leave me your cell number."

She wrote out a phone number on the back of an envelope on my desk. "What time do you want me here tomorrow?" My cell phone began ringing. I looked to see who it was before pressing ignore.

"Nine."

"Great. See you then, Holden."

When she was gone, I collected a few things I wanted to work on further and locked the office behind me. When I arrived home, I dumped the files on the counter and pulled my cell phone from my pocket to return the call. The phone rang three times before there was a tired voice on the other end.

"Hello?"

"Hello, Mrs. Martin."

"Oh, Holden! How many times do I have to tell you to call me Marge?" Her voice sounded a little livelier. "I'm so glad you called me back. I couldn't sleep again. I just think about Olivia all the time."

"So do I…" I trailed off, not knowing what else to say.

"I'm so glad she found you before—she had so few people she cared about…" Her voice faded, and I could hear the tears and the pain through the phone. Three years had not begun to fill the void Olivia left in this world.

"How was the rest of your day, Marge? Did you get out of the house?" I settled down on the couch, ready for a long conversation geared at distracting her from her grief.

Liz Schulte

EIGHT

After giving Olivia space for another hour, I knocked on the door. No reply came from the other side, so I pushed open the door slowly. She was sitting cross-legged in the center of the bed with her eyes closed. A hazy light shimmered around the top half of her body, twinkling like stars dancing around her. She lifted the collar of her shirt to her nose and inhaled deeply; pleasure and yearning showed on face. I cleared my throat to let her know I was here. Her eyes flew open, and she stared at me with a guilty expression.

"How long have you been here?"

"Just a minute."

"I figured it out."

"Figured what out?"

Olivia pulled a foot from underneath her and wiggled around her socked appendage with a smile.

"Ah—so what were you doing wrong?"

"I had to clear my mind. I had too many thoughts before."

"What were you attempting when I came in? The shirt looks the same."

She smiled tightly. "Oh? I must not have succeeded."

Olivia's face didn't wear lies well. "Did it still not smell right?"

Caught, she pressed her hands together and glared. "It *didn't* smell right. It does now."

"What did it smell like?"

"Nothing."

"What was it supposed to smell like?"

She sighed and fidgeted. "Quintus, remember the last time I wore this shirt?"

"Of course."

"Do you remember where I was?"

"Yes." I didn't understand what any of this had to do with odor.

"It wasn't *my* shirt." She looked at me with such directness and intensity I could practically feel her willing me to understand. I thought about what she was saying. It was Holden's shirt. How could I have forgotten Olivia standing in his apartment freshly showered, bare feet, and overly comfortable? I remembered Holden possessively touching her as if he had every right, like she belonged to him. I had put her in his shirt and it didn't smell—like him. I had inadvertently hurled her towards the one person we both needed her to forget.

"Oh," I finally managed to say.

"It's fine," her words blended together in a hurried lump, "really it is. It just threw me off a little to begin with, but I've rebounded. It might even be for the best."

I nodded slowly, grasping for any way this could be for the best. "Do we need to talk about him? I need to understand where you are mentally before we get involved in the training."

"No."

"Olivia—" I broke off as she shook her head insistently.

"There's nothing to talk about. He was part of my old life and isn't part of my current. I just want to forget, and talking about him won't help me do that. My actions may not necessarily support my philosophy," her brow and jaw settled into a determined line, "but we all have moments of weakness. In the grand scheme of things smelling his shirt is a rather minor infraction. I'm done though. No more."

"Can you even say Holden's name?"

Her eyes narrowed, but she said nothing. I shook my head more at myself than her. I wasn't being fair. She was trying, and I needed to remember that for her it was like no time had passed. Whether or not I liked it, she legitimately loved the jinni—anyone could see that—and eventually she would have to deal with that. I needed to be supportive. "I'm sorry. I shouldn't pry. You're doing wonderfully, but I need to be sure that you and Holden are done. You can't be together. Neither side will accept it. You understand, right?"

"It's done."

"Because the consequences could be grave—"

"I said it's done."

"I'll take you at your word," I said, but knew Ezra was right. I needed to keep an eye on her. When it came to Holden she was beyond reason. "Let's get out of here. You could probably use a break."

"Where?" She was immediately on edge and suspicious. She was a lot more relaxed as a human.

"Out. We'll have fun."

"Like a date?" She was already shaking her head no.

"No." This time I replied too quickly. This wasn't a date. It couldn't be a date. I was training Olivia; our relationship was one of student/teacher. That was it. "Just two friends."

She smiled a little. "Okay."

I took her to my favorite restaurant, tucked away from the city. It was the sort of place people spent hours for meals, not like Americans who rushed through everything, never taking the time to enjoy what is in front of them. I wondered if Olivia would be like that. Would she rush through the meal, or would she enjoy it and simply live in the moment? I made our order and smiled at her from across the table. "You must feel overwhelmed by all the change."

"Honestly, it's harder to remember that something has changed, you know? Granted everything looks different, and that helps, but everything feels like it happened yesterday—like I've been asleep."

"It's been over three years."

"Here. It's been over three years *here*, but it didn't feel like that there. They explained the time difference while I was making my decision, so I'd understand that my delay was passing a significant amount of time. I just didn't feel it."

"What was it like there?"

"You've been, right?"

"No, I made my decision before I died. I came back immediately."

"Oh, it was nice, bright, very peaceful and comforting, like being wrapped in your favorite blanket caught between waking and a dream."

"Were you tempted to stay?"

Olivia fingered the single flower in the vase on the table. "It wasn't really so much the temptation as it was not wanting to come back."

"Well, I'm glad you did." I still felt guilty for the part I played in her situation.

"Thank you." She picked up her wineglass and studied its deep crimson offerings, before sipping. I had a feeling she was only partially with me.

"Are you?"

"We'll see." She set her glass down a little too firmly and forced a bright smile. "Okay, enough of this. Distract me."

"Uh, do you have any questions about being a guardian?"

She scrunched her nose in distaste. "I have a feeling we'll be discussing that plenty. Tell me more about the Abyss."

"What about it?"

"What else exists besides the nymphs?"

I leaned forward and rested my elbows on the table so we could talk quietly. "Well, let's see. … There are jinn—as you know. And sprites, witches, warlocks, banshees, elves, gnomes, imps, succubus, goblins, harpies, pixies, sirens, trolls, muses—" I started ticking them off on my fingers as I went, then realized I'd never remember all of them. "There are really too many to name."

"That's fine. I don't know what most of those are anyway."

"Many are part of the faery family tree. With any of the big species, there are several different levels within. For example, you were a born Guardian and I was made a Guardian. I will never rise as high in our ranking as you could. It's the same for them. A nymph can never be a sprite, and a sprite will never be an elf."

The waiter brought by our antipasti with fresh olives, cheeses and meats. Olivia smiled at him kindly and waited until he left to continue. "An elf is considered a faery?"

"Yes, technically at least. They're the leaders of the fae. Elves govern all the different fae tribes throughout the Abyss. The forest elves were selected long ago as the governors of the race, but I don't really know the particulars—it's a very loose form of government."

"You know elves?"

"Of course," I told her, selecting a variety of food for my plate.

"What's a siren?"

"They're the same family as banshees and ghosts. They're souls that have been consumed by their own despair. They are low functioning, low reasoning creatures, and most of them have been confined in the last two hundred years due to the amount of attention they brought to our world. Every now and then one escapes though and wreaks havoc." I noticed Olivia wasn't eating so I nudged the plate in her direction, but she shook her head.

"How are they confined?"

"There are confinement centers within the Abyss—rather like human mental institutions. The centers are blocked completely from earthly contact, so they don't cause problems or draw attention to our existence."

She finally reached for a piece of cheese and nibbled on it deep in thought. "Witches? Is that like Wiccans?"

"No, witches are most similar to jinn. Unlike jinn they are essentially humans who haven't died, but like the jinn they have one foot in and one foot out. They can see some of the Abyss, but not all of it. They have enough power to make minor manipulations on both worlds."

"Magic?" The word from her lips was heavy with doubt.

"After all you have learned and seen, you still have doubts?"

She shrugged as I refilled the wine glasses. "What about vampires?"

"They exist."

"What are they like?"

"Evil."

"Okay, but what are they like? Are they allergic to sunlight? Do they hate garlic and crosses? Do they drink blood? How accurate was Bram Stoker?"

I swirled the wine in my glass before taking a sip, trying to remember which ridiculous legend Bram Stoker tied to vampires. "No. The legends you know will often be wrong. They are allergic to sunlight, but it is not a specific trait to them, all evil creatures are. Their souls have a reddish tinge, so they're easy to distinguish. I doubt they care one way or another about garlic or crosses, and they don't drink blood— they suck the life force from any creature they choose."

"Werewolves?"

"Once bitten by a werewolf, always a werewolf—you never go back to your human form. You'll forever be a wolf, one with animal instincts, human reasoning capabilities, and a highly contagious bite."

"So what keeps any one of these species from becoming over populated and taking over?"

"The created ones— werewolves, vampires, jinn, guardians—are normally kept in check by their own governing devices." The waiter brought our meals and told Olivia he had the chef make it very special for her. I smiled to myself. Her effect on people was already amazing. I couldn't wait to see what she could do when she tried. When he left again and she started eating, I continued to explain. "For example guardians are easy to make, but by our own rules only a certain number can be created every hundred years. But vampires are notoriously difficult to create so there is no reason to limit their numbers. Few vampires choose to create another. Werewolves are kept in check by bounty hunters."

"Bounty hunters?"

"Individuals of any species who are employed to capture or kill anyone who fails to live by the Abyss's one concrete rule: Do not draw attention to our existence. Werewolves have been on the open game list for over a thousand years. There was an outbreak in about 700 A.D. and ever since then their population has been forcibly kept in check. "

"So I could kill a faery and not be in trouble for it."

"Well, I am sure the other faeries wouldn't appreciate it and they could put a bounty on you, but yes, there is no universal law. No one wants to start a war with another species, so in general we all leave each other alone."

"Huh." She thoughtfully twirled her fork in her pasta. I could see her trying to work this entire world out in her head. "Oh. What about zombies?"

I laughed. "No."

She frowned at me. "I was technically dead and now I am alive again. Zombie." She pointed at her chest.

I laughed again. "If you insist, Firefly."

"I do." Her eyes gained an infinitesimal piece of their spark back. "So how do I recognize these creatures from people?"

I glanced around the restaurant; it was mostly humans. "It really won't be much trouble. First, many of the creatures will not look human. Second, those that do look human will be easy enough to pick out. After dinner we can go for a walk around the city and you can practice."

"Cool." She nodded. "Sometimes this all feels like a dream. Something I should wake up from."

"That feeling will go away."

She was quiet for a moment then raised her wine glass to me. "Here's to waking up."

The rest of the meal was uneventful. Olivia seemed happy to sit and talk, never making a sign that she was bored or wanted to go. She had a fast mind that jumped from subject to subject, occasionally blurting out a random sentence that would make me laugh. She seemed completely unconscious of how endearing she could be when she wasn't hiding behind her protective walls. It was like the real Olivia would peek out occasionally, just enough to dazzle me, before she darted back into hiding. Such an odd creature.

NINE

Quintus and I walked the streets of Rome. This wasn't the first time I'd been here, but it was the first time I saw it like this. Creatures of all kinds milled about the cobbled streets and sat in the outdoor cafés. Bicycles and scooters leaned against the faded buildings while music, laughter, and the smell of good food wafted through the air. The older the buildings and structures were, the more they sparkled making the city's lights dim by comparison. Quintus didn't say anything, letting me get used to the glittering spectacle before me. Rome was a hub of activity and cultural blending. We came to a stop in the heavily populated tourist area near the Spanish Steps.

"Guy sitting at the fountain?" Quintus nodded his head in the general direction of the man.

"What about him?"

"Human or non-human?"

"Dancer?" I kidded, before looking closer. He was tall and slender, with large ears and extremely sharp features. He stood with his arms crossed over his chest and his foot tapping against the sidewalk. I chewed my lip, trying to pick out the any strange features. "Human, I think."

"Correct. Woman sitting on the steps."

"Not human—what is she?" The woman appeared to be floating slightly above the step, but other than that she looked like anyone else walking around.

"Ghost."

"Are you serious? She looks so real."

"She is real, the same as you and me."

"Does anyone just stay dead?"

"Most people stay dead, because not everyone has the opportunity to come back—and not everyone takes it if they have it. She probably died before her time." The ghost caught us looking at her and smiled in our direction, appreciating having been noticed.

"What about her?" he asked, nodding towards a little girl skipping along the base of the steps.

"Faery?"

"Wonderful! How can you tell?"

"She twinkles like the nymphs."

"She's a sprite."

"Is she a child?"

"No, they all look like children, but they are a very old race."

"This is insane," I mumbled before I took my own turn pointing out everyone that wasn't human. Quintus showed me the ones I missed, but there weren't many. I could barely fathom that I'd existed my whole life believing I saw everything when there was a whole other world moving right along beside me.

"Quintus!" A female voice came from behind me. I turned to see Quintus enveloped in a hug by a woman I assumed was another guardian based on their similar glow. The man with her gave Quintus a less enthusiastic three pat hug. The couple's gazes flickered over me suspiciously as they greeted him.

"Guardians," I said matter-of-factly to Quintus, as if we were still playing our game.

Quintus smiled brightly, deep dimples pocketing his face. "Olivia, meet Ruth and Henry."

I offered my hand. "Olivia Martin, nice to meet you."

Ruth's expression changed as she watched Henry shaking my hand. "Guardians do not use last names. We keep no ties to our old lives, isn't that right, Quintus?" I let my hand fall to my side before turning back to Ruth smiling at her congenially, but something other than good will clawed at the inside of me. I had enough to deal with trying to keep Holden at bay. The last thing I needed was some catty guardian trying to put me in my place.

"Quintus?" Ruth demanded, forcing Quintus to stop looking at me, which was actually a bit of relief because it was becoming increasingly hard to maintain stoicism with Quintus trying to dissect me at every turn.

"You are correct, Ruth, but I haven't gotten that far in her training. This is only her second day as a guardian. I think we can cut her a little slack."

Henry's face was suddenly washed in interest. "So the rumors are true? *You* are training her?"

Quintus laughed loudly from his stomach, the sound filling the air around us. Holden never laughed like that. He hardly ever laughed, but when he did it was a soft chuckle that seemed to be meant only for me to hear. God I missed that. "Yes."

Henry whistled and Ruth said, "Must be nice."

I looked back and forth between the three of them and mentally counted to ten in hopes that I wouldn't overreact. Why was I so angry?

"You don't normally train guardians?" I asked, struggling to keep my voice normal.

"No, I'm usually in charge of the overall training program. There're too many recruits for me to train everyone personally, so the mentorship is split between different guardians in select areas where the new guardian may excel. We try to match them based on where their talents lay. Someday you'll probably mentor someone," Quintus said as if it was some great prize.

I hoped I didn't look as confused as I felt. Why the special treatment? Why was he training me?

"But you are a *born* guardian, so I guess you're 'special,'" Ruth chimed in snidely.

"You are different," Henry said, his eyes drifting over me in a way that made me want to slap him. I made no effort to hide the fact that I resented being treated like a prize cow at a fair. My light started retracting within me, the more uncomfortable I became.

Henry's eyes widened. "No one ever taught me to do that." He glared at Quintus, as if he'd been cheated in some way.

Ruth narrowed her eyes at me before turned her back to me and faced Quintus fully, as if she could cut me out of the conversation just by not looking at me.

Quintus adopted a kind yet authoritative tone. "Olivia has many talents, most of which are untapped. That is why I'm training her and not anyone else. And speaking of training, we're in the middle of a lesson, so we'll have to excuse ourselves." Both guardians nodded to him that they understood.

"Sorry to interrupt," Henry said, though he still glanced back at me as if I were a marvelous new toy.

"Have you seen Stephen recently?" Ruth asked Quintus.

Quintus shook his head and Ruth sighed. "Is it just me or does it seem like we're disappearing?"

Quintus shrugged. "I'm sure they are just on assignment. Nothing to worry about."

"I guess, but I still haven't seen Jeremiah either. See you later, Quintus." Ruth smiled, and she and Henry strolled away.

I arched my eyebrows. "Who's Stephen and Jeremiah?"

"Other guardians."

"Are they missing? Should we be looking for them?"

"Everything's fine. You just need to focus on training."

I struggled not to roll my eyes, but trusted Quintus knew what he was talking about. "Are all guardians like that?" I asked, nodding my head in the direction Ruth and Henry walked away.

"They're relatively new…"

"Hmph." Unless I was crazy, I knew exactly what Ruth's problem was. Henry was obviously just an idiot, but Ruth had purpose. "So do guardians date?"

"Date?" Quintus's face looked like someone had just grabbed his butt.

"Yes, you know, like go out together, have relationships."

"Well, yes, of course."

"So they're a couple?"

"No, siblings."

"Ah, that makes more sense." I nodded. "That explains her attitude."

"Her attitude?"

Quintus couldn't really be so blind, could he? "Surely, you know."

He shook his head, his face completely blank as if he had no clue what I was talking about. "Ruth *likes* you."

"Of course she likes me. We're friends."

"No! She *really* likes you." His head tilted to the side as he looked at me. "She has a crush," I elaborated.

Quintus laughed. "That's absurd!"

"Quinn, I may not have been a guardian for very long, but I've been a girl all of my life. I know when another girl is sizing up. She has a crush on you, and she thinks I'm competition—that's why she was rude. And her brother, well, he's just socially awkward."

Quintus looked back in the direction Ruth had departed, though she was long gone now, with a dubious expression. "I don't date."

I smiled. "Why not? You're a nice, handsome fellow. Quite the catch."

Quintus's cheeks colored beneath his dark stubble. He was like a big huggable teddy bear. He wouldn't meet my eyes as he started to talk. "I've lived a long time, Firefly. I've fallen in love many times, but it always ended the same, so I stopped dating. I cannot be proficient at this job and maintain a relationship."

I sort of understood what he was saying. Since I'd died, I was certain I'd never be with anyone again. Holden had ruined that for me. He collected my heart and kept it, leaving a gaping hole in my chest. "Who hurt you?"

"It's more a collective thing. I'm just bad at relationships. Our work here always will come first."

"Other guardians should understand that."

"I haven't only dated guardians."

"Really? I guess I assumed..."

"The first time I fell in love, it was with a human I was sent to help. She grew old and died while I continued on as I ever was. Next, I fell for an elf. Our lives were too separate. Where we were once of the same tastes and mind, over time we found we didn't know each other anymore. Eventually, there was nothing left to say."

"Have you ever dated another guardian?"

Quintus gave me a weird look that I couldn't quite interpret, then muttered, "Yes, the last time I fell in love, in fact—a guardian named Catherine. We were together for hundreds of years. We spent nearly every moment together. Everything was perfect."

"What happened?"

"She was killed."

"I'm so sorry. How?"

"A demon."

I closed my eyes remembering how it was. That poor woman. "How do you kill someone who's already dead?"

Quintus frowned. "Not easily. Guardians are reborn under the grace of God—and that's difficult to extinguish. A vampire, for example, could live on one of us for hundreds of years. A demon on the other hand, in its true form, can tear the life from us. It's excruciatingly painful and takes several days if not weeks," his voice cracked with emotion, "but it can be done. A powerful enough jinni could conceivably do it too."

There was something behind his jinn comment, but I didn't acknowledge it. I wouldn't be tricked into talking about Holden. "Did you kill that demon?"

"No. Revenge never gets you anywhere, nor does it make you feel better. Did your revenge for Juliet improve your life in any way?"

I turned away, my throat clenching with tears I refused to spill. Anger and bitterness were quick to fill the hole in my chest. "I didn't get my revenge, did I?"

"You had revenge. You just weren't alive to see it."

"You—you carried through with the plan?" The man who wouldn't avenge the love of his own life carried through with my plan of revenge? Let's just say I had my doubts.

"Holden and I both did."

My stomach plummeted. "I don't want to talk about it anymore."

"Olivia, may I give you some advice?"

"That depends on the advice. If it's about him, no."

"You need to find within yourself the grace to forgive. It's only by that you can heal."

Stubbornness reared its ugly head, and I gave him the stoniest look I could master. "I'm tired, we should head back."

"As you wish."

We walked back towards his apartment in silence, both of us caught up in our pasts until something caught my eye. There was an old man sitting on a stoop in the alley, his light slowly blinking around him like a beacon.

"Are you coming?" Quintus asked, but I pointed towards the man. Quintus came back to me, curiosity filling his eyes.

"He looks strange."

He glanced at the old, smoking man with the blinking soul. "How does he look strange?"

It was hard to tell if he was testing me or if he really didn't see it. "His light is waning. It isn't like other humans."

Quintus's eyes searched mine. "Human souls aren't visible."

I frowned. "You could see mine."

"That's different. You were a born guardian. It was always your path. Most humans come across as little else than neutral."

"That isn't true. It's there, just faint. I see it on everyone and that man's isn't right. He needs help."

Quintus nodded and rubbed his chin. "Then you should help him."

"Me? I can't help him. I don't even speak Italian."

"It won't matter. You can speak English to him, and he will hear Italian, just as you will hear English."

"How is that possible?"

"How did you expect to help people if you couldn't understand their language?"

It was too much. Now I could speak and understand any language? And he expected me to help a complete stranger? How would I get the man to talk to me, let alone let me pry into his life? "I don't know how. Can't I watch you?"

"He was shown to you. You must be the one."

I nodded and slowly walked down the alley, Quintus following a few feet behind me. I guess it was now or never, time to prove I could—or could not—do this guardian thing.

The man took a long draw on his cigarette, savoring the inhalation. I sat down. His mingled scent of whiskey and smoke burned my nostrils. Exhaustion radiated from the old man. He was sick—I could tell as surely as I could smell the smoke in the air.

"Hello."

Startled, his body jerked before he looked at me. "Well, I'll be, didn't even see you sit down, young lady."

I smiled. "Lost in your thoughts?"

He laughed bitterly. "And then some." He took another long drag on his cigarette, "What's a nice girl like you doing at a place like this?"

"Just passing through. How about you?"

"Coming to the end of the road."

"Has it been a good journey?"

"Not particularly."

The old man looked so sad with the quiet acceptance of the path before him. "Not everything works out the way we plan it." I tried not to think about the words before I said them. Forcing my brain to take a backseat, I realized I did still have a heart—and the poor, bruised thing ached with new pain. I let it lead, hoping it knew what it was doing.

"That's the truth, and that's why there's whiskey."

I laughed, but the sadness in the air around us was unmistakable. "Even though life may not work out the way we think it should, there's still," I took a deep breath, "there's still a point. We all have a role to play. Bad things happen to everyone, no one comes through unscathed. It's what you do after the bad happens that develops character."

"What if you're the one who did the bad things?"

"Then you have to find the forgiveness you need, whether it be from God, someone you wronged, or from yourself. Find your absolution. Start over. It's never too late. Mend your heart. Don't tear it to pieces with guilt and regret."

A fat tear traced the deep lines down his face. "I don't know how to start over."

"I'd start by forgiving myself and others. Then find a way to be happy." I took his hand, giving it a gentle squeeze. Energy flowed from me into him, almost like I was giving my own strength only it didn't hurt or weaken me. In fact, it felt wonderful.

Something very near to euphoria crackled against my skin and for the first time I felt I might be able to survive without Holden. Almost instantly the man developed a steady white aura that no longer flickered or faded. I smiled at him, patting the back of his hand. "It was a pleasure meeting you."

"Are you leaving so soon?"

"Yes, I have to go. Get some rest. Everything will be better in the morning. Good night."

I walked back down the alley, literally glowing. Quintus stepped in pace with me, all smiles. "You helped him. How does it feel?"

"How can you be sure I helped him?"

"Your light was surrounding him when you left. It's enough to allow him to see what is right. Whether or not he takes it is his choice."

"So he may not."

"True, but he might. We don't make decisions for people. We guide them towards what needs to be done and if need be, give them a push in the right direction. Well done, Firefly."

I smiled and linked my arm through his, riding high from the buzz. "It felt good."

"Of course it did. It's your destiny."

Liz Schulte

TEN

I didn't like Juliet. She met me at the club the next day and she talked, and talked, and talked—and smiled and flirted until I wanted to shove her in a closet and leave her there. I struggled with whether or not it was worth the aggravation to deal with her at all. Olivia was dead and having the constant reminder of her wasn't going to make my life any easier. Juliet's constant jabs about Olivia would eventually make me snap. I could feel the pressure building every time she mentioned her name in a less than flattering manner. It would've been so much easier just to get rid of her.

But I couldn't do it. I didn't owe Juliet anything. However, Olivia's pain at her death was still as fresh in my mind as it was three years ago, and I couldn't kill her when all Olivia wanted was for her to come back. But the worst part of having Juliet in my face all time? Seeing her live and in the flesh made me think I'd made the wrong choice for Olivia—maybe she would have done okay as a jinni. She would've had us both. I didn't buy for a second that Juliet would actually kill her friend. She may have been mad, but I knew from experience that Olivia was hard to kill when she was standing in front of you all eyes and innocence.

Juliet knocked on my office door interrupting my thoughts about Olivia. "Come in."

"They made a bid." She slid a piece of paper across my desk with a satisfied smile.

I flipped over the sheet and did a double take. "That's for everything? The additions, gutting, and renovation?"

Juliet's eyes twinkled. "Yep."

"We'll take it." I put the paper on top of the other bids she'd collected. When I looked up she was still standing in front of my desk. "Do you need something?"

"You aren't one for praise, are you?"

"If you need your ego stroked, you better run along after Danica."

"You don't know it yet, but you need me."

I shook my head. "Don't fool yourself. You may be useful, but you aren't necessary."

She put on a sorrowful look that I didn't believe for a second. Sure, Juliet managed to acquire an impressive renovation deal for the club, but she was being overly compliant. She didn't like me when she was alive, and I respected her for that. Now she was overly familiar as if we had known each other intimately for years. It put me on edge. She'd been Danica's right hand while she ran the territory. I had to wonder how much of that allegiance was left. Why hadn't she moved with Danica? Why did she want to stay? I hadn't seen the last of Danica, I knew that. She was a jinni and no jinni gave up their territory that easy. She'd come at me. I just needed to know which direction she was coming from.

"I'll prove it to you. Just wait."

"Why do you care? Why are you even still here?"

"I don't want to move, and your plans intrigue me. I want in on the ground level of whatever you're building."

"Then get out of my office and make it happen."

Juliet may have been a plant to scout out my weaknesses, that's what I would have done if I had a legion of devoted followers like her, but I could still use her to bring this business back to life. If she crossed me, not even her connection to Liv would save her.

Thinking about legions of followers made my eye twitch. I didn't belong in this position. I worked alone, had since I became a jinni. I didn't make friends with other jinn, hell I didn't make friends with anyone. I had no following. If Danica wanted to make a move against me, there was nothing I could do about it at this point. Sure Hell was on my side, but they expected their earthly involvement to be minimal. I needed a plan. I needed to become what I never wanted to be, a leader.

I picked up one of my newly organized folders for expenses from the previous year and began entering them onto a spread sheet. I only lasted a couple minutes before the monotony of the task and worry that I didn't have a plan made me put it to the side. I grabbed a few folders and tossed them into my bag and locked the office door. A new location would help me concentrate. All I had to do was come up with a plan before Danica came up with hers.

Outside the front door a human a few inches shorter than me with at least thirty more pounds of muscle leaned against the wall. His head snapped up at the sound of the door, and his icy blue eyes narrowed. "Who the fuck are you?"

He carried himself like a fighter—and it had been a long time since I had a worthy opponent. My fingers twitched towards a fist. The urge to beat something to pulp bubbled inside. I held him in my glare for a few seconds, daring him to make a move, then locked the door behind me when it was clear he wasn't going to.

"Look, I don't care who you are. I need to see that double crossing, dumb Dora who owns this juice joint. Tell me where she is, then scram." The way he spoke like a Humphrey Bogart movie made me rethink my human assessment.

"Gone."

"Figures she'd leave me holding the bag. Where'd she go?"

"She was removed from the region."

"She better keep that way. If I see her again…" He waved his fist in the air. "Who's the big cheese now?"

"That'd be me."

The man scratched his hand over his neatly trimmed ginger beard. "I don't know you."

"That makes two of us."

"Baker McGovern." He shoved his thick hand towards me.

"Holden Smith." The recognition of my name appeared on his face. Apparently, my reputation preceded me. "Now, what the fuck do you want?"

Baker laughed. "Quick to the point, I like that. I was a torpedo for Danica. Nearly got me killed, and she owes me a hundred thousand clams. I was lookin' to settle accounts."

The guy was talking seventy miles an hour and was like a step back in time. The twenties were a good decade for me, but I never picked up all the damn slang. "So you were her muscle?"

"I'm an independent contractor. This was the first time." He shook his head and his eyes flickered towards the building. "Could use some hair of the dog."

"I've yet to hear what you want from *me*."

"I was here for compensation."

"Then you've come to the wrong place. Move on."

"Not from you. Jeez Louise, you're a touchy one. What do you think I am?" His face twisted into a mildly annoyed expression. "I'll get that on my own. I just thought we could shoot the bull since you're the new boss, and I'm currently unemployed."

I wanted to leave, but I needed connections, especially if Danica was itching for a war. I sighed and unlocked the door. We went to the filthy bar. I grabbed a couple of the decent bottles of whiskey and two nearly clean glasses. I poured the drinks and slid his in front of him.

"You don't beat your gums, do you?"

I shook my head, wanting him to get to the point so I could leave.

"That's a good quality for a boss. My old boss, O'Banion, couldn't keep his mouth shut, got himself whacked."

"The O'Banion? Like the North Side Gang?" Baker had a satisfied smirk on his face at my recognition of his name dropping. I shook my head. "We aren't exactly the mafia, are we?"

"Not as well run or as organized, but pretty damn close from where I'm sitting. Let's just say it wasn't an adjustment when I stopped dealing with them and started dealing with you people."

"That's why I'm here, to clean up the mess Danica left."

"I'm surprised they took you off the front lines. You recruit more than anyone."

"How do you know that? What are you?"

"Word gets around—always has in Chicago. You just have to know where to listen. You came out of nowhere too. Where were you before here?"

"Tell me what you are first."

"Shifter. I'm a cleaner, but I thought about getting into hitting, more lucrative, unless you're stiffed."

"St. Louis."

"Can't believe I never heard of you before you showed up in Chi-town."

"Is there a point to this chat?" I didn't want to talk about the past; it would always come back to one person.

"My hands are getting rather idle, and you know what they say about that." He grinned. "I need an occupation for them."

"What makes you think I'm hiring? Especially non-jinni?"

"I haven't heard anything on the street about you being the new boss, so you must be really new or jaws would be waggin'. You need to surround yourself with people you can trust. It's the only way you'll succeed."

"I seem to be hearing a lot of opinions about what I need today." I tossed back the rest of my drink. "Even if you're right and I do need people, what makes you think I trust you?"

"I don't think you're dumb, of course you don't trust me. But I'm your man. Give me a shot. If I don't work out, kill me. I'm not a jinni, so I'm definitely not angling for your position. What do you have to lose?"

"Do our abilities work on you?"

"Only one way to find out."

I sent out some of the despair I saved and waited. Nothing seemed to happen. I touched the skin on his hand, and he shuddered but didn't change his expression. If he felt what I sent, he could handle it, which was impressive.

"Damn, you're strong," he said.

"You could feel it."

"Yeah, I could feel it, but shifters absorb emotion and personality when we change, so we're used to it. I've never felt despair and self-loathing quite like you sent out though."

"Hmmm." My phone started vibrating in my pocket, and I knew who it was. I reached down and hit end before glancing at my watch. "I have to go. Leave me your number, and I'll be touch."

Baker scrawled out his number and studied me with a puzzled expression. "What kind of dame has you wrapped around her finger?"

"Excuse me?"

"Only reason for a man to go running because of a phone call is a woman. I'm not judging, just thinking that must be *some* skirt."

"It's not what you think. Stay out of it."

I ushered him out and called my art dealer back.

"Did you get it?" I asked when Emile answered.

"They countered, Monsieur Falcone," Emile said in a heavy French accent.

"I don't care about the cost. Get me the piece."

"Yes, of course. Three more have been located."

"You don't have to ask. I want them *all*."

"Consider it done."

I hung up. My business ventures had better pay off or I'd have to dip into the retirement fund. I called Marge on my walk home, wanting to clear my mind and talk about the dame who would always have me wrapped around her finger.

Eleven

"So what's on the docket today, oh, captain, my captain?" Olivia leaned against the kitchen counter with her slender arms crossed over her chest as she watched me skeptically.

"We're going to try nudging today."

"Which is?"

"You nudge someone towards the correct path without speaking or making contact with them."

She tilted her head back slightly and her brows furrowed. "How exactly?"

I smiled. "That's what I'm going to teach you. Are you ready to go?"

"Let me check my schedule." She gave me an impatient look. "Looks like I'm all free," she said without moving.

Someone was in a bad mood, but I pretended I didn't notice. I led her to a café where we would find our first project. We settled in at a tiny iron table and Olivia looked around the room taking everything in with a serious expression. I let her go, wondering if she could pick up on the smaller needs as well as the larger one.

"Who are we here for?"

I nodded towards a young woman reading a book in the corner.

"What's her deal?"

"We need her to decide to leave here earlier than she had planned."

"Why?"

"Because that is what we were told to do. Sometimes the smallest change in someone's day changes everything. Perhaps she will be in an accident this afternoon if we don't. Perhaps she will meet someone she's supposed to if she leaves early . . . There is really no way of knowing."

"But what about her?" she asked, pointing towards a morose looking teenager sitting with a group of friends yet not interacting. She had a smoky darkness around the edge of her aura that wasn't right.

"She's not on the list."

Olivia looked back and forth between the two of them. "But she needs the help more."

"That's not our decision to make. She looks like a jinni has marked her, but we can't interfere. We have to trust our assignments are as they should be."

She stared at the other girl a moment longer, then nodded and turned her head back to one reading. "What do I do?"

"Make her feel like she needs to leave."

"Boy," she shook her head, "you aren't very good at this teaching thing, are you?

I laughed. "I like to see what you can figure out on your own. It tells me where your strengths and weaknesses are."

"Okay then." Her face scrunched up and a stream of light floated towards the unsuspecting girl. I had no idea what Olivia was doing, but I was curious about the outcome. The girl snapped her book closed, grabbed her purse, and ran out of the café. Olivia sat back in her chair with a pleased expression. "Easy enough."

"What did you do? Whatever it was it wasn't nudging. Why did she run?"

"I made her feel like she left the burner on at home." Olivia's eyes narrowed. "If you don't like my methods, then you need to tell me what you want. I'm sick to death of your cryptic nature."

"You shouldn't have done that. Now you have altered the course of her day. She didn't just leave the shop; you sent her with purpose. She might not be where she is supposed to be because you planted an idea in her head like a jinni. We do not do that. We only nudge." Her face went dark at the mere mention of jinn, and I hoped my scolding hadn't gone too far.

"Then how would you have done it?" Her nostrils flared as if she was holding back anger.

"You do exactly what it says. You *nudge*. You move closer to the person and send out the thought that she needs to leave. That's all. No light or real energy required. Just a gentle idea that will take root and make her move on. You don't inflict your will on others."

"Something you maybe should have given me direction on," she hissed and stomped her foot.

I sighed and ran my fingers through my hair. "You're right. I honestly didn't know you were strong enough to do that. Most guardians need to be very close to, even touching, someone to help. I don't really know how you did that."

Olivia looked down at her hands and asked so quietly I wasn't sure she actually said it, "Do you think it's something I could've learned from him?"

That was an interesting question. Could she have subconsciously picked up on how jinn use their abilities having been in such close contact with one for so long? Could this have been a special ability of hers or simply a byproduct of Holden? "There's only one way to find out."

She looked up at me.

"Tell me how to do what you did. If it is something you learned by being around Holden then I could learn it being around you." Even though his name made her cringe I wouldn't stop saying it. She needed to move past him and avoidance wasn't helping her do that. "If I can't, it's one of your talents."

"It's the same as the socks—only instead of directing a picture of something tangible, you send an emotion or smell or even an image. I sent her a picture of a house on fire and a thought about the burner still being on."

I chose a person a couple tables away and did as she instructed. When my thought hit the man, his brow furrowed a little but then he shook it off and went back to his paper.

"It didn't stick." I leaned back, puzzling over the issue. Olivia got up and walked out. It took me a moment to realize she wasn't coming back. By the time I made it outside, she was rounding the corner, fists clenched at her sides. I jogged to catch up and fall into pace with her. "What's going on in that mind of yours?"

She shook her head.

"If you don't tell me, I can't help you."

"You can't help me anyway."

"Sure I can."

"Really Quintus? Like you helped me before I was killed?" Her eyes flashed.

"It was different then. I couldn't help you."

She laughed bitterly.

"I tried to help you. I gave you good advice you wouldn't take. I told you to choose your destiny and you would be left alone, but you didn't. You chose the jinni, you chose to fight a demon, you chose—" I cut myself off before I said too much and made her angrier.

"Why didn't you do the light thing and get me out of the apartment? Why did you leave me in there? You could have taken me out at any time."

"No, I couldn't. You were human. I can't transport a human."

She stopped walking and closed her eyes. "I need to be alone for while. I know my way back."

"I don't think you should be alone—" Her expression turned from frustrated to murderous. I held up my hands in surrender. "Fine, fine." I watched her walk away and turned in the other direction. Though I couldn't be sure, I didn't think the way she could push people was Holden's influence. I could almost do it, so I suspected it was an elder trait. Olivia was trying so hard that I didn't want to ask Ezra and raise suspicion. If he already thought she could disrupt the balance, what would he think if he knew of her connection? But my alliance had to fall with my people and not with her. I couldn't risk being wrong. As much as I liked Olivia, I wasn't going to let her hurt the guardians. I made a mental note to mention the exercise on the next check in.

Instead of going home, I went to Paris to visit an old friend who was also on the low council of elders, Jace. I hadn't seen him in many years, but when you lived indefinitely it was easy for time to slip away. I needed someone I could trust to discuss this with, someone who perhaps would be able to see the picture more clearly than I could and who understood elder abilities. I found Jace milling around the Centre Pompidou, his face creased like worn leather and his permanently grey hair slightly longer than last time I had seen him.

Jace's skill with light manipulation was the best of any guardian I had ever known. Normally, however a guardian saw him or herself in death was how they looked after they were reborn. To change your hair required constant focus or it reverted back to as it was. The natural mental image was always the default—yet Jace changed his hair at a whim. He had mastered many things I could not over the years, and I always attributed it to his elder status, so I hoped he would have the answers I needed.

"Quintus, my dear friend. What brings you to Paris? I hear you have a very special trainee." Jace hugged me.

"That's why I'm here."

Jace's eyebrows lifted in surprise. "I'm honored, though I doubt I can shed much light on the issue. You've been training for a great number of years."

"But I never trained an elder. Her talents are more in line with yours than mine."

"Hmm. I did find it curious we weren't training her. Do you know why she was passed to you?"

"Ezra asked me to."

Jace frowned but nodded.

I explained everything that had been going on with Olivia minus the Holden part. Jace stared far off into the distance, drumming his fingers. "That does sound more like me, but I don't know if I can do those things either. However, I would guess they're elder traits. Do you know if she is high or low?"

"He hasn't told me anything. Would you mind trying to influence someone, just to see if you can?"

He shrugged and I watched a light snake out from him as it did from her earlier. His target tried to shake it off as mine had, but Jace persisted and pushed the light until the person got up and left.

Jace's shoulders slumped, and he looked weary. "It's possible, but the energy it takes is phenomenal. How did she recover?"

"That's just it. She was fine. It took her only seconds to achieve her goal, and she had no recovery."

"Amazing. I'd very much like to meet your pupil."

"Do you have plans tomorrow?"

He nodded, so we worked out another time to bring Olivia to him for a bit more focused training. "She doesn't know, so don't mention what she is."

"She doesn't know she's an elder? Why ever not?"

I sighed, not knowing how much I could share. "Ezra didn't exactly say. He said he was worried about her throwing off the balance."

Jace rolled his eyes. "I bet he is."

"What is that supposed to mean?"

"Judging by his actions, my guess is she's high council. Right now they're stalemate on many issues. Since there are only four members, the council is often split on decisions. If Ezra doesn't know whether she'll take his side of arguments, of course he'd be worried about her falling onto his opponent's side."

I laughed. "If they only knew Olivia and her lack of decision making, they would feel perfectly safe in her addition."

"You like this one." Jace's eyes sparkled as he looked at me.

"She's a nice enough girl."

"No, that's not it. You actually like her. I haven't seen you so interested in someone since Catherine."

"I'm simply interested in what she can do. When will I ever have another opportunity to get to know a high elder this well?"

"Plausible excuse, but I'll judge for myself when I see the two of you together. Have you heard the rumors about our missing friends?"

I didn't know what Jace knew, but Ezra was clear. "I'm sure it is nothing. I am not concerned." The lie burned in my throat. I was concerned and hoped the situation was resolved soon.

Jace nodded. "Safe journey, my friend."

"See you Wednesday." I transported directly to my apartment and was glad to see Olivia's light was on in her room, though the door was closed. So much power and so unwilling to use it. I would find a way to get through to her.

Liz Schulte

TWELVE

I was a fraud. I was using jinni methods, my decision had been right. I should've been a jinni not a guardian. I knew it. I wasn't going to be a good guardian. I couldn't even nudge someone correctly. I didn't think I'd be good at hurting people, but I'd been so angry since I got back, maybe I was wrong. Quintus had always been a calm, relaxing presence around me, but I felt anything but calm or relaxed. I was always on the verge of being caught, figured out. How long before they realized they made a mistake and I wasn't supposed to be here.

Did they know what I almost chose? Did Quintus know that if Holden had not been quite so quick on the trigger, I wouldn't be his problem at all? Helping the old man felt great, felt like maybe I was in the right place. But what we did today felt meaningless. I didn't care if I made the reading woman leave or not. I understood what Quintus was telling me and even why we were doing it, but I didn't understand why I had to help her and not the person who really needed my help. . . . Doing that just made me a bigger fraud. I was never going to be an obey-without-questions sort of guardian. I hoped they knew that.

I wandered the streets until I was good and lost, but I didn't care. I didn't want to go back. I sat on a bench and stared out into the ancient city. I wanted to talk to Mom and Juliet. I wanted my life back. I didn't want to be a soldier in the guardian brigade. There were a lot of things I wanted—but I couldn't have any of them, all because of one person.

I welcomed the anger back because it drowned the sadness and gave me the will to master this. I had no illusion I could avoid Holden forever, so when the time came to see him again, I would be ready. I wouldn't be defeated by my feelings for him. It took my constant concentration to keep his thoughts locked out of my mind, and I couldn't sleep much and maintain this privacy. A little grumpiness, however, was better than hearing how he played me or worse falling back into his arms to be hurt again.

A movement to my left interrupted my thoughts. I looked up and saw a young man close on the heels of a young woman who kept looking behind herself nervously. I hopped up without thinking and headed for the man. His light was growing darker as resolve was setting in. I put a hand on his shoulder, and he whipped around startled, knife in hand.

I blinked at the thrill of the rush I felt at the situation. I let my light pour into him, combating the darkness. "Why would you want to ruin your life?" I asked him quietly.

He stood staring at me dumbfounded until the knife fell from his grip. "Where did you come from?"

"It doesn't matter. Killing her won't make you feel any better."

"That's my girlfriend. She just left my friend's place. What will make me feel better?"

"Moving on. Killing her ruins your life more than it does hers. But if you leave her and find happiness somewhere else, then she'll always see what she lost." I didn't know if my argument was a good one or even a pious one, but it was the only thing I could come up with on the fly. I hadn't been prepared to talk someone out of murder. The darkness in him was still strong, the energy I fed him was only enough to keep it at bay. In a split moment I made a decision, I pushed him just like I had the girl in the coffee shop. I sent him the feeling that he didn't love his girlfriend as much as he thought.

He shook his head, but stopped struggling against me. The darkness receded until it was nearly gone. "You're right. You're absolutely right!" He smiled and threw his arms around me and headed in the opposite direction.

"What do you think you're doing?" a voice snapped from the alley fifty feet away. A shadow of a woman approached me. As she came closer, I saw the darkness swirling around her and I wondered if she was a jinni. She was skinny and brittle looking. Her face was stark and pissed off and there was something reptilian about her eyes. Was this what Holden would look like now? "He was mine."

I looked back in the direction the man went and smiled to myself. "Not anymore."

When I turned back towards the woman, her open hand met my face. I clasped my stinging cheek, shocked. I'd never been in a fight in my life. The crazed jinni didn't seem to care as she lunged at me, hands curling around my throat. She ranted on and on about how much planning and work I ruined. I fought against her to no avail, and as I struggled to breathe and my chest burned, anger filled me, lining my spine with steel. One jinni already killed me; I wasn't about to let another do the same. I stopped flailing and hit her as hard as I could on the side of the head. The blow didn't do much besides rock her slightly to the side. She slammed my head against the sidewalk. As a Hail Mary, I sent her a light suggestion to release me and to my amazement she did. She looked at her hands in horror as they blistered.

She fell off of me and scrambled away. "What did you do to me?" she shrieked.

I watched, just as confused as she was, while nasty boils continued to grow over her. I hadn't done anything. I just wanted her to let me go. I had no intention of hurting her, but the fact that for the first time in my life, I wasn't completely helpless smothered any guilt I had. I didn't know what I did, but I was glad I could do it. It made me feel alive, it made me feel as if I had choices all of a sudden, but most importantly it felt right—different, but equal to how helping the old man felt.

I pushed myself up to my feet. "Leave this city and don't come back." I told the jinni before walking away rubbing the back of my head. I felt good, strong. Maybe I couldn't nudge, but I could make a difference my way.

I couldn't tell Quintus what I did because he wouldn't approve, so when I got back to his apartment I was thankful he wasn't there. I closed myself in my room and looked in the mirror. The red scratches and finger prints were beginning to fade, but there were still signs I had been in a fight. I showered and sat on the bed meditating. I pushed back the anger that filled me during the confrontation and used it as a further barrier against Holden.

Something new occurred to me once my mind was clear. Maybe I hadn't picked up how to do this from Holden, but I *stole* how to do this from Holden. He was in my head and I was in his. Maybe I could do what the jinn did simply because of our connection. It made sense that anger would feed the ability. I lay back contemplating this. That was why it felt right— because it felt right to him. There was definitely a piece of me that didn't believe hurting her was okay. Even though she attacked me and even though she was a jinni, part of me had just wanted to walk away and not hurt anyone. If that was the case then the ability was definitely something I shouldn't use. If I drew too much on the connection, it would alert him to my presence and as far as I could tell he had no idea I was around. I was a guardian now, and I should follow their rules, shouldn't I? Hadn't I learned my lesson about messing around with darkness? Whatever it was I couldn't risk using it again.

I sighed, disappointed that my little bit of freedom was already taken away. I cursed the day I ever met him. My life, or after life, would be so much less complicated without him constantly factoring in. I rolled onto my side annoyed in general. I just wanted to go home.

THIRTEEN

Putting Baker on retention may have been the smartest thing I had done. He knew absolutely everyone in the Abyss. He called himself my underboss, which was fine with me. He even drew me a diagram about how I needed to structure the "organization" if I wanted to succeed where the others had failed. He was wealth of knowledge and pegged Juliet as a threat right away which made me like him more. He said I needed to compartmentalize. If one person knew too much about my business, they could take over, but if everyone only knew a piece, then I had security; himself excluded since a shifter could never lead the jinn.

Juliet, at my insistence, was a caporegime, or captain, for the club section of the business. Baker argued that I needed people I could trust in these positions, and I told him I wanted her close so I could keep an eye on her and what she was plotting against me. Plus I liked to be able to control the information she had and could spread. I also had to make sure she didn't get suspicious about my real feelings for Olivia. Perhaps I was being overly cautious, but perhaps not.

He shrugged. "I guess you'd know a thing or two about deception," he said and dropped the subject, though he still kept an eye on her and mentioned anything he saw as out of the ordinary which I appreciated.

We still needed a captain for the jinn and one for the business side of things who would keep me looking legitimate. The jinn captain would have to be another jinni and one who already had soldiers. Baker suggested a human for the business side to find me new investments and corporations to run my money through, so the club and Juliet would be as separate as possible. He chose a human because we could keep the human secret, and he would be easily influenced to do as we want and never rollover. I hadn't exactly been a tax paying citizen before this, nor did I ever intend to be, so I needed someone who could legitimize me if someone started digging.

Baker set off to find us a businessman and my first responsibility was to make a connection with a jinni. Baker knew a few jinn who had beefs with Danica and directed me to their local hangouts, but jinn were a notoriously closed group. We didn't trust each other; we trusted outsiders even less. I had no idea how to do this. I didn't make friends, and I sure as hell didn't reach out to people. The thought of asking for help made me cringe. I sat sprawled on my couch, staring at the wall, trying to decide how to approach this. If another jinni came to me for help, I would see him/her as weak. I couldn't afford that; our relationship needed to appear mutually beneficial. If a jinni came up to me and struck up a conversation, I'd be suspicious and think they were angling for something I had that they wanted. I wouldn't trust anything the jinni said or did, and I certainly wouldn't enter into a partnership with said jinni. How would someone get me to help them?

The sound of the clock ticking on the wall was like a metronome. I couldn't think of anything but the sound of it, as I tried to figure out what I had always avoided. What could I do that other jinn couldn't do? Just like humans, some jinn were better suited for some areas of life. Not every human could be a doctor and not every jinni could work the subtle influences where I excelled. I needed to find a brute out of the possible candidates Baker chose. Someone I could help and would want me to keep helping him. If I made myself indispensable, he would protect me and my interests with his life.

The first jinni I went to scout was Mears Olsen. He looked like a mean fucking giant. He was enormous. He was at least half a head taller than me and had to go a good 350; he didn't look soft either. His head was hairless and his black eyebrows came to a point in the center of each brow giving him the constant appearance of being pissed off. Part of me wondered if I could take him and was itching to try. Mears was surrounded by leather clad lackeys the whole time I watched him in the biker bar. I couldn't figure out what his specialty was until half way through the night a brawl broke out like none I had ever seen. It wasn't punches being thrown—people were being stabbed with pool cues, four or five guns were fired into the crowd, and tables were set ablaze while he sat in the center and laughed. His eyes connected with mine when he noticed I wasn't participating. He tilted his chin slightly, acknowledging that he knew I was a jinni. I stood slowly and finished my drink before I walked over to him, easily dodging the mayhem.

"What do we gain by this?" I asked him as I sat at his table and a barstool flew past me through a plate glass window.

"Who da fuck cares?"

I shook my head and stood up. "Clean it up now or suffer the consequences."

Walking outside, I pulled my phone from my pocket. He wasn't right for the job. He was a brute, but he had no sense, no game plan, no big picture. He was an idiot. I texted Baker that Mears wasn't going to work, then sensed Mears behind me, wrath still radiating from him.

I side-stepped his slow swing easily without even having to look back. He had so little control I could tell exactly where he was at any moment. I could have fought him blindfolded. He was slow and sloppy, obviously depending on his looks to frighten people. He pulled a switchblade out of his pocket and I shook my head.

"You should have stayed inside and did as I told you."

"Come on, pretty boy. I've been needin' a new bitch."

He took a clumsy lunge at me, and I disarmed and hamstringed the big fellow before he even realized he was outmatched. He lay on the ground bleeding and holding the back of his knees. I squatted beside him, laid hands on his bald head and sent a blinding pain that made it feel like his skin was being peeled off with rusty, dull razorblades. I let him jerk and spasm until his eyes rolled back in his head, then I let go. "Next time you cross me, you'll wish I sent you to hell."

"Who are you?" he croaked, his voice hoarse from yelling.

"Holden Smith, your new regional commander, and I'm not impressed." I walked away satisfied with the encounter. I may not have found my new captain, but I'd established dominance, and he would think twice before challenging this pretty boy again. Asshole.

The next contestant was Phoenix Harbolt. I found him in a Goth punk club. I took my seat amongst the plastic-garbed, eyeliner-wearing menagerie of people who all wore identical woe-is-me expressions. In fact, I'd felt that heavy burden of self-pity and discontent blanketing the room as soon as I walked in. It was subtle, but intense and relentless. Already Phoenix was more interesting than Mears, and I hadn't even laid eyes on him.

I sat casually observing while people wallowed in self-pity and paid for the right to do so. He didn't even have to go look for targets. They sought him. I finally caught sight of him at the back of the room with an arm around two girls wearing black lipstick and not much else. He was short, probably no more than 5'8, with a sharp nose, a hair lip, and heavy eyebrows. I waited to see what he would do, how he would perform, but nothing changed. He simply maintained the room's despondent feeling and I bored quickly. I followed one of his patrons as they left the bar, curious about how strong the influence really was. Did Phoenix just make them depressed while they were in his presence or was it lingering? What was his recruitment and mortality rate? Why did other jinn follow him?

I caught the girl I was following by the arm and smiled at her letting some of my own energy flow. Her scowl immediately vanished, along with the downtrodden posture. "You hang out there a lot?" I asked, pointing back to emo heaven.

She nodded. "A couple times a week, but I never saw you there. I don't know how I could have missed it." She ran her fingertip down my chest.

I gave her a quick once over, but she wasn't worth my time. I was only interested in wholesome these days. Olivia had spoiled me. I turned and walked back into the club, ready to throw Phoenix a curve ball. I stood opposite of where he'd been and let the lust gates crack open. Slowly but surely it spread out from me and towards him. The petting and groping spread across the room and threatened an orgy, but slowly the wet blanket of despair became heavier and heavier until it started to put out some of my fires.

I released another small amount of sexual passion and once again took the upper hand. Minutes later, when lust had firmly taken over, and I was about to leave, I felt a strong assault directed solely at me. Olivia's face popped into my mind, and I wanted to fall to my knees and weep at my loss. I didn't want to wear eyeliner or anything, but it was a strong attack, especially on a jinni of my age and strength.

I walked Phoenix's way. He scanned the crowd with irritation, trying to find me while his two female companions made out.

"You're welcome for that, by the way," I said, nodding towards the two girls.

He looked down at them as if he hadn't noticed, then back at me. "Holden Smith, I presume."

"Does my reputation precede me?"

"I heard you were in the area and lust was your strength. I took a guess."

"So, you are what? Sloth?"

"I prefer *acedia*."

"What's the point of all of this? What's your gain?"

He shrugged. "Why go looking for people when they can find me and bring their friends, then pay me for the opportunity? I can throw one stone and hit a whole lot of birds."

"How's your recruiting?"

"Not as good as yours, but I do all right."

"I can imagine. Your group control is marginal and shallow, but that was an impressive individual attack. If you were more focused and hands on in your assaults, I bet you could double your recruit stats for the month by the end of the week."

"Why are you here?" he asked, annoyed.

"I'm the new North American commander. I'm checking out the talent." I started to walk away, not sure about him. He didn't seem strong enough for a captain, but he was intelligent.

"What's in it for me if I double my recruits?" he asked as he caught up with me at the door.

"What do you want?"

Phoenix tilted his head back and thought for a moment. "A mentor."

The words, "I don't mentor," stuck on my lips. I wanted to say it because it was the truth, but then again, teaching the kid a few tricks would be a small price to pay for an ally. "How old are you?"

"85."

I nodded. "If you double your recruits, I'll teach you some things. Come by and see me."

I left and headed to my final stop, Isaac Cicero. Cicero was the hardest of the three to get to. He ran with society, the rich and jaded. While most jinn lived outskirts, Cicero was right in the thick of it. I charmed my way into the private party then blended the best I could while I looked for him. Before I could make a complete round two bouncers, vampires if I had guess, took me by either arm and led me to a back room where Cicero sat behind a large desk.

"You weren't on my guest list."

"True."

"Since you are a fellow jinni, you have two minutes to tell me what you want before Frik and Frak remove you from the premises."

I shook my head. "That doesn't work for me." I twisted my hands around so I could clasp their wrists, and I directed all my energy into one long and glorious release with the single thought of pain. As I held on, boils rose on their skin and their mouths moved in silent screams. When I had enough, I reached down and snapped both of their necks, leaving two ashy piles on the floor.

Cicero leaned back in his chair and swallowed hard. He wore a shiny silver suit, had a slightly receding hairline, and had on a pair of sunglasses. "What is it that you want?"

"I don't want anything." I sat down in the chair across from him. "I'm the new regional commander."

"Ah." Cicero studied me from behind his glasses. "Very interesting you chose to come here."

"Why is that?"

"My talent isn't flashy enough for most jinn."

"I understand the benefits of understated. Holden Smith." I offered him my hand.

He took his feet off the desk and shook my hand. "It is nice to meet you, Mr. Smith."

"Likewise."

"What are your plans for the region?"

I smiled slightly. "The organization has gotten sloppy. I plan on cleaning it up, putting in new hierarchies. Many changes have to be implemented to produce the results Hell desires."

"And why did you come to see me?"

"I'm looking for people who can understand my vision for the future of the jinn."

His eyebrows rose above his glasses and his lips twitched. "And you are here to ask me?"

I shook my head. "Nah, like you said. I'm just looking." I stood up. "Have a good evening, Mr. Cicero."

Cicero needed me. His power and friends were strong, but he wasn't. He would benefit from my protection, but could I benefit from his influence?

FOURTEEN

I couldn't figure out what was happening with Olivia. She was quiet for the entire week, only speaking when asked direct questions. Her eyes seemed far away all the time, but she still put in the effort to learn everything I told her. She had a lot of trouble mastering nudging which frustrated her and made it even harder for her to do it. I kept explaining she had to relax and find her inner peace to nudge with any consistency, but still it evaded her.

Her mastery of light manipulation was light years ahead of where other new recruits were after only a week or so, however. Maybe it was her photographic eye, but she seemed to have no problem recreating whatever she saw in wonderful detail. I anticipated light travel wouldn't be much of an issue for her either so I planned to tackle it as soon as we got her acceptable at nudging.

"You are going to meet someone new today," I said.

Olivia's head snapped up from her coffee like she had forgotten I was here. "Who?"

"A good friend and fellow guardian, Jace."

"Why?" Her eyes narrowed as she studied me.

"I think his talents align closely with yours. He is very proficient at light manipulation, and he can even do the direct influence like you."

Her entire face lightened. "How do know?"

"I went to see him after you left that day. I figured if any guardian could explain what you did, it would be him."

"And this is the first I'm hearing about it?"

"You haven't exactly been in a talking mood, have you?"

Olivia nodded and looked down. "Sorry. I have a lot on my mind."

"I can't force you to talk to me, Firefly, but I think you should consider it. I can help you."

She blinked and leaned back in her chair. "When do we leave?"

I winced. "Would it be easier for you if someone else trained you? Perhaps I was not a good choice?"

She shook her head. "It's not you. I just need to deal with some things on my own. If it makes you feel better, I wouldn't talk to anyone about it. You're fine. I don't mean to be difficult."

Relief filled me. I didn't want her to go. As difficult as she could be, it was nice to have her around. I had been alone too long and Olivia and her moods were a breath of fresh air in a room that had gone stale. "Well then, shall we be on our way?" I held out a hand to her. She laid her soft hand in mine, and it occurred to me that I might miss transporting her places once she could do it herself. I dismissed the notion immediately—Olivia was, and could be, no more than a pupil to me.

Jace was waiting for us in a wine bar off of the Boulevard de Port Royal.

Olivia looked around the new city, a small smile toying at her lips. "I love Paris."

"After you." I motioned her inside. She walked directly to Jace's table, recognizing him as a guardian.

Jace looked startled at first, then smiled widely at the two of us. "You must be Olivia. Well, I'll be, I thought you were human," he said, ignoring her outreached hand as he hugged her. Olivia had been repressing her light all week. I didn't know why, and she didn't want to tell me.

Olivia hesitated a moment then hugged him back. "It's nice to meet you. I haven't heard anything about you."

Jace laughed. "Yes, Quintus has done a good job of hiding you from the rest of us as well."

She glanced back at me, then returned her gaze to Jace. "That may not be entirely his fault. I haven't been feeling overly social."

Jace patted the chair next to him and motioned me to sit down across the table. "It's completely normal," he told her. "It takes time to adjust to life like this. The human in you just wants everything to be as it was, but nothing is the same."

"Exactly."

"This means you don't feel much like you belong. I felt like an impostor the first several years as a guardian. I still feel like that occasionally."

Relief washed over her and some of the tension in her shoulders eased. Jace hit the nail on the head, but how could Olivia not feel like she belonged? She was born into this. I didn't understand her at all.

"And here I thought I was the only one," she said.

Jace patted her hand and looked over at me. "She's lovely. I can see why you like her."

Olivia frowned at me and her shoulder stiffened again.

Jace looked back at her. "No, dear, I only meant that Quintus thinks highly of you. I've known him a long time. I can tell when he thinks a recruit has promise."

"But I'm not a recruit. Apparently, I was born."

Jace flicked his eyes at me, and I shook my head enough for him to know not to say anything. "Yes, you were and you'll be wonderful. I hear you already have impressive talents."

Olivia blushed. "I don't know about that. I can't even nudge."

Jace moved his hand like he was brushing her doubts from the air. "There are more important things than that. We all have our strengths. I would like to see yours. Can you demonstrate?"

"What?" She looked back and forth between the two of us suspiciously.

"The suggestion of course."

She pressed her lips together. "You can do it too, right."

"Yes." Jace nodded to her.

She rolled her neck and looked around the bistro until her eyes honed in on one person. She took a nervous breath and a stream of white light no bigger than a piece of yarn threaded its way through the room to a middle aged woman sitting along the window. It wrapped around the woman three times and a second later she had her phone in her hand, dialing. Olivia broke eye contact and let the light dissolve. "That's it," she said with a shrug.

"What did you do?" I asked.

"Had her call her daughter."

"Why?"

"She was upset about something having to do with her, so I eased those emotions and pushed her to call."

Jace still watched the woman. "How do you know she was upset with her daughter?"

Olivia shrugged. "I don't really know. That's just what it felt like. It was vague but there."

He finally looked back at her. "And how do you feel?"

"Fine."

"Not tired? Drained?"

"No. Why? Should I be?"

"I don't know. Can you explain what you do?" Jace smiled widely at her then at me. "This is marvelous." He seemed excited to be learning a new trick, while Olivia looked horrified.

"You said you could do this. You said—" her eyes filled with fear and she shook her head.

"I can, just not as well as you. Tell me your technique."

She looked hesitant and chewed on her lip, but nodded. "Are you sure this is normal?"

"It isn't something everyone can do, but you aren't everyone else, are you?"

"It can't hurt to try, Olivia."

"Yeah, right." She made a ponytail holder appear in her hand and pulled her hair back from her serious face. "I focus on the person and study their aura to see how it looks wrong. Then I reach out for their mind, feel their stronger emotions and blend my own thoughts with theirs. Does that make sense?"

It didn't make any sense at all. I couldn't see human auras or feel their emotions enough to decipher where they were directed, but Jace nodded slowly and looked around the room. He pointed towards a blond man in the corner. "Like him?"

"Yeah," she said. "Do you see it too?"

"Tinged in red, angry about something." Jace stared at him with his own serious expression. "I can't really tell what." A wider band of light came from Jace and went towards the guy. When it reached the man, unlike Olivia's which wrapped around the person, Jace's light went right into his chest.

Olivia nodded encouragingly. "It's fading."

"But it's so draining."

"You're sending too much."

"I don't know how to control that."

She looked at me helplessly.

"How do you control it?" I asked her.

"I don't know. I just do."

"Pull back, Jace. We'll talk through it," I told him.

Jace turned back, deep frown lines creasing his tanned face. "It's the fine tuning I'm missing. How are you so proficient so fast?"

She shook her head, her cheeks coloring. "I have an idea." She took Jace's arm and directed her attention to the man. "Can you feel what I'm doing?"

He closed his eyes while she sent her suggestion. When she finished, Jace nodded. "I think I understand."

We left the bistro in search of other people, and Jace practiced all afternoon until he was doing well enough that he stopped questioning Olivia and she started questioning him.

"If you see the auras as I do, do you ignore those who need help unless they are *assigned* to you?"

"I wouldn't know how to help them. You seem to sense their emotions far more clearly than I am able. I can only see a little coloring here and there."

She nodded. "Is that a born thing?"

"Probably," I answered quickly before Jace could tell her he was born too.

"Is it possible that it's not? That it's something else?"

"What else could it be?" Jace asked her.

Olivia walked off without answering. I assumed it must have something to do with Holden since that was her gut reaction to anything having to do with him, but I couldn't imagine what he could have to do with this. Jace looked at me and I shrugged. "She gets moody sometimes."

"Definitely an elder trait." Jace laughed and we walked behind her. "She would be an excellent companion for you, Quintus."

"You know I cannot."

"Why the devil not? She's smart, nice, you like her, and she would be a powerful ally someday. A little moody, but I know none so patient as you."

"Her destiny is greater than me."

"Yes, but she can make up her own mind. She's in the position to choose whomever she wants."

"Then she won't choose me."

"Perhaps because you haven't tried."

I watched Olivia and wondered if maybe Jace had a point. Maybe the best way to help Olivia forget Holden was to give her another option.

FIFTEEN

I read the article for a second time just to be sure before I stormed towards Quintus who was reading at the table. I slammed the paper down in front of him. He looked up and raised his eyebrows.

"Right here." I pointed to the small article on the bottom corner of the page.

Quintus set his book to the side and looked at the newspaper. He read for a few moments, then looked up at me. "That's very sad."

"That's it? That's all you have to say?"

"What else would you like me to say?"

"That you were wrong. That you should have let me save her. That would be a place to start."

Quintus looked at the paper closer. "The girl from the coffee shop." I nodded to keep from yelling. "It wasn't our place to interfere. We can't save everyone. She had been marked by the jinni and it's difficult to undo—even for someone with experience. Plus we had no directive to interfere."

"But why not?"

"I don't know how those we help are chosen, but I'm sure there is a big picture we just can't see. We must follow orders. There aren't enough of us to help everyone who needs it."

"I don't care about orders. I wanted to help someone in need. That's what I agreed to do! I didn't agree to come back and fall in line and be a good little soldier. You can't be happy doing this either, can you? Why can't we help the people we encounter who need help? Why can't we look for those missing guardians?"

Quintus looked at me carefully and tilted his head back. "Olivia, this is the way we do things. It has worked for many, many years. I understand your frustration, I do, but give it time, and I am sure the reasoning will come to light. Don't rush into judgment until you are more acquainted with our ways."

I couldn't even respond to him. He was so confident and calm and sure of his answers. Surely Quintus had to see my point. Surely he had to care more than he let on. I rubbed my fingers between my eyes. "You don't mean that."

"Just give our ways time. Learn them and understand them before you condemn them. If you still disagree, then you can solicit change."

"But how do *you* feel?"

"I have not thought much about it in a long time."

"I can't believe you. Don't you question anything?"

"Of course, but I am not so arrogant to think I know better than the elders."

Arrogance? I didn't think my desire to help people who clearly needed my help when I had the means to do so was arrogance at all. It made sense to me. The only thing that didn't make sense was why I couldn't. "Who exactly are the elders? When do I get to meet them? I want them to explain this whole process to me."

Quintus cleared his throat uncomfortably. "Not for a while yet. You need to complete your training and establish yourself a bit more first."

I sighed. We had worked on nudging since the day with Jace. I hated it, but was gaining ground. I hoped the rest of the lessons would go smoother than this one, which had become the bane of my existence, or I would never get to meet them.

"Give them a tap on the shoulder, don't hit them with a sledge hammer," was what Quintus constantly told me in his ever patient voice. I took a few deep breaths. I was so quick to fly off the handle these days. I would do as Quintus said and give being a guardian a chance before I set my mind against it.

"I'll consider your advice." I sat down in the chair next to him and pulled a knee up under my chin. "You haven't told me much about the guardians."

"Haven't I?" Quintus picked back up his book as if to begin reading again.

I waited for him to continue, but it became clear our conversation was over in his mind. "Am I boring you?"

"No, not at all. There just isn't much to say that I haven't said. We are a simple group." He started reading again.

I rolled my eyes and went back to my room. Lying back on the bed, I tried not to think. I needed to get my emotions under control. Quintus had to think I was insane. Half the time we were almost friends and the other half I could hardly stand the sight of him. I needed to stop dwelling on what I'd lost and move forward.

I wondered if having more alone time would make everything easier, but at the same time the idea terrified me. The last time I was alone I managed to pick a fight with a jinni which was bad, but there were worse things I could—and possibly would—do.

Alone I'd have no distractions from memories of my last hours, which liked to visit when I least expected them. . . .

No, I was lucky that Quintus was always around. I could barely shake him, which wouldn't have been bad if he wasn't always so cryptic. Who were these elder people and why wouldn't he tell me about them? He went on and on about every other creature or race in the Abyss, but about the one race I actually belonged to, he barely said a word.

My day with Jace still had me puzzled, too. Jace could sort of do what I did, but not exactly. It gave me hope it wasn't a jinn thing, but I still couldn't be sure. To top it off, Quintus had been acting stranger than normal, more awkward and uncomfortable, which made me wonder if he had the same suspicion. All of this led me to one question: why was Holden still messing up my life?

Just thinking Holden's name brought him closer to the surface—not where I wanted him to be. I wanted him as far away as I could get him. I wanted to never have to think about him again. A knock on my door pulled me from my thoughts. "Come in."

"Do you want to go do something?" Quintus asked, dimples in full effect, hands in his pockets. "Something that has absolutely nothing to do with the Abyss or guardians?"

"You have no idea how much."

"Great! I have been around long enough that I forget sometimes how stressful it can be. It won't hurt you to take a night off. It might even help."

"What do you want to do?"

He shrugged. "You're the expert at being human. What would you like to do?"

"You're more familiar with Italy."

"We can go anywhere you would like, except St. Louis."

"Let's go to New York."

"New York?"

"Yeah. I haven't been there in a while and I don't know anyone there, but it's an awesome place to people watch and window shop and you know, just be yourself." Plus nothing there reminded me of Holden—even better.

"New York it is." He held out a hand towards me.

I climbed off the bed. "One sec." I envisioned something more appropriate than yoga pants and a t-shirt, but still comfortable. I settled on jeans and a long sleeve black Henley. Then I took his hand and let him take me to New York City.

As soon as we arrived and the head rush passed, I let go of him. I knew it was ridiculous, but I felt like I was cheating in some way, especially when Quintus' touch lingered.

We meandered down the busy streets, just looking around. Someone stopped and asked me for the time, but I didn't have a watch. When he walked away Quintus asked, "Why do you do that?"

"What?"

"Repress your light all the time."

"Oh, do I?" I asked innocently. I knew I did it, and I had no intention of stopping. I looked more normal and felt more normal without the constant reminder of what I was. I felt safer like this, and safety was something I sorely needed right now. "I guess it's more natural for me."

"That's so unusual." He smiled. "I never know what to expect with you." His hand reached towards my shoulder, but I dodged him by feigning interest in a window display we were passing.

And so the evening went. We made easy small talk, which was nice. I didn't ask Quintus any personal questions because I had no intentions of answering his. He didn't try to touch me again, which was appreciated. He just hung out with me and I felt given enough time and distance from what happened, Quintus and I could become very good friends. Night was beginning to fall as we strolled into Central Park. I loved studying the people as they passed by. It made me feel like very little had changed. We sat on a bench near an ice skating rink and watched the skaters twirl by, laughing and smiling.

After a little while though, I started to feel like an outsider looking through the window of people living the life I wanted. The thought so depressing, I nearly asked Quintus to take me home—but then he made two sets of ice skates appear.

"Want to give it go?" His warm whiskey colored eyes twinkled, and I wished I felt something, anything, for them. "I'll teach you, but you have to let your light free."

"Why?"

"So you won't be seen and I can catch you if you fall."

"I don't know, Quinn."

"Come on, it'll be fun."

I agreed, not really believing it would be fun at all. We laced up our skates and headed for the ice. Immediately my feet sent danger signals to my brain that made my fingers dig into Quintus's surprisingly firm arm for support. He laughed and patiently helped me move around the rink. After the first lap I was more secure and we went a little faster for the second lap.

Quintus was patient and true to his word, he caught me every time I was about to fall.

If only he were as good at teaching me how to be a guardian as he was at teaching me to ice skate, I thought wryly. Before I knew it, I was having fun despite my hang ups. I didn't notice my light, I didn't worry about whether or not I would be a good guardian, and I didn't think about the fact that I had recently died.

We laughed and enjoyed ourselves, which filled me with warmth that made it easier to let my own light shine even brighter. And I never once thought of Holden.

SIXTEEN

"Just choose one." Baker gave me an impatient look I chose to ignore.

"I don't want either of them. They're both too weak."

"Cicero has the appearance of strength."

"But it's all appearance. Kill his muscle and he's like a kitten. He can't have my back."

"Then go with Phoenix."

"Too young, too inexperienced. I need a leader not a trainee." I shook my head. I needed someone like me, but I would never trust someone like me. "I made the connections. They'll both seek me out and want my friendship. I don't need a captain for the jinn yet. I've been taking care of them, and I will continue to take care of them."

"But that's not how it's done—"

"That's how I'm doing it," I cut him off.

"Well, you're a stubborn son of a bitch—" Baker looked at his watch, "who never sleeps. Maybe you can pull it off. At least groom Phoenix for the position."

I made a noncommittal noise and rolled my neck and shoulders as the figures on the spreadsheet in front of me began to swim.

"You know, I haven't seen you do anything fun in the weeks I've known you. You're always holed up in this office or at your apartment or glued to that damn phone. I thought jinn were carefree and reckless."

I glared at him.

He held up his hands. "Not that I'm complaining. You kind of remind me of the old days, but I do think we should go out and blow off some steam tonight." He lifted his red eyebrows. "Or do you gotta go home and see your old lady?"

"I've told you, there's no one who has me wrapped around her finger."

"Agree to disagree."

"You're lucky you're useful, or I'd have killed you long ago for being annoying." I shook my head. Baker was growing on me. "Xavier is opening tonight. I need to stop by."

"Great. They have drinks, music, foxes, and I happen to know the owner."

I frowned. "Baker, you're unequivocally not allowed to work my club. Do you understand?"

"Scouts honor. I won't work it, just have a little fun."
****

It didn't look like the same place anymore. I stood outside of the club, admiring my plans having been brought to life. Diamonds was no longer, now stood Xavier. I had more than tripled the size of the original location by expanding to its two neighboring buildings. Chicago's newest night spot was opening tonight and the town was abuzz with anticipation. The complex featured multiple bars, a dance club, and private party facilities.

Juliet had somehow managed to get the newspapers to not only promote the club, but to laud it as a miracle-enterprise that had turned the whole neighborhood around. Press, red carpet, lights, and hopefully droves of people would fill the area in a couple hours. I had numerous jinn lined up to keep bad elements from the club's vicinity. They'd direct criminal traffic to different areas of the city, so there'd be no problems for the yuppies, socialites, and minor celebrities I was depending on to make admittance to Xavier the most lusted after ticket in the city.

The employees were all young, fresh-faced, and beautiful—mixed with a good sprinkling of new jinn who knew their purpose was to make sure everyone believed they were

having the best time here. New jinn because they were easiest
to mold. The ones who had been around awhile dealt too much
in violence. They wouldn't create the atmosphere or the
clientele wanted. I slipped through the back door and headed
up four flights of stairs to my new office. I had no intention of
participating in the circus that was already beginning to form,
though Baker expected me to later on. And much to Juliet's
annoyance, I refused to let her tie me to any of this. I didn't
want my picture in the paper, and I didn't want articles
mentioning me. I would remain completely anonymous in the
venture. If it succeeded, I would have a target on my back.
There was no need to make it easier for them to find me.

My new office was expansive, with a private bar, restroom,
two couches, and a beautifully handcrafted desk. I looked out
the window to see a long line forming outside of the building;
relief flooded me. Unfolding the latest newspaper with a large
article about the club, I settled into my chair and began reading.
Juliet's devotion to the club launch didn't lessen my suspicion
about her, but it did make me more forgiving of her annoying
personality. The jinn numbers were growing and most everyone
was adjusting to the new order of things without any major
problems. Some of the older jinn and the Danica loyalists were
causing the occasional hiccup, but mostly everything was going
better than expected. However, Danica still hadn't made her
move and I still had no idea where she'd strike first. It worried
me, but I chose to put it out of my mind.

We were in the process of changing jinn thinking from
self-centered to group oriented. As I knew personally, one of
the biggest downfalls for jinn was that once you had everything
and there was nothing else to want, you were overwhelmed
with boredom because everything was always the same. But
seeing your actions as part of the whole and having a unified
purpose? It opened up endless opportunities. Even I wasn't
bored anymore.

It amazed me to no end, but I was pleased. The project
had given me new purpose, a *challenge*.

I refolded the paper, tossed it into the recycling bin and reviewed the monthly statistics I compiled for Malphas, whom I expected to arrive at any moment. A sharp knock sounded at the door, without waiting for a response, Malphas and his jinni companion walked into the room.

"Malphas, Nicola." I nodded.

"Holden." Malphas said and sat on the couch. Nicola stayed by the door, clipboard in hand and no expression on her face. "What do you have for me?"

I handed him the spreadsheet. He took a few minutes flipping through it. "Marked improvement."

I nodded.

"It has brought some notice to us. Expect an increased guardian presence, but don't let it slow you down."

"It won't be a problem." Guardians didn't concern me; it wasn't like they ever posed much of a problem with their gentle, unobtrusive methods. They were too meek to ever make a difference.

"See to it."

"Next month?"

He nodded and Malphas and Nicola left without another word, typical meeting. Everything was going according to plan. I could handle the guardians when they came, so long as Quintus didn't come with them. If he did then, well, I wouldn't be responsible for anything that happened to him. I had no particular grudge against him, but I wasn't about to do him any favors either. Those times were long gone.

I lay back on the couch and closed my eyes. With all the work to do, it had been days since I slept. I was drifting off when a little rush of frustration hit my mind—then was gone the next instant. *What the hell?* I opened my eyes I was still alone in the room. *What was that?*

Again, I closed my eyes and began to slip away. This time I was hit with another sensation, a deeper more permanent feeling that I was very familiar with: sorrow. Overwhelming sadness, longing, and despair braided their way through my mind. It had been a long time since I felt any of those emotions in this magnitude. The thin layer of frustration did nothing to disguise what was churning below.

But these weren't my feelings, I was sure of it. I had only ever been able to feel the emotions of one other person in this place so deep inside of me—but it couldn't be her—not after this long.

I concentrated to block them from my mind. Someone was doing this to me. I was under attack. The emotions stubbornly stayed put. They were buried so deep within, I wasn't sure how to push them back out. I panicked at the thought that I couldn't get rid of them.

"No . . ." I might have groaned the word aloud. I didn't want these feelings back. I practically resold my soul to make them manageable the last time. I couldn't do it again.

"Holden." A hand stroked my face, tearing my thoughts back to my external world. I grabbed it by the wrist opening my eyes. Juliet sat in front of me, stunning in a navy cashmere dress.

"What are you doing in here?" Suspicion filled me, though I knew she wasn't strong enough to do this.

"Do you want to sleep through the entire opening?"

"Has it started? How are the crowds?"

"See for yourself." She nodded towards my window. I released her. Outside the club was swarming with people vying for the chance to get in and news vans, everything I hoped.

"Great, I'm going to go home."

"You're leaving? You don't want to stay?"

"Not really. Baker will be by later, make sure he has a good time."

"Baker," she frowned and spit out his name. "I'll never understand you."

"There's nothing to understand."

"Why is it you work a hundred hours a week, but don't want to reap the rewards? Why is that every week you receive one phone call that you don't answer, but leave shortly after you receive it? How come you never cut loose, Holden? You never reach out and take what you want. Always so controlled, always so secretive. How come you turn down every advance I make?"

Juliet being my assistant was a two way street. Yes, I was able to keep an eye on her, but apparently she'd been keeping an eye on me as well—slightly problematic. "Because I control being a jinni, it doesn't control me."

She ran a hand down my arm, "But it's so much more fun over here."

Another wave of despair crashed over me. I needed to feel anything, but it. I grabbed Juliet roughly, kissing her without any thought of civility or gentleness, with brute survival instincts.

She bit my lip, drawing blood, then pulled back from me and licked my blood off her lips. "I knew you had it in you. Give me a chance Holden. You won't regret it."

I rolled my eyes and grabbed my jacket. She stood dumbfounded in the center of the room. I paused at the door. "Are you coming?"

She looked over at me her eyes wide and a small smile on her lips. "Not yet."

Juliet was at my side a moment later. I had zero interest in her, but I wasn't about to let myself get sucked back into that place it took me years to scratch, claw, and fight my way out from.

If rough, mind-numbing sex with someone I didn't like or trust was what it took to keep me free then so be it. I was sure she had an angle—sure since day one. There was a reason she was here and it wasn't for my benefit. Yes, she had helped me and did a wonderful job, but I wasn't a fool. There was more to this seduction than sex on her part, way more—

My phone rang, interrupting my inner rant. There was only one person who would be calling me at this hour. I hit end on my phone to stop the ringing without taking it from my pocket.

"Never mind," I told Juliet, removing her hand from my arm. "Something more interesting just came up."

"I'd love to know who calls and sends you running."

"It's not like that."

"What's it like?"

"None of your fucking business." Juliet narrowed her eye as I walked out the door. "Face it, Juliet, you just aren't my type."

The phone call trumped any needs I might have. I'd battle my demons alone later. Marge would always take priority. She was my last living piece of Olivia. I would take better care of her than I did of Liv.

I went straight home and grabbed Olivia's camera out of my closet before hitting send on my phone. Marge answered after two rings.

"I'm sorry to keep calling you," she said without saying hello.

"You never have to apologize for that. How has your day been?"

"Horrible. Everything's going wrong. It started this morning, when I couldn't get my hair dryer to turn on. I discovered none of the outlets in the entire house worked. I called an electrician, but he can't see me until next week. Then tonight I realized that meant the refrigerator and freezer aren't running so I have quite the mess on my hands. Then while I was cleaning that out, a big storm blew through and knocked the tree in my front yard down onto the garage." By this point Marge was sobbing. "My car—"

I could see the problem. Everything went wrong, and she had no one to help her. I wondered what Olivia would have done. "What can I do to help?"

"Nothing," she sniffled. "Just having someone to talk to is enough.

Marge continued to talk for the next thirty minutes about all the horrible things that had happened and how she didn't know how she would manage it all on her own. She talked about maybe selling the house, that it was too much for her to deal with by herself. Though I didn't understand it, I knew I didn't want her to sell Olivia's home. It was where Liv grew up. It needed to stay just as it was.

After she hung up, I continued thumbing through pictures. I stopped fighting against the fresh pain. Instead I let it wash over me. How the hell could she not come back? If not for me, then why didn't she do it for her mom? How could she have been so selfish?

A new thought occurred to me. Maybe they wouldn't let her come back because of me. What if our relationship was the abomination Quintus said it was? Would they punish her for loving me?

"Olivia," I said aloud, wanting to feel her name brush against my lips. I felt a surge of panic, then most of the sadness in my mind receded. It was impossible to tell if the panic was mine or someone else's. I was losing my mind.

I put the photographs back in her bag. Enough of this. I'd go mad if I sat there much longer. I texted Juliet that I wouldn't be in the next morning, then grabbed my keys and headed for my car. I drove all night and pulled up in front of Marge's house by 6 a.m. with coffee and bagels. She sleepily answered the door, dissolving into tears the moment she saw me. The woman hung from me as if her legs had no strength left in them. I walked her to the living room and deposited her in a chair.

"You didn't have to come, Holden," she said with a shaky breath, when she finally regained control with a little help from me. It took more effort on my part, but while training others I learned I could use my abilities to calm not just incite— something I wished I knew back when Olivia was alive.

"I know I didn't have to. I wanted to. I want to help. You go do what you would normally do, and I will take care of everything."

Marge took my hand in her thin, frail one. She had lost so much weight since Olivia died. She looked like a child playing dress up in her mother's clothing. "Why are you doing this?"

"Because Olivia would have wanted me to help you, and you remind me of her."

"You're just the sort of man I hoped Olivia would find. I'm sorry the two of you didn't have more time together." She looked like a new round of tears was about to start.

"I wouldn't trade our time together for anything." I gently squeezed her hand. "Get dressed, get out of the house. Everything will be back to normal when you come back, I promise."

Marge nodded and slowly walked out of the room. I drank my coffee and went over my plan on how to fix this. By the time I finished my coffee and hers, she was back downstairs, dressed up and looking more alive. I sent her to meet her friends in my car and set in making phone calls. By 9 a.m. I had the adjustor and electrician out to the house. Next came the tree removal, a tow truck, and a contractor. By the time I left, I had a rental car, the contractor was working on the garage, and the electrician had fixed the power issue. Being able to make people bend to your will had its benefits.

I left Marge a note that I would be back, that I needed to get out of the house for a while. I didn't feel Olivia's presences there like I used to. The house had a solemn, death-like atmosphere. Perhaps Marge should sell it. I would buy it from her and Marge could move somewhere that didn't feel like a funeral home. I drove to Olivia's old apartment, wondering if she was a ghost. Maybe she haunted the spot she died. The thought was too tempting to pass up. I parked and went directly to her door. No one was in the hall, so I picked the lock and slipped inside. I walked around the living room, taking in all the differences. Whoever lived there now had changed things. The furniture wasn't where she had it, so I moved it to where it should have been.

I pictured her bleeding and helpless at Vetis' hand. I let the scene play in my head, hoping it would attract her ghost, but nothing happened. She didn't come, and I wasn't really surprised. I knew in my heart she would never be ghost.

I went to her bedroom. We hadn't spent much time together there, but just knowing it had been hers was something. I pictured it as it used to be, and suddenly I felt her around me. I paced the room, trying to figure out where the sensation was coming from. Her voice drifted in from the living room.

"Liv?" I went out, but no one was there—however it smelled like her. I could feel her in the air. Christ, she *was* a ghost. I stayed, trying to get her to come back, but she didn't. When I finally left, I put in a call, making it known that if the apartment came up for rent again I wanted it.

I went to the bar I'd visited when Olivia was falling apart in my bed after Juliet died and I didn't know what to do. I still didn't know what to do, though this time I was the one falling apart. I felt helpless and I hated it more than ever. Whatever this overwhelming sadness was, it screamed Olivia and refused to leave.

I sat down, hoping I would get the same relief I got last time I came here for help.

The same bartender from all those years ago still stood behind the bar. He barely glanced up from his paper. "Whiskey?" he asked.

"Good guess."

At my voice, the bartender finally looked up. "You've been here before." I met his piercing blue eyes with a flat look. There was no way he remembered me.

"Have we met?"

"Your girlfriend's best friend had just died. You insisted she—your girl—was different than other girls. You still believe that?" He slid the drink in front of me.

"She was one of a kind."

"Are you still together?"

"No."

"She got wise to you, eh?"

"She was murdered." I tapped the glass for a refill.

"Murdered! Well, if that's not a three-toed, one-eyed opossum. I'm sorry to hear that."

What the hell was this guy talking about? Part of me couldn't believe he'd been helpful before. Perhaps I had given him too much credit.

"It was a few years ago."

"What are you up to now?"

"Criminal mastermind," I said dryly, but the bartender didn't laugh. Instead he looked back down at his paper. "You have an opinion about that?" I asked.

"I think it would be in my best interest not to comment."

"I was only joking," I mumbled, and I had been joking—though it was true. For all intents and purposes, I *was* a criminal mastermind.

"What do you think she would think about that?" He still didn't look up from his paper.

"Olivia liked jokes," I said, but I knew what he meant. Olivia wouldn't like my new profession or what I was doing. She wouldn't like the hurt that I caused or the people I destroyed, but she didn't come back so she lost her say.

"Death doesn't end everything," the old bartender said and flipped to a new page. "I wouldn't write off her good opinion just yet if I were you. You've changed since I last saw you—maybe not for the better." He tapped his finger on the bar top.

"Excuse me?" How could he possibly know what I was thinking?

"Just call them like I see them."

I didn't want to mention the mind reading, just in case I was misunderstanding him. "How am I different?"

"Last time you were here you had a spark, an energy, to you. It's gone. Now you seem like a shark."

"If there was anything there, her death took it."

"It didn't take it. You've just done your damnedest to stamp it out."

"How do you know any of this?" This bartender definitely wasn't all he seemed.

He smiled. "I'm just a student of life."

"Like hell."

"Don't lose hope, Holden. Life may surprise you yet," he said before he fucking vanished.

I looked around the bar and it wasn't a bar at all, just an empty room that was for rent. The kind of power it would take to pull off an illusion of this magnitude on a jinni wasn't possible. What was that guy and what did he know? Though it was too late, I wondered if he could tell me whose feelings were in my mind.

I picked up the stool I'd been sitting on—the only piece of furniture in the place—and smashed it against the wall. I hated this convoluted bullshit. I hated not being in control and not knowing what I needed to do. Fuck this, I didn't need it. Olivia was gone and no one had a hold over me. I would finish up with Marge then I was out of here, I had a region to run.

SEVENTEEN

I thought about what Olivia could do all the time. She saw human souls and could pick out ones in need—she was amazing. I didn't know if the elders could even do that. The difference she could make was staggering. She was a shining star of hope in a world that was in very real danger of losing all hope. Guardians always fought an uphill battle; our job wasn't easy. As people became more jaded and guarded, they were harder and harder to guide—but now we had her. She had new methods she could teach us, she had new abilities she could share, and she desired to do both. She would change everything.

A smile spread over my face as I lay in bed, imagining all of the wonderful things she would do and I would witness. I hated having to tell her no, but I needed to get her through the training and Ezra out of my hair before I gave her the freedom to do as she pleased. All I had to do was keep her from going back to *him*.

Just the thought of Holden evaporated the smile from my face. It concerned me that she wouldn't talk about him. Every night I half expected to wake up in the morning and find that she'd left, run right back to him as she had before. I couldn't understand the draw. He was a murderer and a jinni—both should have been enough to assure her repulsion.

This morning I was once again convinced she was gone, and it took everything I had to not open her door and check. Instead, I waited in the kitchen staring in the direction of her room. Olivia, eventually, shuffled out, her hand covering a large yawn.

"Morning." She rubbed her eyes and sat in a chair, pulling her knees up under her chin.

"Good morning!" My voice betrayed my happiness at her still being here. She shut her eyes and yawned again. "Did you sleep well?"

She grimaced. "Fine."

I figured this was about Holden. Every awkward moment was generally about him in some way. Olivia's moods had evened out some, but Holden was still an extremely touchy subject. I didn't know what to say or what questions I could ask without making her storm off or shut down, so I focused on what I did know. "Today I'll teach you how to transport."

Her eyes opened and something resembling interest sparked in them. "You mean we're finally done with nudging? Praise the Lord!" She rolled her eyes good naturedly. "Let's start."

It was good to see her excited about something guardian related. Our occasional night of human fun was the only thing that brought her out of her shell, and I loved seeing her happy and so alive. "Don't you want breakfast?"

"Oh. Um, sure, I guess." She came into the kitchen and grabbed a piece of bread and a small glass of orange juice, then boosted herself on to the countertop. "So tell me what I have to do."

"We can start when you're done, no rush. We have forever."

She tore off a chunk of the bread and plopped it into her mouth. "I can listen while I eat. No need to waste time."

I shook my head, but consented. "It is really a rather simple concept. Basically you focus on the address the same way you focused on changing your clothes this morning. If you have been there and you can picture the location along with the address, it helps get you closer. If I am going to a new location, I'll normally make it within a couple blocks of where I need to be, but if I'm coming home, I can show up in my apartment."

"So once I focus my energy and picture and think of the address, then what? How do I go there?"

"You disperse. You have to come to grips with the fact that your body isn't the way it used to be. You look the same because that's the image of yourself that your soul carries with it, so it's how you put yourself together. But you do not have an actual body. You are light. All you have to do is release the hold."

She chewed on her bottom lip and rubbed her hand over her arm. "I have skin. I can feel it beneath my hand. Is that just because I believe I can? Is it not actually there?"

"No, you have skin because you created it. Just like the clothing you are wearing. It is real—it can be torn or damaged—but it was created with light."

"I don't understand any of this." She picked up a steak knife out of the drainer next to the sink and twirled it in her fingers. "If I cut myself, will I bleed?"

I shook my head. She raised an eyebrow, then dragged the knife down her arm.

"Olivia!"

Pain twisted her face, and she watched light gleam from the slice. "This is so weird." She looked up at me. "It stings."

"You just wounded your soul, probably not the best idea."

"Huh. Should I get a Band-Aid or something?"

"You can mend it."

The skin stretched and braided itself back together as she stared with wide eyes. "This is so not right."

"But you do it so well." I laughed.

"How exactly are we killed?" she asked, still staring at her arm in horror.

"Not the most uplifting of subjects."

She finally tore her eyes from her arm. "But I want to know."

"A soul can only take so much damage before it cannot repair itself. We are resilient, but not undefeatable. Imagine having pieces of your body sliced off, like being peeled, until you lost so much of your essence you could not go on. It could take days, weeks even, depending on how strong the soul is. That's what it would be like. Do you understand?"

Olivia looked away. "I think I have a vague idea." She hoped off the counter. "Let's do this."

"So do it. I told you how. Give it shot."

"Where should I go?"

"Go to your room."

"Is there an address for that?"

"You know it well enough. Just picture it."

Her eyes closed, her cheeks twitched, and light surrounded her, but she didn't move from the room. "It's not working," she complained.

"You're not dispersing."

"I'm trying, but…"

"You put yourself back together multiple times. It's the same thing, just opposite."

"But I don't know how I do that—it just happens."

And so it went for days. She stood in the kitchen, trying to transport no more then twenty feet. We tried different exercises, discussing what she needed to do, and I even transported with her so she could pay attention to how she came back. Each time we transported, she came back together faster and faster, but she made no progress with pulling herself apart. Olivia didn't give up. I doubted she even slept. She was consumed with figuring out how to transport. I never saw anyone throw themselves into something with the determination she had. It was amazing and a little concerning.

I tried to talk her into taking a break, but she flat out refused. Weariness ground her down as each day passed. Her face began to look drawn and stretched, and her temper was nearer to the surface, as her attempts grew weaker.

"Just let everything go," I snapped at her.

"You aren't helping!"

"What's holding you back? Why can't you do this?"

"Just leave me alone, let me work on it."

"It's Holden, isn't it?"

"Shut up."

"Just say his name, Olivia. *Holden*. Tell me Holden isn't what's keeping you from doing this rudimentary task." I moved closer and closer to her, speaking calmly, though the air around us was thick with Olivia's unrest. She shook her head and looked away. "Say it." I hoped goading her would push back her walls, force her to let go.

"Leave me alone!" she shouted, but I advanced.

"You want to get away? Then transport. Or are you afraid Holden wouldn't like it? How is he constraining you?"

"No."

I grabbed her by the shoulders. "How would he feel about me touching you? How would Holden feel if I—"

Light filled the room and blinded me. When it receded, Olivia was gone. I went to her room, but she wasn't there either. Crap.

EIGHTEEN

I didn't know why Quintus was being such an ass. I was trying. It wasn't like I didn't want to transport, but I just couldn't let go the way he insisted I needed to. I knew exactly where it would take me if I did. It didn't matter what I was thinking of, only one place was constantly on mind, and I didn't want to go back there. I tried everything I could think of to get that image of home out of my head. I didn't sleep or rest. All I did was work night and day until I was completely fatigued and frustrated. Suddenly Quintus was challenging me and moving closer and closer. Then he had me in his grasp and the only thing I could think of was getting away. I did it without even trying. One second Quintus's face was dangerously near mine and the next I was standing in my apartment. My feet were in the same spot I'd sat that night. I stared at the floor thinking I should be able to see the blood. The place I'd taken my last breath should be marked in some way. Tears filled my eyes, but I didn't let them fall. I looked towards the door. My gaze caught on the rafter where Juliet died.

I heard shuffling in the bedroom. It wasn't my apartment anymore. I couldn't stay. I tried to transport, but nothing happened. More movement came from the bedroom. *Concentrate, Liv, concentrate. Breaking and entering isn't anonymous.*

I squeezed my eyes shut, trying to will myself out of the room. But nothing happened. The floorboard by the bedroom door squeaked. The handle turned. "Shit!" I pushed out with every cell, wanting to go anywhere but here.

Quintus's apartment faded in around me. I bent down, hands on my knees. I did it. I could do it! I let my breath slow. I survived. I went home and survived. I was strong. It didn't break me to see where Holden killed me or where Juliet died. I could do this.

"Where'd you go?" Quintus's calm voice came from the living room.

"Home" was on my lips, but I couldn't bring myself to say it. Not going home was one of the few rules Quintus had given me. "To the beach."

"Huh."

I couldn't tell if he believed me or not. I tried not to look guilty as he came into the kitchen.

"I was worried about you."

"I'm fine. I'm better than fine—I can transport now. What's next?"

Quintus ran his fingers through his hair. "A break. You're going to rest."

"I don't want to rest."

"You don't have a choice. Tomorrow morning we are going to a guardian coffee shop. It is time you start socializing with your peers."

His mood seemed off, but my thoughts were in such disarray I couldn't think about it.

****

I trailed behind Quintus, holding air in my cheeks and trying to find the energy to be social as he walked into the coffee shop. I had decided that I liked training. It was the best distraction there was. I didn't care if all we did was work. I liked to work. When I was working Holden could be ignored, he was easier to block out, and I didn't have to feel.

Quintus and my fun nights were okay, but they were starting to make me miss Holden, which made me feel weak and fragile, something I avoided. Needless to say, meeting other guardians wasn't high on my priority list. In fact, if they were like Ruth and her weird brother, it didn't make the list at all. I liked Jace, but so far he was only guardian I had met who was tolerable.

I didn't need self-righteous, goody two-shoes critiquing my every step. Quintus had been telling me from the start that this was where I belonged, and I even believed him every now and again, but most days it felt like being here was all a big mistake. None of this felt natural. It felt concocted, insincere. The more used to this world I became, the more everything felt off, or, at the very least, like I was sorely misplaced. I didn't have the pacifist attitude they all seemed to have. I was having a lot of trouble with the "that's just the way things are done" lifestyle.

Born into it or not, perhaps some people were never meant to be guardians—that thought made me really want to talk to the elders. I needed to see if I could change my mind, but I didn't want to ask Quintus. He was trying so hard to connect with me and to make sure I was happy, I couldn't bear to disappoint him, and so I trudged along behind him into the café.

The coffee shop had exposed brick walls and large windows with wooden frames painted Kelly green. The furniture and china were mismatched and worn, but well taken care of. Small sitting areas were arranged around coffee tables and the barista glowed behind the counter. About fifteen guardians were scattered about the room, some talking softly in small groups and some sitting alone with a book.

"Quintus." A man in grey dress slacks, a white collared shirt and a light blue pullover came over, offering Quintus his hand.

He shook it firmly. "Heinrich, how have you been?"

"Well." Heinrich's eyes fell to me.

I met his gaze, then let my eyes drift from him. Everyone in the room seemed to be staring at me, which made me shift and cross my arms in front of my chest. What was their problem? It was like I was a guardian repellant.

Heinrich leaned in and whispered something to Quintus who then glanced back at me. I could feel my cheeks turning red and anger started to bubble inside. I didn't need this. About to turn around and march myself out the same way I came in, Quintus laughed.

"She's not a human. Olivia is the newest guardian. Olivia, this is Heinrich, a very old friend of mine." He spoke loud enough that everyone in the room could hear. All the oglers trickled back to their previously scheduled programming.

Heinrich looked properly embarrassed, so I smiled slightly and nodded. "It's nice to meet you."

"Likewise." He turned back to Quintus. "What are your thoughts on doctrine 214C?"

His question alone made my eyes glaze over, so I moved away and plopped down on a beige overstuffed chair and crossed my legs. I didn't belong with these people. They were stuffy bureaucrats, and I was ... pathetic.

Holden immediately drifted into my thoughts. What would it have been like if I had listened to him and not gone after the demon? Would we have been happy? Did he ever really want me? His thoughts at the time said yes, but he was a master at manipulation, so how could I be certain? Especially when he so clearly didn't choose me in the end. I missed him with every fiber of my being and hated him with every cell. Holden hurt me more than I would have ever thought possible. The image of him silently aiming the gun at me flashed in my head for the millionth time. I flinched at the memory before I shoved it away.

"I have to let this go," I whispered, hoping saying it out loud would make me do it.

"Let what go?" a voice came from beside me.

My eyes popped open, and I met the gaze of a tall, lanky, goofy-looking guy. His hair was light brown and floppy, his nose a little too big for his face and his chin a little too small, but all in all he looked like a nice sort of fellow, perhaps 18 or 19. I didn't know what to say, so I frowned and shook my head at him.

"Why do you look like a human?" He leaned back in his chair and watched me, a smile twitching on his lips that nearly reminded me of Holden only there was nothing dangerous about this guy. His legs bounced up and down, and his fingers drummed on his leg as he waited for my reply.

"I don't know." I couldn't keep the sadness from my smile.

"You're a guardian, right?"

I nodded and released my light to prove it. "I'm just more comfortable not displaying."

"That's so cool." He leaned forward, studying the glow around me and pushing his wire rimmed glass up.

I grinned as his enthusiasm, despite myself. "How old are you?"

"Old enough," he quipped.

I gave his lanky, not quite filled out physique a once over and cast a dubious look his way.

"Okay, so maybe not as old as you, but I totally dig cougars."

I laughed from deep in my belly. The kid was crazy. "What's your name?"

"Marshall. And yours?"

"Olivia. It's nice to meet you, Marshall. How long have you been a guardian?"

"Since 1999." His face twisted in a grimace. "Car accident."

"Three years ago, gunshot to the head."

He nodded at me slowly. "So you're like hardcore? Wouldn't have guessed it."

"What does that mean?"

"The people who died like crazy, violent deaths are always like the hardcore guardians. All strict and rules oriented." He wiggled his fingers in the air like rules were a magical notion. "Like their traumatic deaths make it harder for them to remember people have to live their lives."

"I'm too new to be concerned with rules. I don't even know them all."

"But you said three years?"

"I didn't come back right away."

"Why not?"

"Do you always ask this many questions?"

He looked up in the air and tilted his head to the side. "Pretty much. Plus I had nine chocolate bunnies before I came here so I am on a sugar high."

I laughed again. "Personal reasons. How do you like being a guardian?"

"It's pretty much awesome." He looked down for a second. "I do wish I could see my friends and family, let them know I am okay, but I guess that's the nature of the beast."

"Hmph." I looked down at my hands thoughtfully. This kid had every right to be upset and give up because he never had a chance to live, but here he was still going along, doing all right.

"How about you? Are you happy to be a guardian?"

"I liked being human more." My eyes met his for a brief moment, and he nodded like he understood. Maybe all guardians weren't so stuffy. "I feel like such a misfit here."

"Don't feel so bad, there's a whole group of us who don't quite fit management's idea of an ideal guardian. I mean look at those two," he gestured towards Quintus and Heinrich. "I'd be surprised if either of them could find their ass with both hands."

I smiled at him. "Quintus isn't so bad. He is a nice guy."

"He's a suit."

"A little stuffy, I give you, but he's a good person—"

"But that's just it. Guardians aren't people. Don't forget that. Our brothers and sisters have been disappearing for a month at least, and no one in management even seems aware it's happening. They're blind or they don't care."

Mention of the missing guardians piqued my interest. I had yet to get Quintus to acknowledge there was even a problem. Maybe this kid would know something more. "How many are gone?"

"At least twenty."

"Have you told anyone?"

He shrugged, looked at his watch and stood up. "Duty calls. Watch your back, Olivia. It was nice meeting you. We should hang out—I'll tell you how it really is. " He gave me a half wave as he loped out the door.

Marshall seemed nice, bit of a conspiracy nut, but nice—and he didn't make me feel inferior. I made a silent promise to get to the bottom of these missing people no matter what Quintus thought. It wasn't long before another guardian starting inching her way towards me. Soon she was sitting on the couch staring at me. I gave her a tight smile, disliking all the attention.

Before I knew it most of the guardians in the room had moved closer. They all talked at once, kept shooting glances my way, and questioned me like I had committed a crime.

I was too frustrated to answer most of their questions.

"Is it true you are a born guardian?"

"How do you repress your light?"

"Can you do any other cool tricks?"

I fumbled for answers, but I didn't know any. I plastered a smile across my face, as my brain screamed for help. I just wanted out of there.

"When will you join the others?" asked a pretty blonde with a beauty contestant smile.

"What others?" I asked her, just as Quintus stepped in the middle of everyone.

"Okay, I know you are all excited to meet Olivia, but we have been working really hard on training, and she isn't up for answering your questions, so I am going to ask you to return to your tables." Everyone got up and moved back to their spots, grumbling.

"You seem to be getting along well." He sat in the seat closest to me. "Are you having fun?"

"A blast." I rolled my eyes. "I love being interrogated."

"They're just curious."

"Aren't we all?" I frowned. "So what's the deal with the missing guardians?"

"There aren't missing guardians. People get sent on assignment and sometimes it takes a while before they can complete their mission. They'll be back." Quintus sounded defensive, and his eyes looked worried in direct opposition to the smile on his face.

I shrugged. "That's good. Marshall seemed worried."

"Everything is fine, I assure you. I would tell you if there was anything you needed to worry about. Trust me."

I looked at him for a long moment. Trust was hard to come by. Quintus didn't exactly have a history of being open and forthcoming. When I was alive, he didn't tell me about guardians until it was too late. But what would he have to gain by not telling me? I sighed deeply and nodded.

"So apart from the abnormal amount of attention, what do you think of Brewed Awakening?"

"Seems nice. A little more hipster than I would have guessed for you people."

Quintus laughed, a nice, natural sound. "You *are* one of us."

"What keeps regular people from coming in here?"

"The same thing that keeps them from seeing us. This shop exists on a different plane. It looks like an empty building to anyone on the street."

"Can only guardians see it, or can other species in the Abyss see it too?"

"Sure, they can see it."

"So why are only guardians in here?"

"Because it is a guardian place."

"Do you ever just hang out with other people and races, or do guardians pretty much stick together?"

"We mostly stay around one another because we understand each other. There aren't any rules about it. You can make friends with anyone you like, but you cannot expose us to humans, and you must understand that other creatures in the Abyss will never fully understand you."

I wasn't sure *Quintus* fully understood me. I didn't feel comfortable with the guardians, not liked I hoped I would. Everything felt awkward and forced. Maybe in time, but at that moment I would have very much liked a friend who had no part in any of my last few weeks as a human. I missed Juliet so much it felt like my chest was collapsing, but I forced a smile and nodded to Quintus like everything would be okay, like I didn't want my best friend and my boyfriend back.

Get over it, Liv. You made your choice, now make the best of it, I tried to encourage myself. If I could just have something to hold on to, something that reminded me of who I was, so it didn't feel like I was losing myself completely, all of this would be so much easier.

"Is there any chance I could get a camera?"

Quintus shook his head. "Not for a while. You need to wait until your human connections are gone before you start photographing again. No ties to your human life, remember."

"How could I forget?"

"I know it is hard, but it will pass faster than you think." Quintus patted my leg, and I tried not to scoot away.

"I'm ready to go."

He gave me a sympathetic smile. "You remember how to get back?"

I nodded and transported away before he could say anything else.

NINETEEN

"What could pull off an illusion strong enough a jinni couldn't see through it?" It had been bugging me since I got back.

Baker scratched his beard and thought for a few moments as I drank my scotch. "Is that a trick question? Nothing comes to mind. Why?"

I didn't want to tell him I'd been deceived twice, but I couldn't stand not knowing what it was. I had to find whatever was behind the illusion. I was certain it had information about Olivia. He told me not to discount her good opinion just yet. Why? What did that mean? Could she still come back? Was she back? It was hard to think about anything else. I finished my glass and nodded towards Will, one of the most promising new recruits we had, and he refilled my drink. "No reason."

Baker didn't look convinced.

I took another languid drink and considered whether it hurt me to share this. Finally I decided it was worth the risk. If she was back, I'd be leaving this life anyway, so what did it matter? "I have contracts upstairs that I need you to pass off to the accountant. Come with me," I told him, getting to my feet. I didn't want to talk in front of Will. I liked Will. He was a good kid with a calculating head on his shoulders, but that also made him dangerous if he knew too much. Besides he was our best bartender by far, and I'd hate to have to kill him.

Baker followed me up without complaint, then sat on the edge of one of my couches. "So something pulled off an illusion that fooled you—what was it?"

"If I knew, I wouldn't have asked you. I would have taken care of it already."

"Where were you?"

"St. Louis."

"What were you doing back there?"

I narrowed my eyes. "I had business."

"Whatever. I mean, where were you?"

"In a bar."

"What was the illusion?"

"The bar."

"Huh." He leaned forward, bracing his elbows on his knees. "What sort of bar was it? Were there other patrons? Were they fooled too?"

I thought back to both times it happened. There was a sprinkling of other people in the room, but I didn't pay much attention to them. "I think they were part of the illusion. The only person I spoke to was the bartender. I think he is whatever did this."

"Strong enough to fool a jinni? No idea. Normally, I'd say a leprechaun, but it would have revealed itself after a good joke, a kelpie, but you were nowhere near the ocean, or Kitsune, which are definitely not known for being in Missouri. What'd it look like?"

"I don't know, a normal human man."

"Old or young?"

"Middle aged."

"Hm, probably not Kitsune." Baker studied me closely. "Are you sure you aren't just over tired. I mean I just saw you here in Chicago yesterday, then you drove all the way to St. Louis, then back here again. When's the last time you slept? Jinn don't need a lot of rest, but you do need some. Maybe your defenses are down."

"My defenses aren't down."

Baker shook his head.

"Even if they are, this isn't the first time I was in that bar or have spoken to that man. I was there once before, around four years ago, and trust me, I was well rested then."

"So it fooled you twice? Did it reveal itself the first time?"

"No."

"What exactly happened?"

This was pointless. He didn't know any more than I did. "Nothing."

"I'm trying to help you, guy, but I need something to go on."

"Advice. He gave me advice."

"About what? What sort of advice?"

"That's all I'm telling you."

"Ah, it's about the skirt, isn't it?"

"How many times do I have to tell you—"

"Yeah, yeah, yeah, there's no skirt." Baker straightened his back. "Well, there's only one thing to do. Tell me the address. I'll see if I can get a read on the joint."

I didn't see harm in giving him the address, except that it took him so close to my old life. I didn't want Baker or anyone poking around there. "Let me think about it for a while."

"Jinn are so paranoid."

"You would be too, if everyone was out to get you."

"Even the skirt?"

"Just get out. I'm done talking."

Baker laughed, but stood up and headed for the door.

"It's on South 9th in Soulard." This gamble had better not backfire on me. "And I know it goes without saying—"

"Not a word about this to anyone or it won't matter how useful I am."

"Exactly."

Baker shut the door behind him. I didn't let myself think about what he would find out or whether or not this man could lead me to Liv. Instead I headed over to Phoenix's Goth paradise. Before I could get out the back door, Juliet was headed in wearing a cat-who-ate-the-canary smile. Her head jerked when she caught sight of me.

"I thought you wouldn't be in today." Her hands twitched nervously.

"Yet here I am. You're late."

"I had other business to attend to."

"Like what?"

"None of your business." She tried to brush past me, but I caught her arm.

"That's where you're wrong. You're my responsibility; all you do is my business. This isn't a democracy, and you aren't free." I said, backing her against the wall.

"Just finished off a new recruit. Jeez, Holden, take a joke."

This time I did let her push by me, though my eyes followed her until she was out of sight. I didn't trust her at all. I made a mental note to tell Baker to have her followed, and left the building.

Punk rock pulsated through me as I wove my way to Phoenix's table and his newest collection of tattooed and pierced co-eds. When he saw me, he tilted his chin in acknowledgement. "Anyone look to your taste, Holden?"

I shook my head and Phoenix dismissed his groupies.

"What brings you here, old man?"

I took a seat in the curved booth across from him. "Just stopping by to check on you."

"You aren't going to ruin my atmosphere again, are you?"

"Hadn't planned on it, but you can never tell. How's training coming along?"

"Good." In exchange for my showing Phoenix some of the cooler advanced tricks, he agreed to head up the lower level training. I generally tried to stop by on training days, wanting the new ones to know me and hopefully develop loyalty among them. "You didn't come by today."

"I had other responsibilities."

Phoenix draped his arms across the back of the booth. "Being the leader must suck."

"It isn't as much fun as it sounds, no."

"But you're good at it. I already notice a difference. It's amazing what a little organization can accomplish. If we started this fifteen years ago, the city would be ours now."

"Perhaps. I hear there's going to be an increased guardian presence because our advancements haven't gone unnoticed. Have you encountered many guardians?"

"Not one. You?"

"A few."

"Are they challenging? They sound like pushovers to me."

"Not necessarily challenging, but don't underestimate them. They have an appealing message. People like to be happy more than they like to get revenge or hurt people. It could be a problem, and decreasing productivity isn't an option. Make sure our people are ready."

"What are we supposed to do to them if we can't touch them?"

"Be a stronger influence. Guardians are gentle with their message, but it sticks better than ours, so just make sure you aren't cutting corners and keep after the people. If you run into any real trouble, let me know."

"Never had guardians hanging around when Danica was in charge."

I gave him a hard look.

"Must be doing something right."

"We'll see, I guess."

I passed along the news to Mears and Isaac as well. The jinn population of Chicago would be ready for whatever the guardians could throw at us.

****

A few weeks later I was sitting in my office when my door slammed open. Phoenix stormed in, the door denting the wall.

"You said they weren't strong in their suggestions."

"Have a seat."

His face still raged with hate.

"What happened?"

"A bitch guardian stole my mark. I've been working this kid for three months easy, and over one lousy lunch she undid everything I did. And to make it worse, I can't even get a good foothold to start over."

I frowned. There was no way a guardian should be that strong. "Do you know who she is? Her name?"

"Why would I know that? It isn't like we were hanging out, becoming *besties*." At the word besties he clasped his hands in front of himself and gave me a tight smile that made him look homicidal.

"I'll see if I can track her down."

"What can you do about her? There's a truce."

"Everyone has a weakness. Even guardians. It's just a matter of finding and exploiting that weakness to our advantage."

Phoenix grumbled and stewed, but seemed okay with my solution.

"Has anyone else had issues?"

"No." He crossed his arms over his chest.

I laughed. This was an ego issue—and there was no room for egos in the jinn world. We may think highly of ourselves, but if someone beats us, we find a way to best them the next round. "Get out of my office and get back to work. I'll check into the guardian. Let me know if you hear anything that will help."

I'd just started back into what I was working on, when that pain rushed me again. Damn it, this had to stop. Baker had to find whoever was doing this to me. I couldn't do it. I couldn't fight my pain and this pain.

Olivia, I thought, reaching out with my mind, just in case.

I closed my computer down, locked up, and started for home. Eventually the pain subsided. The night was quiet and tranquil. Then something like a sigh moved through my mind and a flash of a person who moved like Olivia turned the corner about a block in front of me.

Before I knew what I was doing, I was running after her, stupid heart thumping in my chest.

TWENTY

Melancholy hung over Olivia, though she put on a good front and pushed through it. She worked harder than any new guardian I've ever seen, but as I got to know her better, it was clear she was unhappy. No matter what she learned or who she helped, she never moved a step away from her past. Olivia remained anchored to a life she could never have again. I admired the fact that she refused to give in and try to go back—though that had to be a huge temptation. She demonstrated her strength of will and character every day by not succumbing to what had to be a constant pull against her. Every new guardian had their breakdowns. The moment they insisted on seeing their families one last time, to go home for a visit, or do whatever it was that reminded them of who they were. Olivia wore her past like a band around her arm, always stopping herself from moving forward. I couldn't tell why she did it. If she didn't want to go back, why wouldn't she let it go? She didn't request to speak with her mother, she never spoke Holden's name, and she didn't even blink an eye in the direction of St. Louis. She grieved alone despite my best efforts.

Olivia excelled at empathy, but was less proficient at forgiveness. She could dissect a situation faster than anyone I had ever known, but she wouldn't lead the person she was helping. I decided she would never be happy until I let her help the people she saw who needed help. So long as we kept it quiet, I thought, what could it hurt?

It only took a day of her searching out and helping people, however, before it started to cause fights. She insisted on either shoving them with her mind to exactly where she wanted them to be, or presenting them with paths and letting them choose their destiny. There was never just a nudge in the correct direction. She insisted it was their right to choose what path they wanted, unless she saw something in their aura that made her frown. In that case, she shoved them hard with her mind towards her desired outcome. I tried to make her see that it was our job to direct them to the correct path, but not force them. By evening, we agreed to disagree, as her method appeared to be as effective as my own, perhaps more so even.

My meetings with Ezra hadn't slowed throughout her training. We averaged at least once a week. Some weeks he just listened. Other weeks he questioned me about her state of mind and progress in certain areas. His exact interest in her or what he was looking for remained a mystery. His questions often appeared to be random or about insignificant occurrences. He didn't appear to care that her ability to identify people needing guidance was growing, as was her ability to directly suggest paths. Yet he did ask if she was suffering from nightmares and if she disappeared for any length of time without explanation. I answered his questions to the best of my abilities, but I had no idea what signs he expected me to report to him.

Holden was her only secret that I kept from him because it had nothing to do with her present life. She was obviously making a valiant effort to deal with that on her own, so there was no need to bring an elder into the situation. It was impossible to say what was going on in her head with regard to him. Whether she was hurt, angry, still in love . . . at this point, it was anybody's guess, but so long as she stayed away from him, I would stay out of it. Most of the time, Olivia was friendly and directed every conversation back to me, while rarely volunteering anything of a personal nature. Something about her calm face and curious eyes made it easy to forget that our conversations tended to be one sided.

Olivia strolled into the kitchen, dressed and ready to begin working, while I was eating breakfast. "What am I learning today, Obi Wan?" she asked, sitting down at the table with me.

"Nothing." She waited patiently for me to continue. "What you need is practical experience."

She wrinkled her nose. "Haven't I been getting practical experience?"

She had a point, but only because she recognized people who needed help while we were out practicing—what else were we supposed to do? Ignore them? "This is different. These will be your assignments, not people you choose."

"Like I'm going to be graded?"

"No, we receive assignments that tell us who, when, and where. Our job is to show up. No one grades us. If you fail, people get hurt. If you succeed, people are saved. It's as easy as that."

"Holy crap. No pressure or anything." She chewed on her lip.

"You'll be wonderful, and I'll be there if you need me."

"Who decides which person is worthy of our attention and which one we ignore?"

"The high elders."

"Oh, *them*. I don't suppose you would tell me what criteria they use? State secret?"

"I have no idea."

She mumbled to herself before redirecting her attention to me. "Where do we go to get our assignments?"

"We already have them."

"What? How?"

"They were dropped off." I pointed to a piece of curled paper on the counter.

"The elders I'm not allowed to meet came here to drop off the assignments?"

"No, it was a carrier. They have more pressing matters."

She jammed her hands against her hips. "Am I ever going to get to meet them?"

"Eventually, though I can't say when."

She made a derisive sound.

"I know how frustrating it must be for you, but trust me, it is for the best."

"That argument is the biggest piece of—"

"Olivia," I cut her off with a warning tone.

She sighed. "Where are we going?"

"Illinois."

She frowned. "But we're in Italy. They couldn't find anywhere closer? There are plenty of people in this city who need help."

"We can be assigned anywhere. I just happen to live in Italy. Which reminds me—you can get your own apartment, anywhere, anytime you want. You're proficient enough at transporting that you don't need to live here for the remainder of your training."

I probably should have mentioned it to her as soon as she successfully transported, but I had gotten used to having her around. It wasn't until my latest meeting with Ezra and he asked me where she decided to move that I realized she didn't know she could leave.

"I don't have any money," she said flatly. "Do I get a job or how does this work?"

"Apartments are provided along with modest bank accounts. You just have to put in a request for a city and a furnished apartment will be arranged for you."

"So I can go anywhere?"

"Absolutely. May I suggest somewhere you feel comfortable? Somewhere you feel you belong? Rome has always been my home, so it's a pleasure to come back after a long day. If you go somewhere unfamiliar, it's harder to adjust."

"Can I think about it for a while, or do I need to decide now? I assume St. Louis is out of the question."

"Eventually you can go back, but not yet. You have to wait about a century before you can reside there again."

She nodded. "I'll think about it."

"No rush. I like having you here." I smiled and she looked down at her hands, gone behind the walls again. After several seconds of awkward silence, I handed her the piece of paper with the address and the name of the person we were to help in Illinois. She read the words carefully. "Are you ready?"

She nodded. An instant later we were on the cold streets of Highland Park, Illinois, a suburb of Chicago. Olivia studied her surroundings as if memorizing them. "You should make yourself a coat," I pointed out to her.

"I'm not cold," she said off-handedly.

"Of course you're not, but it's for appearances. There's snow on the ground. You'll standout without a coat."

A second later, she resumed her inspection of our whereabouts, wearing a calf length red wool coat, white gloves and a scarf. I looked down the street lined with shops and people milling around the sidewalks. It wouldn't be easy to find him in this mess.

"Coffee shop," Olivia said.

I looked at the coffee shop behind us. "How do you know?"

"I can see him."

"Which one is he?"

"The fidgety, pale one with colored hair at the table has a troubling aura."

We walked through the door together. She immediately headed towards him, but I pulled her into the order line with me. The young man was marked by a jinni, and it was a deep well cultivated mark. I was very curious to see how well she would go up against this, but I was surprised this was her first assignment. It didn't seem they were going to take it easy on her.

"The cases you are assigned will be different, Firefly. Not quite as easy as walking up to them and striking up a conversation. You need to assess the situation."

She glanced around the room. "I need to talk to him sooner rather than later."

"Why?"

"His aura is becoming volatile and really smoky. The situation will get a lot worse and fast if I don't."

Deciding not to question her instincts, I let her go. Olivia learned best by doing. If this was a mistake then I could probably handle it. She walked over and sat at the table with the nervous young man. He was obviously startled by her forwardness, but soon visibly relaxed. Before I ordered our coffees, I heard him let out a short barking laugh. I glanced back and she smiled at him. The boy no longer appeared agitated or bothered. By the time I picked up our order, he and Olivia were walking towards the door together. When they stepped outside, she waved to him as he walked down the street. I waited a few moments then joined her on the sidewalk.

"What happened?"

"Crisis averted for now. He was going to open fire in the coffee shop, I think. His ex-girlfriend is working here."

"How did you change his mind?"

"I noticed him," she said simply, but her words struck a deeper chord with me. She noticed me not too long ago too, and my life had changed from that moment on. Sometimes just noticing someone could change everything.

"So you are done?"

She shook her head. "There's still a chance he'll end up here. I think a jinni's been working him, a powerful one too. I said I'd have lunch with him, hopefully reverse the damage."

"How can you tell it was a jinni?"

"His emotions seemed lacking in something … sincerity maybe. His aura had a grey smokiness to it like the girl in Rome, and it sort of made my skin crawl."

She didn't identify jinn victims the same way I did then. I saw them as voids, just like I saw jinn. I wondered briefly what she would see when she looked at a jinni now, and with my next thought, prayed she would never meet a jinni face to face. It wasn't easy to undo the web that jinn wove around humans. Olivia's tendency to shut down when anything Holden related was mentioned, apparently didn't extend to jinn. She appeared to be fine working against them. I would let her work off her instincts and see where that got her, rather than trying to give her advice she wouldn't take. "What do you want to do next?"

"Ummm, yeah … following him might be for the best."

The boy worked a few blocks over at an electronics store. We watched him all morning, but everything seemed fine. I was silently thankful the jinni that had worked him didn't come by to prod him. The diner where Olivia agreed to meet him was bright and colorful, but looks were often deceiving. I needed to check the restaurant for jinn before she went in. I wasn't ready for them to see her yet, and she certainly wasn't prepared for such an encounter.

"I'm going in first. I'll get a booth close by. Wait a couple minutes before you come inside," I told her.

The diner was moderately busy, but it wasn't too much trouble to get the booth across from the one where the young man nervously waited. I didn't see a jinni in sight. It was safe for now. Olivia walked through the door, looking completely human and beautiful. Snowflakes stuck to her hair and a wide smile covered her face when she saw the boy—a smile that seemed like it was just for him. I felt a seed of dislike for this young man take root.

"Nathan! I'm so happy you came," she said, sitting down across from him. Nathan's face lit up and a shy smile fluttered across his jaw, crinkling his eyes.

She spent the entire meal talking to him about nothing. They spoke of television, music, and movies, but never anything important or relative to our mission. All the while her light braided itself around his chest, thick as a rope. She didn't appear to be struggling, but she also didn't appear to be concerned with the mission. Outwardly she just looked like a nice, interested young woman who had never known the darker side of life. As their meal neared its end Nathan suddenly reached across the table and seized her hand.

"I'm so happy I met you. Today should have turned out completely different, you have no idea, but somehow it became one of the best days I ever had."

"That's the funny thing about days. One day, or even a whole month or year, can be absolutely awful, then you wake up some morning and everything's better. That's why you should never give up. Life is good at changing faster than you can blink."

"You're right. I never would've believed that until now. But I know, I know everything will be okay. I don't know why, but I feel like I should thank you."

Olivia smiled at him. "I'm glad to hear that, Nathan." She waved her hand in front of his face just like I'd taught her and his eyes glazed over.

I followed suit, taking care of the rest of the room for her before we left. In a couple seconds, they would all snap back, completely rested and with no memory of us, only the feelings we'd generated. Our job here was done, though I had no idea if she had fixed the problem.

"Are you satisfied?" I asked her when were outside. "Do you think it worked?"

"Yeah, I think so."

"How did you do it?"

Her eyes met mine for a moment, then she walked away. After a few steps in silence, she finally said, "I made him feel something real. The dominate emotions he was feeling were thin. So I wrapped him in the light, though I didn't shove him, I promise, and then I just spoke with him like a normal person. I let him feel what it was like to have a new friend—that hope and encouragement you feel when something new and exciting is happening. I figured if I left him with a real emotion it would be stronger than the fake ones."

I could not have been more proud of her progress. "Why didn't you just overpower their suggestion with your own?"

"I don't know if I could. The negativity and false thinking had taken root and was strong. I thought the only way I could battle it was with something real, something they couldn't compete with."

"That's as good of a theory as any I've heard, Firefly. I'm impressed."

"Thanks," she said, but didn't seem happy. We walked a little further in silence. I waited, hoping she would let me in on what she was thinking about, but after a few minutes it was clear she wasn't planning on talking about it.

"Are you ready to go?" I asked and she nodded.

Back in Rome, she collapsed onto the couch and tapped her foot impatiently, accented with the occasional sigh.

"Is something bothering you, Firefly?"

"Why was I assigned a person marked by a jinni?" she asked bluntly.

"I don't know." I watched her closely for a reaction.

"Do they know?" She tugged on her lower lip.

"Not from me." I felt sorry for her. "They're probably just testing to see how good you are. There is a lot of interest in your success."

"Why?"

I had said too much. "Because every guardian's success is shared by all."

She rolled her eyes and stared out the window. "Well, at least it was interesting."

That wasn't the response I expected. I thought at the very least she would be mad I didn't tell her more about the elders, but instead all I got was *interesting*. "What's interesting?"

"Just seeing what jinn involvement looks like," she said half-heartedly. I nodded for her to continue, but she didn't.

"It wasn't like that with you and Holden," I told her, taking a stab at what she was thinking.

Her eyes met mine, cold rage behind them for just a moment. "You have no idea what it was like with us."

"I'm just saying your emotions didn't appear to be hollow, like the other jinn created feelings."

"And I'm just saying it's none of your business," she snapped. "Jesus, Quintus, don't you ever learn?"

"Fine." I started walking away. Obviously this was a mistake.

"I think I want to live in Chicago," she said before I made it out of the room, her voice sounding more normal.

Her declaration cleared my mind of any thoughts. She was really leaving. I searched for an excuse why she couldn't go, but came up short. Chicago was a little close to St. Louis for my liking, but she seemed to be fine with the not going to St. Louis part of the rules. I realized I had been hoping she had been in Rome long enough to want to stay. I cleared my throat. "Why Chicago?"

"I was trying to think where else I would feel at home. Then today it was so nice to be back in the Midwest, I thought why not. While I like to travel and I like to visit other places, I'm a Midwest girl at heart. I feel the most comfortable there. Outside of St. Louis I've probably spent the most time in Chicago, so I think it will be okay. And I don't have any close friends or family there. . . . "

Damn, she even thought her decision through. "We'll put in the request for you tomorrow."

"Great. It'll be good to settle in somewhere, start my life."

Her words felt like daggers. I watched Olivia lay her head back on the arm of the couch and prop her feet up. She inhaled and exhaled in slow deep breaths as if expelling pent up tension. "Are you happy?"

"I'm getting there." She smiled at the ceiling. "Thank you for putting up with my moods. I know I haven't been the most fun these past months. And sorry I snapped at you."

"I don't know; I've had fun."

She laughed, her whole face lighting up. For just a moment she looked like the girl I'd watched in the park that day. "You, my friend, have low expectations for fun then."

I joined her laughter. "Maybe I do, but I have enjoyed our time. I had forgotten what it's like to ..." My voice trailed off. I didn't know how to finish my thought in a way that wouldn't make her run away.

She tilted her head so she could look at me. "To not be alone?" she said, all the humor melting from her face.

"Exactly."

Olivia searched my eyes. "You should start dating again, Quinn. Just because you were hurt doesn't mean you should stop. You're a nice guy. You shouldn't be alone." She let her head fall back to the arm of the couch.

"That's good advice. You should think about taking it."

She smiled sadly, but didn't look at me. "Yeah."

"I'm serious, Olivia. At some point you have to let go."

"I have let go. I carry no hope. I have no delusions. I've let go."

"Then why does it follow you around?"

"It's just the way I am. I was never good at handling failure and this is so much worse than just failing. Murphy's law beat me with a stick."

"You didn't fail, Firefly. You are here now."

She shook her head. "You don't understand."

"I know you're in pain, but no one is meant to be with just one person. You're not defined by him."

"I know. He's evil. He manipulated me more times than I can count, and I never want to see him again. You were right about everything. I should have distanced myself. I get it, I do. I'm not the same as I was then and probably never will be that person again. I'm little wiser now." She chewed on her bottom lip. "I hope. But it doesn't change the fact that I'm sort of broken now. I don't think I could ever trust anyone again."

"That isn't true." I stepped towards her, but Olivia stood up abruptly.

"I'm still wound up. I'm going for a run."

"Do you want me to come with you?"

"You hate jogging."

I shrugged. I did hate it, but I would make an exception for her.

"No, that's okay. I just want to clear my head. I'll be back in a little while."

The door shut behind her and I sat alone in my apartment, which had always been a refuge for me from the stress of work but now seemed empty without her. I wondered if Holden knew she was back. If he did know, how could he stay away? Perhaps he didn't care anymore. If only I could know for certain whether she had really let him go or whether she'd just buried him deep inside, then I could know how to help her. Every time we started to talk about it, she ran away, clammed up, or stormed out. If I knew for a fact she had let him go, I could dare to hope—

I wandered into her room. It smelled like her, clean with a hint of something sweet. She had done nothing to the room to make it look like her own. Everything was as I kept it. I ran my fingers over her pillow and opened the closet. There was only one shirt hanging in the closet, a men's black button down. The one I had made for her, Holden's shirt. Was it a memento of her love or a reminder of how close she came to danger? I shut her closet and left the room.

I wished the jinni had kept his filthy claws out of her. She was too good for him—but I didn't have time to dwell on that. I felt the tug of Ezra's summons. An instant later I was in his private office. Twice in one week. Didn't he have better things to do?

"Sir?"

"How did today go? How did she do on her assignment?"

"Very well, I think. It was a hard assignment for a new guardian. I take it you know she was assigned someone marked by a jinni. But she handled it deftly."

"Excellent. No problems?"

"No. Why would she have problems?" I wondered if Ezra knew more about Holden then I thought.

"The jinn in that region have a new commander. His changes to the organization have been felt. They are becoming better at what they do, which is becoming a problem for us. I'm glad to hear she could handle it. Many other guardians have been losing their people."

"She said she made him feel a real emotion and left him with that because it would be stronger than the hollow ones he was filled with."

"How?"

"She talked with him, sir. She was a friend to him I believe."

"With a human?" His eyebrows shot up which was Ezra's equivalent of running around the room, flailing his arms in surprise. "Interesting."

"She has decided where she wants to move."

"Where?"

"Chicago."

"Really?" He drummed his fingers across the desk. "Did she say why?"

"She has spent time there and wants to stay in the Midwest." I had a flash of hope that Ezra would turn down the transfer and she would have to make another choice.

He nodded and appeared to be mulling it over. "That's as good a place as any for her, especially given her success with the jinn's webs. Yes, I think that will work out perfectly. We are planning on making a more concentrated effort in North America, so the more guardians we have on hand there, the better."

"We're going to put in the request tomorrow." I buried my disappointment.

"No need, I'll take care of it."

"Uh, thank you, sir, but you don't have to—"

He waved off what I was saying. "I have work to attend to, as always. Quintus, thank you."

"You're welcome."

"Does she know you come here?"

"No, sir."

"Good." And with that I was sent back to my apartment. I heard the shower running. Olivia was back. I chose a book from my shelf and was just sitting down when there was a knock at the door. I answered to find no one there, just an envelope taped to it. The envelope held an address in Chicago and two keys.

"What's that?" Olivia stood behind me with wet hair, baggy pants and a t-shirt.

"Your new apartment, I think."

"I thought we were going to apply for that tomorrow."

"I had some time so I thought I would surprise you." I didn't like lying to her. "I didn't expect it to happen so quickly."

"May I?" She held out her hand for the envelope, a small smile twitching her lips.

"You want to check it out?" I asked her.

"Yes."

It was a nice apartment, a really nice apartment. It had a great view and had to be expensive, the perks of having an elder make your requests for you, I guess. The furnishings were modern and sleek. The main level was a big open space with floor to ceiling windows, a large sitting area with a huge flat screen TV, and a dining table that could easily seat ten people. The kitchen was one step up and expansive, with a double oven, gas top stove, and a refrigerator paneled to match the cabinets. Off to one side of the apartment was a stainless steel stair case hovered over the floor and led up to a loft bedroom and bathroom.

Olivia whistled. "Impressive. I really don't need all of this, but wow."

"Do you like it?"

"Obviously, who wouldn't? So can I stay here tonight?"

"Of course, it's yours." She smiled. "Do you want me to get your things from my apartment?"

"No, don't worry about it. I'll come back with you and get them."

No more than twenty minutes later she stood in front of me, small overnight bag in hand. "I guess I'll see you in the morning."

"You're really leaving me, Firefly?"

"Only for a few hours."

I gave her a hug though she stiffened underneath it. "We'll see each other in the morning, Quintus," she said, pushing away from me.

"Would you like to have dinner tomorrow night?"

"Sure."

"Great, it's a date." Worry immediately etched her face and she started shaking her head, but I cut her off. "You said I should start dating, and I decided you are absolutely right I should." I flashed my best smile, willing her to agree. "I choose you."

She looked deep into my eyes, searching for something, but I had no idea what. Finally she sighed. "Yeah, let's give it shot."

Perhaps not as excited as I was, but it was a start. I grinned and she gave me a tight smile before fading into light. *It was a date.*

Liz Schulte

TWENTY ONE

"There was nothing there," Baker told me as I answered the door to my apartment.

"I told you it was an illusion." I stepped back so he could come inside.

"Yeah, but I should've felt something. Some trace if that kind of mojo was used."

"What did you feel?"

"Nothing at all. It was completely clean as if nothing had been there from the Abyss, ever."

"Damn it."

"I'm at a loss, boss man. The only solution I can think of is highly unlikely if not impossible."

"What's that?"

"Well, there are beings that can supposedly, if they're real, visit you in your mind. They wouldn't leave a trace, because they were never there. It could have made you see whatever it wanted you to see because it was controlling the old melon, if you catch my drift."

"And what are these so-called beings?"

Baker shifted uncomfortably and stared at the ceiling. "Angels." He shook his head. "Believe me, I know how stupid that sounds, but I don't have any other guesses."

I paced away from him. That wasn't as crazy as he thought. Angels, guardians, they were all connected and whether or not I liked it, I was now connected with them through Liv. Could an angel really have visited a jinni, twice no less? The first time made sense. They were helping Liv through me. But the second time, what was the gain? Olivia wasn't here anymore, why did they care? Could this be revenge for Liv?

"Shit," I said aloud.

I could feel Baker's eyes drilling into the back of my head. "Why in the hell would one be tormenting me?"

"Are you on the up and up or have you been hitting the giggle water? Angels? Seriously? They could snap their fingers and make you sizzle. They wouldn't torture you—you aren't worth their time, if, in fact, they're even real."

Baker was right. It didn't matter why the angel was bent on driving me crazy. Angels were untouchable. If it wanted me to go insane, I would and there wasn't a damn thing I could do about that.

"Thanks, I'll take it from here. I have another job for you."

"Wait, you have to tell me what's going on."

"The less you know, the better. I need you to start tailing Juliet. She has something in the works, and I need to know what—it's the more immediate threat. I'll tell you the other story someday." *If I live that long,* I thought.

"You have more problems—"

"I can't do this now, Baker. I have to think."

Baker mumbled to himself the whole way out about angels, and he kept glancing back at me as if trying to determine if I was crazy or incredibly unlucky. It was an excellent question. I heard voices that weren't there, chased after flashes of dead girls walking down the street, and drank whiskey with angels in my head. Three very real strikes on the crazy train—unless Olivia was back, a thought I couldn't dare to let myself hope.

If she was back and didn't want to see me, she would at least ease her mother's mind. It was only right. Olivia would never be callous. Even if she couldn't outwardly reveal herself to her mom, she would have the ability to calm her and lead her to a better place, but Marge had remained the same, therefore Olivia remained dead. Which meant something was after me. It was now a matter of determining if this was something Danica sent or if I was being punished for my time with Olivia. I didn't really care what it was. I would rather them kill me than torture me with her.

"What are you waiting for?" I growled, turning a slow circle in the center of my apartment, ready to be struck down by lightning, but nothing happened.

I shook my head and pressed my palms against my eyes. I had been good too long, too caught up in the club and business ventures. I felt that familiar clawing at the door as the jinni begged his way out, wanting to take my frustration and play. But I didn't want to hurt anyone tonight. I didn't feel like it; I'd rather feel something than nothing. I let the dull aching pain that was always there rise up around me. The jinni could wait.
****

I went out the next day to take the edge off before I went to the club. I hadn't slept in a week and was exhausted, so I hoped to make it an early night. I wandered the streets and sent out feelers for someone ripe for the picking, someone who wouldn't require a lot of time. Bankers, business men, sales clerks, boring. I stopped outside of a church and considered. It would be a lot more fun, but—I looked at my watch—a lot more time consuming. It wasn't a luxury I had. I noticed a police officer on the corner talking to a lady walking her dog. Who didn't love a dirty cop?

I went up to him, studying his actions and testing the water as I went. I sent a little rage in his direction to see how he responded. His cheeks turned red and his jaw clenched as I neared. Finally he snapped and got in her face, yelling at the top of his lungs, jabbing a finger at her.

"I don't care what your excuse is! Pick the poop up or get rid of the dog!" He furiously scrawled out a ticket and threw it at her, before sending the dog a disgusted look and marching off in the opposite direction. Not bad, but not something I could work with either. I ignored the stunned woman and followed him. I hit him with a little greed about a block later, but that didn't stick either. All he did was keep the extra change the vendor gave him, not exactly hell worthy. Gluttony wasn't much better. By the time we reached the station, I wasn't sure I would hook him. He shook hands with a superior officer outside of the building, and I tested him with a little envy. That seemed more effective. I almost went with it until I decided to be a bit more creative. I sent a healthy dose of pride and envy his way. The pride would reinforce the envy and vice-versa, leaving him completely at my disposal whenever I chose to swoop down and show him how to take what he wants. I went to the club, jinni happy and mind settled for the time being. I still had plenty of trouble inching its way towards my door, but at least I didn't have that nagging beast clawing at me from the inside. I still had time to figure things out.

After wallowing in self-pity for a bit, I decided that if I was still standing, there was no way an angel was after me. It had to be something else, something Baker wasn't familiar with. I just had to determine what and I'd be golden. I also concluded that whatever it was, it wasn't out to hurt me. If anything, it seemed helpful, like it wanted to be an ally of some sort. Too bad it knew too much about Liv to be allowed to live. I went up to my office and called Baker.

"Yeah?"

"Anything to report?"

"Nah, she hasn't done much interesting. She hung around some warehouse for a while last night, but I never got a good look. Some low level thug jinn carried in a glowing crate, then she left. I think she suspects something."

"Any idea what was in the crate?"

"Nada."

"It would be in our best interest to know."

"The place is locked down. Give me a day or two to figure out how to get in. I can't exactly shift into a jinni, I'd be pretty easy to pick out of a crowd. You're the leader. Go there and demand entrance."

"Not until I know more than they do."

"Let me take this tomato for a ride, and you can be done with her once and for all. She got nice gams, but that's the only thing she has going for her. She's a regular Mrs. Grundy."

"Do you realize I only understand about half of what you say when you talk like that?"

Baker laughed. "You slay me, boss."

"I'm gonna slay you," I mumbled, shaking off my irritation. "I don't think it's an angel. There has to be something else, something you haven't heard of."

"Not to toot my own horn or anything, but you're all wet. There ain't no creature I don't know about."

"Obviously there is, and if you give me one more sentence based in slang, I will beat you with this phone when you get back."

"But I haven't slept. It's always worse when I don't get some shut ey—sleep."

"Try."

He sighed and was silent for a while.

"So, any other ideas? If it were an angel, I'd be dead right now, agreed?"

"Yes, but I swear there's nothing else."

"There has to be. And if Juliet has made you, then tag in someone she isn't familiar with and head back here."

"Okie dokie." He hung up before I could complain. Nervous energy fluttered its way across my stomach and again I knew it wasn't mine. I didn't do *nervous*. I focused on it to the best of my ability, but it seemed to lead nowhere. I hated whatever this thing was. I just wanted to be left in peace.

About thirty minutes later, Baker barged into my office and flopped down on my couch. "You're a genius, boss. Well, I'm the genius, but you pushed me in the right direction."

"What are you talking about?"

"Loki."

I shook my head at him.

"Norse god, shape shifter, likes to inject himself in problems he has no business being in."

"Sounds like you."

Baker snorted. "I'm nothing compared to this guy. Now the only question is, if a loki has taken an interest in you, then what sort of mess have you gotten tangled up in?"

My jaw clenched. After she had been gone for this long, why would I still be of interest? "This has to do with the dame, doesn't it?" I held up my hand, but he charged on. "I know, I know— 'There is no dame,'—but who do you think you're foolin'? We both know there is."

I shook my head. "She's dead."

"Human?"

I nodded. He didn't need to know the details.

He gave a half-hearted shrug. "Hell boss, this is the Abyss. No human has to stay dead. You know that."

"She didn't come back."

"What's her name? I'll look."

There was no way I was giving Olivia's name to Baker. I trusted him as must as anyone, but that wasn't saying much. "If she were back, I'd know it," I said, maintaining my calm demeanor. Baker started to object, but I shook my head in a warning.

"Man, this chick must've been the cat's meow."

I felt a smile tug on the corner of my mouth, a gesture Baker didn't miss. I shook it away. "How do I kill a loki?"

"Not to pry or anything, but it doesn't seem to want to hurt you."

"Doesn't matter. It knows too much."

"I'll have to research. Gods don't exactly advertise their weaknesses." He scratched his beard. "I'd worry more about Juliet than anything else if I were you."

"Agreed. We need in the warehouse. We need to know what's in the box."

"She seems smart. I haven't seen too many cracks in her armor, except for one big one."

"What's that?"

"You."

I leaned back in my chair and considered. Letting Juliet think she was close to me would bring me closer to her and Danica's plan. I tapped my foot on the floor. She was annoying, but not insufferable, unless she started talking about Liv—*Liv*. "No."

"Holden—"

"Not an option."

"You have the strangest hang ups for a jinni."

"Nevertheless, we need a better path."

"Kill her. It takes her out of the equation, then kill Danica too. Voilá, no more problem."

"But who steps up to take their place? I know what I'm doing with her. I know who to watch. If I can beat them at their own game, then I show strength and others won't challenge me—right away. If I sneak around killing them but leaving the army, I make no advancement in the eyes of the jinn."

Baker stood up. "I'll keep someone on her. Maybe we'll stumble across another opening."

Liz Schulte

TWENTY TWO

What am I doing? What am I doing? What am I doing? I was beginning to wear my carpet thin with pacing. This certainly wasn't the first date I had been on. Why was I so nervous? Maybe it was because Olivia seemed so unsure, or maybe because it was the first time since Catherine that I wanted to go out with someone. Or maybe it was because I knew I shouldn't. She was my trainee, and I shouldn't blur our boundaries. It would only complicate our relationship. However, her moving panicked me in a way I thought I was too old to feel. I longed to have her near me, and it wasn't until she was gone that I realized how much.

I glanced at my watch. I still had twenty minutes. I resumed pacing. Why did I choose her of all people? She was still in love with the jinni. She may not have wanted to admit it, and she might be trying to move past it, but she was, without a doubt, fixated on him. In fact, she had probably been from the first time I met her. Her heart had never been open, yet here I was hoping beyond hope she would give me a chance.

If she wasn't willing to try, she wouldn't have agreed to this, I assured myself.

That was true. Olivia was never anything but completely frank. If she believed she had no interest, she wouldn't have said yes. Enough! No more worrying. Tonight we would just have fun and see what happened. I nodded to myself; that was a reasonable plan. And then it was time.

I opened my eyes at her door. Taking one last deep breath, I knocked and waited.

Olivia answered in a red dress with a plunging neckline. Her hair was down and flowing in rolling waves around her slender shoulders. She looked breathtaking and a little nervous which calmed me.

"You didn't say where we were going. I wasn't sure how I should dress."

"You look lovely."

She smiled. "Thank you. Would you like to come in?"

"Sure." It had only been a day since I'd last seen it, but it already looked like a different apartment. All of the furniture had been changed, and it had a decidedly more "Olivia" feel to it. No longer modern, nor was it like her last apartment. Now it was warm and soft.

"You've done a lot to the place."

"Yeah, I worked on it last night. I haven't figured out if I want pictures or paintings on the walls yet. I'll have to stop by a bookstore and flip through some books. The only images I can visualize well enough to create are my own."

"Your abilities are becoming quite impressive." I was amazed at the detail she created in one night.

She shrugged. "Not bad for an illusion."

"It's better than mere illusion."

"Don't you ever just want to hold something real, something you didn't have to manipulate?"

"I haven't really thought about it."

She smiled again, though her eyes dimmed slightly. "I'm sorry. I never offered you a drink. Do we have time? What are the plans for the evening?"

I checked my watch again. "Would you rather walk to the restaurant or transport?"

"Walk."

"Then we probably don't have time. I have reservations at the Signature Room and tickets to the theater. If that is acceptable to you. Otherwise there is a popular new night club that we could check out."

"No, it sounds perfect."

"Shall we then?" She nodded and we walked out the door like any normal couple headed for a night on the town, and I guess, for one night at least, that's what we were.

Dinner was nice, but Olivia was quieter than normal. By the time we got to the theater, however, she was more like her normal self. The more I spoke with her about nothing of importance, the more her stance eased and the nervous weight also lifted from me. The show seemed to change her mood completely. She watched the actors with undisguised interest and for more than a brief second she looked like the person she once was. When the show was over, old Olivia wasn't quick to fade away. She was too vibrant, had too much life to keep hiding from the world because of one broken heart.

Walking her home, she linked her arm through mine and something in my chest tightened.

"Thank you, Quintus. I had a good time."

"Are you sure you wouldn't have rather gone to that new club?"

She laughed. "Not even a little."

"You were quiet at dinner."

She looked away. "I know. I'm sorry. "

I didn't say anything else. I didn't want to ruin the evening by pushing the subject again. We'd had a good time, and I was willing to leave it at that. I had an eternity to show Olivia that there was more to life than Holden.

"It's just that this is all strange. I don't do well with change," she whispered.

"I want to see you happy, Olivia."

"I know you do. Is that why you asked me out? You think I'm unhappy?"

"No ... Well yes, but no."

She smiled. "So which is it?"

"Both. I asked you because I wanted to go out with you. And I was hoping it would also make you happy."

"Quinn, you're the nicest guy I've ever met, but when I said you should date, I didn't mean me. I'm—"

"You're the first woman I've wanted to date." I cut her off before she could list all the reasons I already knew about why she wasn't the right girl for me.

She chewed on her bottom lip. "Why me?"

"Who can say for certain, but I realized when you were leaving that I'd miss having you around."

She smiled sadly. "It's the human condition."

"What is?"

"Loneliness."

"We're not human anymore. Besides, I think it's more than that."

"Really?" She looked the other direction, her arm retracting from mine.

I tightened my grip to prevent her from sliding away. "I don't know how to explain it. You're different."

"I hear that a lot."

"Look, I know you don't love me—yet. I know you still want him. But in time that *will* change. In time you may grow to love me. We know we get along, right? I'm not exactly repulsive, and as you said, I'm a nice guy. It wouldn't hurt to give this a shot."

She shook her head, but she was smiling.

"It's true, Firefly. Just promise you will think about it before you say no."

We continued on silently until we came to her building. "Well, here we are," she said in too high a voice. "I did have a nice time, and I'm sorry I was quiet."

"No apologies—it was wonderful. And next time will be even better" I felt Ezra calling me, but I ignored the pull, wanting her to agree that there would be a *next time.*

"We'll see." She stood on her tiptoes and kissed my cheek softly. "Good night."

"You'll think about what I said."

She nodded and shut the door.

I let Ezra's call take me away. This time we met in a bright white room with a large table in the center and nothing else around us. Ezra sat on the edge of the table waiting for me.

"I'm sorry, sir, I was … in the middle of something."

"Never mind that. I called you because I have a mission for you and Olivia. As you know, I have done my best to keep the disappearances quiet and out of general knowledge, but there has been a steady string of information leaked from what can only be the highest ranks. Our missions have been jeopardized as well as the lives of those who serve. It must be stopped."

"What can I do?"

"I haven't been able to flush out the traitor, but I finally have a good lead. I have received information that the informant will be meeting with the new North American jinn commander who has been capturing guardians and selling them over to the demons for his own advancement."

"Why would they do that? None of the species have ever been at war with one another. We have always managed to co-exist. The truce—"

He brushed off my words and continued. "The jinn aren't interested in co-existing. They want to eliminate the guardians and prey on human souls, uncontested. With this leak it would be easy enough for them to do so. Have you heard about George, Stuart, or Emily? And most recently, Jace."

The air rushed from my lungs. I could hardly believe it. "No. I just saw Jace. He's an elder."

"He disappeared last night. All missing and more I'm afraid. All of your lives are in grave danger."

It was maddening. They couldn't target us. It had never been done before. Who was this new leader? How did he think he could get away with such actions? Stuart and Jace were friends of mine. Hatred fought its way in around the edges, though I tried not to let it. I had to remain calm. "What's our mission?"

"I want you and Olivia to go to the meeting location and find out who the guardian is behind this. Report back to me with no delay. Do not attempt to intervene or apprehend. Just watch and gather intelligence."

"You cannot expect Olivia to go. Please, sir, I'll go alone. She is a novice. This is far too dangerous. As you said, the traitor is someone high in our ranking. Olivia could be caught or worse." I knew I wasn't supposed to argue with our orders, but I couldn't let her already fall into peril.

"She must go. She has uncanny abilities as you yourself have reported. I'm convinced she is necessary to the success of this mission. She may be the one weapon they will not anticipate, giving us an edge. I have kept her existence as quiet as possible for just this reason. I know I need not tell you this, Quintus, but we may never have another chance to discover who the informant is. It is a matter of life or death, or I would not ask."

I didn't want her involved in any of this, but how could I stop it? Ezra was right. It was a matter of life or death, and Olivia wouldn't appreciate being sidelined in such a matter. However, exposing her to more jinn seemed like the worst idea imaginable. Ezra didn't know anything about Holden, so he couldn't possibly know why this was a horrible plan. I considered telling him for half a second, but couldn't bring myself to betray her like that. Against my better judgment, I held my tongue about the affair and asked the only question I had left.

"Who's this new commander?"

"Oh, his name is Hollis … No, that's not it. Holdus … Hold…" Ezra tried to work out the name with little success, as my stomach turned inside out.

"Holden?" I asked weakly.

"Yes, I believe that's it. How did you know?"

"I've heard of him."

"Have you? Intriguing."

It was hard to tell if Ezra really found it interesting or whether he was just eager to get on with things.

"Here's the date, time and general location of the meeting. We're depending on you, Quintus. Do not fail us."

"I won't, sir. I'll see you soon." I transported back to my apartment, fuming. Holden! Holden was the new commander.

Holden was dead set on extinguishing our race. I'd expected more from him even if he was a jinni. He may not owe me any loyalty, but he damn well owed it to her. Maybe Ezra was right. Maybe Olivia was the best person for the job. If any of their bond was real, if any of it still remained, perhaps she could get through to him. Maybe she could stop this war before it ever had a chance to start. As far as I knew, Holden had no idea she was back. There would be a huge element of surprise. Maybe Olivia didn't have to see him at all. If I could just talk to him, tell him she was here, maybe he would stop. He had to listen to sense. What would either of us gain from a war? I called Olivia to let her know we wouldn't be meeting the next day. I had something I needed to do.

Tracing him was easier than expected. I'd already deduced that he must be living in Chicago. After a few informative visits to some of my more established guardian friends in the area, I discovered the new club I nearly took Olivia to was also the newest jinn hotspot. After that, finding his address wasn't very difficult. Olivia had moved right into the heart of his realm. She only lived a few blocks away. How could I have let this happen? I should have been keeping track of his whereabouts. I once again failed to protect her.

Standing outside of his door, I loathed to reopen this chapter but had no choice. I knocked. There was no answer. I knocked harder. Part of me felt the urge to walk away, to deal with him later when I had a clearer head.

If you don't confront him, Olivia will, I reminded myself. The stern words worked. Anything was better than the two of them seeing each other again. I knocked a third time with enough force to rattle the door. The door yanked open and Holden appeared, surly and threatening—pretty much exactly as I remembered him.

"I swear if this isn't important I will pull your liver out through your nose and feed it to you—" His cold eyes met mine mid-threat and recognition flashed in them. He used his hand as a shield from my light and grimaced. "Do you have a death wish?"

"We need to talk."

"The fuck we do." Holden started to shut the door on me, but I put out a hand to stop him.

"It's about Olivia." Her name nearly lodged in my throat. I hated to even say it to him. He couldn't have her again, but the effect of just her name was what I had hoped for. He reopened the door looked at me with a hard expression.

"Olivia is dead. There's nothing more to say." He sounded weary.

It was as I expected. He didn't know. It was now or never. If I told him, he would let me inside. If I kept it from him, hope of a peaceful end was lost. In good conscience, I could hide Olivia no longer. "She's not."

He shut his eyes and his jaw tightened. "I hope for your sake that you're not playing games right now. I *will* kill you, Quintus. I owe you nothing."

"But you owe her."

Holden beckoned me inside, his face an icy mask of indifference. Still shielding his eyes, he asked, "Can you not control that insidious light?"

"Your soul has grown darker. My light didn't bother you this much before."

He ignored my comment. "What do you want?"

"I want you to stop. I know you don't care about humans or anything other than yourself, but at one time, you may have cared for her. If you insist on starting a war with the guardians, she will probably die. You owe it to her to allow her a chance at a happy life."

He stood in complete stillness and stared. "You're saying Olivia is alive. Where is she? How long?"

"Not long."

"When?" he shouted, all feigned nonchalance melting away. Underneath was raw emotion that hit me like a baseball bat to the gut. He was a mass of exposed nerves.

"Less than a year."

"*A year.*" He shook his head and paced across the room, before sinking down onto the couch with his head in his hands.

"No one bothered to tell me. She's been back for a fucking year, and I was kept in the dark. After all I did, I was denied this knowledge." He looked me directly in the eye. "Why?"

He couldn't be serious. He couldn't have expected to be kept in the loop on this. He was a jinni for crying out loud. "You had no right to know. She's a guardian and you are a jinni. If anything, she needs to forget you, to move on with her life. This is Olivia's second chance, and I intend to let her have it. What did you expect, Holden, to live happily ever after? Did you think you could go out and condemn souls all night while she works all day to save them? Would that have made either of you happy? You have nothing left to say to one another. The chapter in her life that involves you is over, and thank God for that. Leave her alone, but do this one last thing, I implore you. If you ever cared for her, please do not start this war."

He was across the room in a blink, his hand crushing my throat. "I didn't have a right to know? No right?" He spoke slowly and dangerously, his grip tightening. "You will not use my love for her against me. What we had transcends everything else."

"If that is so, then why did she not tell you she was back?" I managed to croak out.

Holden shook his head as if trying to dislodge what I just said. "She loves me." His hand loosened slightly.

"She *loved* you. She's not the same person," I lied. He couldn't have her, not then, not now, not ever. Immediately he renewed the crushing force on my trachea with greater enthusiasm.

"I don't know what war you speak of, but if you come here again to use Olivia to your advantage, I'll rip off your arms and gut you. Kill you slow. Do you understand me?"

I nodded because I could not speak. Holden dropped me to the floor. "Get out."

The pain raging through me had nothing to do with my damaged neck. I made a mistake. Holden wouldn't help us. We would have to stop this on our own.

TWENTY THREE

Quintus was a really, really *nice* man.

Quintus was a *good* man.

Quintus didn't *lie* to me.

Quintus was handsome and had the most adorable dimples I'd ever seen.

So why didn't I want him? I sat miserably on my bed, trying to decipher what in the hell was wrong with me. Tonight would have made any girl happy, but since I got back home, the only thing I felt like doing was crying. I crawled out of bed and wandered into my closet. It still held only one item of clothing: Holden's shirt. I stripped from my nightshirt and slid my arms into the garment. My eyes closed and my other senses took over. The soft stroke of the expensive material against my skin and subtle traces of his smell made me light headed. I almost believed he was waiting for me in the next room. I wanted to hear his voice, feel his touch.

The sound of my phone ringing brought me back to reality. I answered it, not at all surprised to hear Quintus on the other end of the line. It wasn't like Jace or Marshall or those other two ridiculous guardians called me.

"Do you know what time it is?" I asked, annoyed he would call so late. Or was it early?

"You don't sound like you were sleeping," he said practically.

"That's not really the point. What did you need?"

"We won't be meeting tomorrow. I have some other matters of business to attend, so you have the day off."

What was I supposed to do with a day off? The idea scared the hell out of me. I had no friends, no family, no money. . . . Was I supposed to sit and twiddle my thumbs all day? Resisting the temptation to peek into Holden's mind was hard enough at night. I might not make it a whole day. "No one needs saving tomorrow? Couldn't I do an assignment alone? Or can start looking for the missing guardians."

Quintus cleared his throat. "Someone always needs our help, Firefly, but you aren't ready to be out on your own, and I cannot be there. As for the guardians, I told you, it isn't a problem."

"What about Jace?"

Quintus sighed. "Take the day off. Relax. Have fun. These days are few and far between."

"I'm counting on it," I mumbled.

"Pardon?"

"Nothing." A whole day. I guess it was time to see how much temptation I could take. Cold loneliness over swept me. "I'll see you the day after tomorrow then."

I went back to bed and slid between the covers. Another night of dreams of being tortured and shot. Oh boy.

The next morning when I could stay in bed no longer, I sat up stiffly. It was barely dawn and I'd only managed to sleep a couple hours, but I was thankful they were over. I dressed for a run and left the building in the soft light of the breaking day. I jogged to Michigan Ave then north towards Lake Shore Drive and the beach. Following the shoreline I strove to clear my mind of all thought.

I will beat this., I am stronger than this. I repeated the mantra over and over again until the words fell in time with my steps. I ran harder and harder, letting the burning in my lungs overshadow all other feelings and loving every moment of it. When I could run no further I stopped, hands pressed into my knees as cool air gushed in and sweat ran down my neck. Slowly I straightened and began walking back. The sound of the water stirred something peaceful and accepting in my core. I didn't have to do anything other than deal with what was in front of me. If Holden discovered I was back, I would deal with it. If he never discovered it, then slowly, piece-by-piece, I would let him go. If something grew out of my friendship with Quintus, then so be it. I wasn't looking or asking to be in love again, but Quintus was my only friend. If this was what he wanted, I would give us a shot. The only thing I could control was my number of connections in this world. I never had a lot of friends, but I intended to change that. It was time to come out of my shell.

By the time I made it back home, I gave up completely on the idea of going back to that coffee guardian place. I didn't want to hang out with guardians, though I did like Marshall there wasn't a guarantee he would even be there. This was Chicago. Surely there were more than just guardians here. There were plenty of people, supernatural and not. I could make my own friends. There was no rule they had to be guardians, at least no rule that was relayed to me. Once I showered and changed, I hit the streets like in my photo hunting days. I quickly dismissed my desire for a camera. Today wasn't about that. I wasn't going to hide behind a lens. I was going to meet people. Introduce myself. Be outgoing.

I walked slowly down the street, people watching. Now that I had grown used to seeing the Abyss, it was easy to ignore it. And if I didn't acknowledge the Abyss, I didn't see the supernatural people—they were mere glimmers in the corner of my eye. It was too easy to fall back into my human inclination to ignore them, just as I had always done. Today, however, I was determined to see them, to find my place among them. It was amazing just how many there were in Chicago. About every third person I passed wasn't human. All of them looked at me suspiciously as I watched them.

"Not a friendly lot." I mumbled to myself as a strange horned creature gave me the stink eye. Maybe making friends wasn't going to be as easy as I thought. Being social had never been my strength.

"You'll have to excuse them. They aren't used to humans watching them so openly," said a voice behind me.

I turned to see a pretty girl, with long amber colored hair and skin so bronzed it nearly shimmered, leaning against a nearby building, arms crossed over her chest. She wasn't human, I was sure of that, but I couldn't quite place what she was. Her face was too smooth, her eyes too cat-like, and her voice too purring to ever be human.

"I'm not human," I said, looking directly into her feline eyes.

She approached with a graceful gait and circled me like I might be lunch. She sniffed the air on either side of my shoulder. "You look human, smell human, if you aren't human, what are you?"

"Bored," I said giving her one of Holden's patented expressions. "What are you?"

"Hungry," she said with a wide grin. "Do you want to get lunch?"

I had no idea what to make of this person. I couldn't tell if she was a threat or just curious. "Do you invite strangers to lunch often?"

Her shrug was the most graceful movement I had ever seen. She made me feel like a frumpy troll next to her smooth liquid motions. "I can already tell I'm going to like you. Human, or whatever are, not many people would have the balls to stare down the whole of Chicago's Abyss. You're fearless. I like that in a person."

"Olivia," I said, holding out my hand to her.

"Femi." She took my hand in a surprisingly firm grasp. "You aren't human, are you? I can feel it in your skin." A pleased smile spread across her face.

"I told you I wasn't."

"People lie." She released my hand. "You really do look like a human. Out with it already."

I smiled at her impatience. "I'm a guardian."

"Bullshit." She laughed. "I can recognize a pain in the ass, holier than thou guardian a mile away. I'm not fooled, try again."

I joined her laughter, but didn't feel it. I had suspected I was a bad guardian; now she had confirmed it. I wasn't nearly holy enough. *Perhaps I would have been better off as a jinni*, I thought for the umpteenth time. "What makes you think I'm not a guardian?"

"Well, you're talking to me. You don't have a stick up your ass. But most importantly," she tapped my shoulder, "no light."

Right, I'd forgotten about that. It felt so natural to keep it repressed I did it all the time, without thinking. I focused and released my will, letting the light halo my skin—but not so much as to make a spectacle of myself. "Is that better?" I asked.

Her greenish yellow eyes widened, as if seeing me for the first time. "You weren't joking." Her hand reached out towards me, but stopped mid-air. "May I?" she asked, suddenly seeming nervous.

"Sure."

Her fingers grazed mine and her eyes widened even further. "Holy shit," she said under her breath, then smiled at me. "You're not like any guardian I've ever seen, are you?"

I pulled my light back, uncomfortable. Would it kill anyone to just let me fit in for once in my life? "I guess not."

She nodded, regained composure. "That's cool. I'm rare too."

"And what are you?"

"Have you heard of Sekhmet?"

I shook my head.

"Yeah, not many here have. She's the Egyptian warrior goddess of healing. That's what I am."

"You're a goddess?" I had little doubt my own eyes were as wide as hers had been.

"No, the first of our kind was. We are now simply called Sekhmet. We are born of her power and follow her will."

I nodded. A warrior goddess of healing? I couldn't even begin to understand what that meant. "So what is it you do?"

Femi laughed. "I'm a bounty hunter. Not much call for warrior goddesses anymore."

"Oh. How does one become a bounty hunter?"

She looked at me skeptically. "How long have you been a guardian?"

"Not long."

She nodded as if that explained everything. "Bounty hunters can be any race. My people don't have much to do these days. Many of my sisters have stayed in our homeland, but I've always been more open-minded. The only thing I ever wanted to do was get out and travel the world. Becoming a bounty hunter was the best thing I ever did." Her eyes shifted from mine as she scanned the street. "I thought new guardians always had a partner."

"I do. He has other business today, so I got the day off," I said without enthusiasm, making Femi laugh.

"Not fond of days off?"

"Not really. I don't know anyone. I'm bored out of mind."

"Well, you're in luck. It just so happens I'm free today. We'll make the rounds, but lunch first. My treat."

"The rounds?" I asked, as she pulled me down the sidewalk.

"Yeah, to all the good Abyss hotspots. Didn't your partner teach you anything?"

"I guess not," I said as she yanked me into a bar crowded with unusual creatures. Femi walked up to a table where two wrinkly, grey skinned creatures were sitting. She narrowed her cat eyes at them and they scrambled out of the booth. She looked back at me, flashing a pleased grin.

"Booth savers!"

"Looked more like intimidation to me."

Femi laughed. "Maybe it was. They're hobgoblins. Tricky little devils, love to pick on humans. They slip up a lot, so bounty hunters tend to make them nervous."

I nodded, looking in the direction they scurried. Why didn't Quintus tell me about places like this? All I got to see was coffee bars. This was so much cooler. I scanned the room.

I didn't see any other guardians, but they were probably all working. "What do they have to eat here?"

"Everything. They cater to all walks of life." Femi leaned back in the booth, openly studying me, but not in a creepy way. She looked at me as if she was trying to piece together a puzzle. She reminded me of me in certain ways. "Why aren't you like the other guardians?" she finally asked.

I shrugged. "I never really fit in during my life. Why would I expect my death to be any different? I'm destined to be alone."

She ignored my pity parade. "That's right. You were human. What's dying like?"

An image of Holden pointing the gun at me, cold resolve in his eyes, flashed in my mind. "Painful."

She grimaced. "You went bloody, didn't you?" Her headed tilted slightly to the side. "Yeah, you're a fighter. I can see it in your eyes. Do you remember any of it?"

"Every last moment."

"What happened?"

"It's a long story."

She rested her chin on her hands. "I have time."

"I'll give you the Cliff's Notes; I was tortured then shot in the head."

"That . . . completely sucks."

Laughter overtook me. She was right! It did suck, but it was even worse than she knew. What was I doing here? Making friends wasn't helping. If anything sympathy made it worse.

"You don't look like the type to have gotten yourself into such a mess."

"It's hard to say if I found it or it found me."

A waitress came over and Femi ordered fish and chips, while I just got fries. Once the waitress was gone Femi began studying me again until her eyes sparked and she perked up again. "It was over some guy, wasn't it?"

I kept my face passive, but my heart thumped hard in my chest. "What makes you think that?"

"There's something sad about you. You seem cool and reserved on the outside, but underneath that you have anger and sadness. A woman scorned vibe."

"You can see what I am feeling?"

"I have some talent towards healing. In order to heal something you have to know what ails it. And I've gotten better at reading people's eyes over the years. Your eyes have a lot to say. So how did this guy fit into the mess?"

"I don't really want to talk about it. You know, thank you for lunch, but I can't do this." I started to stand up, but Femi caught my arm.

"Sit back down. I didn't mean to pry. Curiosity comes with the territory."

I sat back in my seat fiddled with the napkin in my lap. "I'm sorry. I'm just not ready to talk about it yet."

"Hell, don't apologize. I should know better than to ask about something like that."

She let me have a couple minutes to regroup during which our food arrived. I twirled a fry in my fingers, then dipped it in ketchup. "Why do guardians not talk to Sekhmet?"

"Excuse me?" she said, an eyebrow quirked.

"You said that was one of the ways you knew I wasn't a guardian, I was talking to you."

"Oh. It's just Sekhmet have a long history of siding with the winners in conflicts. We feel no tie to good or evil or any other labels guardians like to put on things. We believe the world naturally changes and evolves, and we back the winners."

"Or do the people win because you back them?"

"That's the guardian point. They disagree with many of our choices throughout history, so it's a mutual avoidance on either side." Her eyes narrowed. "Do you have a problem with it?"

"No, I actually think I understand. Not about siding with the winners, but about making decisions they don't approve of. Let's just say it's slightly amazing I am sitting here now."

"You certainly don't seem like the others."

"What are they like?"

"You should know. You're one of them."

"I've only met five. I'm not an expert. My partner, Quintus, another to help with training, a conspiracy theorist who seemed nice, and two who were, well," I searched for the right words, "*different*. It probably isn't fair to judge all of them based on that sampling."

"I've heard of a guardian named Quintus. He's been around for ages. Cute, dimpled, Italian—maybe."

"That's him."

"He must not be as cute as I've heard if you're still moping around about some other guy."

"He's every bit as cute as you heard." I sighed not sure how to explain. "Have you ever wanted something with every last fiber in your body and soul? You know you can't have it, you know it isn't good for you, you know 10,000 reasons why it would never work, yet it's all you want."

"No," she said, "but it doesn't sound fun."

"It isn't."

"That guy really did a number on you." She took a large bite of fish and didn't wait to swallow before she began talking again "You know what you need? A girl's night out. Does your friendless ass have plans for tonight?"

I laughed. She was brash and nosey, but I liked her. "No."

"You do now. We're going to hit so many clubs, have so much fun you won't even remember that guy's name by morning."

"Sounds perfect." What did I have to lose? I needed friends, and Femi was all but offering to be my friend and introduce me into this bizarre world. After lunch she took me to one supernatural hub after another. I saw creatures I could never have imagined, and she explained everything as we encountered it. Femi stuck to my side and scared away anyone who looked like trouble. My mind wandered to whether or not Holden would like her. Our last stop of the night was the new club that had just opened on the south side, Club Xavier.

I sensed them immediately. The club was swarming with jinn. Femi seemed oblivious to them as she flirted with the jinni bouncer and pulled me over to the jinni bartender, but I knew I shouldn't be there.

I pulled everything within myself as tightly as I could. If I could manage not to draw attention to myself, then maybe I'd make out of all right. I didn't touch the drink she handed me. The last thing I needed were dulled senses when I was surrounded by manipulative hell spawns. I had the same reptilian, skin crawling feeling about them as I did the jinni I encountered in Italy. However, despite my natural abhorrence for them, I still caught myself searching the room for Holden. I knew the chances of his being there, out of every other place in the world were miniscule, but a thin string of hope threaded its way through me.

"You okay?" Femi asked, interrupting my latest Holden scan.

"Yeah, I'm great."

"Let's dance." She propelled me to the dance floor. "This is so much nicer than the pit it used to be." Femi shouted over the thumping music.

We danced for several songs, until I began to loosen up. It was fine, I could coexist with jinn. There was no reason to get uptight about them. Guardians and jinn had coexisted for thousands of years. It didn't mean I planned on advertising what I was, but I didn't have to be scared either. If something happened, I could always transport out. Or if worse came to worst, I'd do the blister thing again. I didn't believe the jinn knew I could do that.

A cool, hard body pressed up against me from behind, and my heart nearly stopped mid-beat. It couldn't be—it couldn't be him. I had been watching for him. I held my breath, my heart squeezing in my chest, and turned slowly. I didn't know if I would slap him or kiss him, if I let my feelings run away. Either one would be a mistake. I had to stay cool. The face that met mine was not the perfectly chiseled face I expected. I couldn't stop the rush of disappointment that flooded me.

The jinni before me was young and preppy. His blond hair was perfectly tousled and his cornflower blue eyes screamed,

"Trust me. Take me home to meet your parents." He laughed at me as he pulled me closer. "What I wouldn't give to be the person you expected."

I felt a gush of energy pour off of him. It felt slimy and unnatural. Is this what it felt like when Holden used his powers on me? I wanted to push him away, shower immediately. I forced a smile to my lips and pushed back. "But you're not."

A new, stronger wave hit me, as he pulled me back in, pressing his lips against my ear. "Are you sure about that?"

I didn't know how to get out of this without making a scene. If I were a human as I was pretending, I'd be swooning by now, but I only felt repulsed. His lips felt like snakes against my ear. All I wanted to do was get away from him. What choice did I have? I pushed him off of me. "No means no, jackass."

His eyes widened as he looked at me with new appreciation. "Well, aren't you full of surprises?" He leaned into me again. My hands balled into fists, ready to fight if he laid another finger on me. Another hand grabbed my shoulder and yanked me away from the jinni.

"None of that tonight," Femi said, poking him hard in the chest. The jinni narrowed his eyes and took a step towards her. Femi smiled with a lazy regard that could only be seen as a warning. "You don't want to upset me, jinni. I'll eat your heart."

"Stay out of this. I saw her first."

"Your tricks don't work on me. I see you for what you are. A stupid, lonely boy who knows he made the worst mistake of his life agreeing to any of this. You want to make everyone else suffer as you do, and I don't want your soulless vessel anywhere near me," I said moving closer to him.

His lips curled back in anger. I knew I should let Femi handle it, but I was tired of being quiet, of biting my tongue. The time for passively watching from the sidelines was over. I'd make my stand and nothing was going to push me around. I gathered energy for a strike against him, but Femi held out a restraining arm.

"No more. We need to go before he loses control and starts a riot," she said, watching the jinni like a hawk.

The two of us walked out of the door, heads held high. I felt wonderful, victorious. Jinn didn't frighten me, I could take care of myself, and when I saw Holden again, all of my feelings for him would melt away. I was sure of it now. He'd be just as revolting to me as any jinni in the club. I glanced at Femi as we walked down the street. Her manic grin probably rivaled my own.

"Girl, you're crazy. What do you think you were doing, pushing his buttons like that?"

"Standing up for myself for once in my life, and it was wonderful!"

"Do you know what jinn do?"

I nodded. I knew all too well what jinn did.

"As I said, you're crazy."

"I'm crazy? Do you know what they would've done to me if they knew I was a guardian? That was a jinn club you took me to. We aren't exactly cool with one another."

"Ah, shit. I didn't even think about that. I'm sorry. I'd heard about the club and thought it sounded fun. Plus it's geared more towards humans, so I thought you'd like it. I forgot about the guardian thing."

"No problem. I did have a good time."

"Yeah, right up to the point where you were felt up by the jinni."

"Even that. I wouldn't change one moment of tonight. It was just what I needed. I'm so happy I met you today." I said, smiling at her.

"How on earth did you become a guardian?" She laughed.

"Born into it."

"I didn't know you people could be born."

"Not many of us are."

"And everything's starting to come together."

I laughed at her. "You think you have me figured out?"

"Sure. You're different because you were born a guardian. Makes perfect sense."

"I'm different for a lot of reasons, not the least of which is I was born a guardian. You don't know the half of it."

"Yeah, right. Everyone thinks that."

"I almost became a jinni instead of a guardian. Does everyone say that?" I asked innocently.

Femi stopped dead on the sidewalk. I could feel her éyes boring into the back of my head as I continued walking. I didn't feel like myself tonight. I felt free more open, like I could do anything I wanted to do. I hadn't forgotten Holden like Femi had promised, but my shell of loneliness was breaking. It was great to have another girl to talk with, but it made me miss Juliet.

Femi quickly caught up with me. "Are you serious?"

"I rarely ever lie."

"Then this is a story I have to hear."

"Remember that guy you asked me about earlier?"

"The one you're so uptight about?"

"I'm not uptight!"

Femi raised an eyebrow in disagreement, but didn't say anything

"Whatever. He was a jinni. I met him while I was still human and fell in love with him."

"They manufacture feelings like Hershey's does chocolate. It should have dissipated when you died. Do you just feel dumb now?"

"No. This wasn't manufactured. I was *actually* in love with him. Like give up everything to be with him sort of love."

"So what happened? How did you end up a guardian?"

"He shot me in the head."

"What!"

"Only after a demon tortured me."

She started to speak several times, but stopped. Finally she shook her head. "No wonder you didn't want to talk about it over French fries. I should have bought you a bottle of tequila. So you were tortured by some demon, shot in the head by the man you loved, then what?"

"Isn't that enough?"

"Plenty, but where in this did you almost become a jinn?"

"That's where the story gets complicated." I rehashed the finer points of the end of my life for Femi, without using names. The less specifics she knew, the safer she'd be.

Femi never responded like she was judging anything I did or said, just listened actively and eagerly to everything I said—and didn't shy away from telling me when she thought one of my decisions was dumb. Before I knew it we were back in my neighborhood, and I'd told her more about my life than I'd told anyone in a long time.

"I don't know why I'm telling you all of this."

"Because you might explode if you keep anything else bottled up in there."

"Death by secrets." I laughed.

"Exactly. So have you seen him?"

"No."

"Are you still—" She gestured back and forth between our heads. "Can you still, you know?"

"Hear his thoughts? I believe I can, but I haven't done it. I'm not ready to open myself up to that again."

She whistled. "Damn, I've been alive a long time, but I've never heard of anything remotely like that. Aren't you tempted?"

"Constantly."

"Do you want him back or do you want revenge?"

"A little of both."

"If you tell me his name, I can find him for you. Then at least you'll know where he is, and you can avoid him or kick his ass, whatever floats your boat."

"No, it's best if you stay as far away from this as possible. Plenty of people have already died because of me. I'm not interested in adding anymore tallies to that list. We'll see each other when—" My vision went black and blind fury drenched my mind. I felt Holden everywhere, and he was livid. My legs gave out and the sidewalk rushed toward me. I clutched my head against the assault. He knew I was back. He'd found me.

The pain released my hold on my light, and it wrapped around me, protecting me from the mental barrage. My vision came back spotty, but at least I could see. His anger continued to course through my veins. He wanted to make someone pay.

Femi's hand connected with my face, making my check burn. "Olivia. Snap out of it," she demanded, hauling me to my feet.

"He knows I'm back," I said weakly and stumbled forward. "I need to get home."

Femi helped me to my apartment and wrung her hands nervously in the doorway to my bedroom while I crawled beneath my covers, still fighting against his rage—but he was so strong. Too strong.

"I don't know how to help you," she said.

"I'm fine. He just caught me off guard. My defenses were down. I just need quiet."

"That bastard. I'll kill him if you want."

"Get the light on your way out, please—" It took all of my energy and all of my concentration, but I managed to fight Holden back out of my head, but not before I felt the hurt that was feeding the fury.

Liz Schulte

TWENTY FOUR

I stared at my door. I wanted to move, but my feet were planted. They didn't want to move an inch for fear this dream would end. I wanted to smash things, relieve the anger that lined my veins like ice. And rejoice that the evil inside didn't win. I wanted to fall to my knees and thank God for returning her, and curse Him for keeping her away. My heart felt on the verge of bursting and collapsing. She was alive, and I was as alone as ever.

My mind was blank. I couldn't react. Every past clue I had dismissed was real. What I worried was delusion was true. The enormity of these thoughts threatened to swallow me. It was her, not my imagination. My mind reeled at the notion. It was her pain, her despair. She had said my name. She was the light in my mind. She really could have been the girl on the street? She came back ... just not to me. She was no longer *my* Olivia.

I sank to the floor, resting my forearms on my knees. Everything had been going so well, except for the fact that the universe seemed determined not to let me sleep. Olivia had stopped occupying my every thought. Work had become tolerable. I had even found purpose.

She didn't even tell her mother she was back. *Her own mother.* My mind couldn't reconcile what I knew of her actions with the person I loved. Why didn't she at least let me know? That's all I needed—just to know she was alive and well. Her safety was all I ever cared about.

I sat stunned for hours. My phone rang, but it barely penetrated the fog and I didn't answer it. Olivia was back. I could still see her if I wanted to. Finding her couldn't be too hard. I was a jinni for Christ's sake—finding things came with the territory. I could talk to her, get answers. She owed me that. At the least she should explain herself. Why would she let me suffer, her mother suffer? No, now that I knew she was alive, I doubted there was anything that could keep me away from her. I could devote the rest of my existence to finding Olivia, winning her back. And if I decided on that path, there was not one creature of the Abyss who would keep me from her.

But I was always the one going to her. She never came to me, not in all the time I had known her. She came into my subconscious, but I pursued her. Her pain mirrored my own sense of loss, but she had all the power to end the suffering— she had to have known that—yet, she ignored it. She chose to live in agony rather than come to me. I let that realization sink in. Olivia truly didn't want to be with me. I would have crossed Heaven, Hell, and Earth to be with her, and she couldn't even pick up a phone. No, I wouldn't force her to see me again. If she didn't want to see me, it was time I took a hint. Since the day I met her she was always the one who left me. I wouldn't chase Olivia for the rest of eternity. Either she would come to me or become a memory.

I never would've imagined that knowing she was alive, but didn't want me, would be worse than her being dead. I pulled myself from the floor, having no idea how much time had passed. The anger won. All bets were off. The door slammed behind me and my feet hit the pavement at a determined pace. If she didn't want me, if she wanted that ridiculous excuse for a guardian, then so be it. I wasn't waiting around for her anymore. I was done. Maybe I didn't even want her back. No way could she live up to my memory of her—romanticized nonsense. But she owed it to *me* to tell me to my face, damn it. Not to send her puppy over to piss on my floor. I should have killed him, sent her back my own message.

My knuckles rapped impatiently on the door in front of me.

"Holden, what are you doing here? I tried to call you when you never came into the office. I left the club early tonight," Juliet yammered, hair slightly tousled, probably from sleeping.

"Are you alone?"

"Yes," she said suspiciously.

I pushed her roughly against the wall, my mouth covering hers. What I lacked in passion, I made up for in force and anger.

How could she not tell me she was back?

Juliet bit my lip, snapping my attention back to her. I leaned back slightly, and she smiled. "I knew you'd come around."

I ripped open the front of her nightgown. Buttons clattered against the floor. "Don't talk." I turned her around, pinning her hands above her head while I searched my mind for Olivia. She had to be here somewhere, hiding. My free hand trailed down Juliet's soft skin along her side before curling around her front yanking her back against me.

"What are you waiting for?" Juliet asked breathlessly.

"Shut up." I growled. *Come out, come out wherever you are, Livi.*

God, even her name hurt. Finally I found her little hiding place. I found the dim light and pain that had been hiding from me for a year. A. Whole. Fucking. Year. I watched the light as I took her best friend, hoping somehow she could feel it. I took out my anger on Juliet with each thrust, and she begged for more. Olivia became dimmer in my mind, but never disappeared. It was no good. Juliet wasn't the one I wanted. Hers was not the skin I needed to feel beneath mine. She was a cheap imitation. I could fuck her for a thousand years and still every part of me would remain unsatisfied. Olivia was the only one. Juliet moaned, her body contracting. Olivia flared in my head, her presence rebounding and surrounding me for an instant before it shut off again. It wasn't even a contest.

Juliet tried to convince me to move into the bedroom, but who was I kidding? I was done. I'd done what I came to do. I put the final nail in the coffin of our relationship, closed the lovesick chapter in my life. Brushing off Juliet's hand, I stalked to the door. "I'll see you at the club tomorrow," I said and walked out. I had lost count of the days since I last slept. I needed sleep.

When I awoke hours later, my mind was sharper and more focused. Originally all I'd taken from my conversation with Quintus was that Olivia was back, and she didn't want me. However, there was more to what he'd said. He seemed under the impression that I was starting a war.

I fought to recollect his words. Something about killing guardians. . . . I had no idea what he was talking about, but I had a feeling Juliet, the warehouse and the glowing crate Baker saw had something to do with it. But why would Danica start a war we couldn't possibly win? Not that we would lose, exactly. . . . The battle would just rage on for centuries and never go anywhere. It would be bad for business on both sides.

It didn't add up. Malphas would've mentioned something about it if he knew, wouldn't he? And why did Quintus think I was behind it? I was responsible for the region. If someone within my area was killing guardians, I'd have to answer for it to my superiors. Surely, they couldn't be happy about war. A guardian here or there wouldn't ruffle any feathers, but a full-blown assault would upset the balance.

Could this be Danica's ludicrous plan to get her job back? Surely she knew Hell would punish her for an unsanctioned war that would draw human attention to us.

Then again, it was possible that this had nothing to do with Danica—or at least not Danica alone. Maybe something had changed, something powerful enough to set all of this into motion, something bigger than any of us. All I had to do was figure out what it was and how to stop it.

I lay back in bed, letting my mind work. Two things that I knew of had changed: Olivia became a guardian and I became the regional commander. Was this attack about me or about her? Quintus had indicated Olivia was special. Could her arrival have sparked this fuse? Only one person would benefit from seeing me fail and that was Danica. Who would benefit from Olivia's demise? Danica wasn't smart enough to pull something like this off on her own, which was clearly where Juliet came into the picture, but I didn't know the gain. Juliet hated Olivia. Could all of this be about killing Liv? Would such an elaborate plan be worth it? I had my doubts. What were they trying to accomplish and how were they pulling it off?

No matter which way I let my mind run, nothing made sense. A war in no way benefitted either Danica or Juliet, and I had no idea how they were capturing guardians. Obviously, there was a master plan. I just needed time to figure it out, to push in a little closer.

I called Baker and didn't wait for him to say hello. "I know what they're up to. I just don't know why."

"Where the hell have you been, boss? I called you, left messages, stopped by the club and your apartment. . . . "

"It doesn't matter. I know what they're doing."

"That's good because things are getting strange."

"What does that mean?"

"More jinn are guarding the warehouse, another glowing box was brought in, and get this—two guardians are staking out the building from the roof across the way. Whatever she's up to, it's in the majors."

"They're starting a war."

"Come again?"

"You heard me right, a war between jinn and guardians."

"Why?" Baker sounded as shocked as I was. "Bad business."

"Can you find the Loki for me?"

"Maybe."

"Find it. It knows something. I think it was trying to warn me."

"You want me to stop following Juliet?"

"No, I'll take care of her."

I hung up and set out to find Juliet. She'd finally earned my undivided attention. She was leaving her apartment as I arrived. I followed her to a café where she bought coffee and a pastry.

She browsed some shops, caused some fights, and didn't seem to be in a rush. After several hours of mindless shopping and instigating, she went over to the club. I watched her for a while before I ran back to my apartment to change and shower. Half an hour later, I was back at the club and headed up to my office, ignoring Juliet trailing behind me.

"Are we going to talk about last night?" she asked when I tried to shut my office door on her.

I looked at her steadily. "What do we have to talk about?"

Juliet's mouth fell open, and she stumbled over her words. She'd never make it as a jinni.

"Look, sweetheart, you'll never make it in this life if you can't detach. We had sex, that's all. It'll probably happen again if you don't get psycho. But we're not in a relationship. Hell, I don't even like you most of the time."

Her eyes narrowed and her chin tilted upward—still so much pride. That would be her downfall. When I changed, my pride was the first to go. You do what you have to do to survive. I crossed my arms, waiting for her to storm off or come at me.

"You cold son of a bitch." She spat at me, looking like what she really wanted to do was punch me in the face.

I grinned widely. "If you want someone to cuddle with and call your boyfriend, find a fucking human."

"How on earth did you ever get Olivia to go out with you? She should have hated you. You're everything she disliked in a person."

Well, she does now. "She was a mark. Things are different with a mark. You know that. I can be whatever they want me to be."

Juliet ran her tongue slightly over her lips and walked towards me slowly. "Then you can be whatever I want you to be."

I looked down at her with my own half smile, and leaned in until my lips were nearly on her ear. "But it would be a waste of my time," I whispered and walked back to my desk. "Don't you have work to do?" Juliet frowned, but left.

I worked in my office for a little while, then went down to the club. This afternoon told me absolutely nothing about Juliet except she was lonely. I needed to find something. If she wasn't the traitor, I needed to get rid of her. She was too unstable. If she was the traitor, I needed to maneuver closer to her. Find out who or what was behind all of this.

When Juliet was nowhere to be found, I asked Will, the bartender, where she'd gone. He pointed me towards the back entrance. She was pacing in the alley, softly talking into her cell phone. I moved back into the club and sat where I'd see her return. Thirty minutes and ten girls surrounding me later she walked back inside. Now was the real test.

Juliet was headed in my direction. She cut through the gaggle of women, receiving dirty looks every step of the way. "Glad to see you decided to join us on the bottom," she said with a pleasant smile, but suspicion-laced eyes.

"Where have you been?" I asked, having no intention of defending my actions.

"Over on the strip side," she replied smoothly. She was definitely hiding something.

"Is everything going well?" I asked blandly not looking at her. How was I going to get her cell phone?

"Of course I have it covered down here." She looked at me then back upstairs as if showing me where I belonged which made me laugh.

"In case you've forgotten, this is my club." I said, sliding her against me.

"And in case *you've* forgotten, I run your club and run it well."

I met her eyes and let lust pour from me. Her cheeks colored, and her breathing became shallow as she willingly moved towards me. My hand folded over her hand that still clutched her cell phone, when I felt a vibration in my pocket.

Damn it. It had to be Marge.

I pulled everything back in and released Juliet, who looked dumbfounded by my sudden change in mood. I'd have to get her cell phone another day.

TWENTY FIVE

It was an understatement to say that my meeting with Holden didn't go exactly as I had hoped. His reaction to Olivia being alive wasn't wholly unexpected—I'd known he would be upset. What I'd counted on was there being some remnant of the love he'd seemed to genuinely have for her once—but no. I shouldn't have told him. And now I had to tell her that Holden knew she'd come back—and that he was unhinged and killing guardians.

What would this do to Olivia's progress? Maybe I didn't have to tell her. Maybe she was better off not knowing. Something happened when you put the two of them together. Like dynamite and flame, only destruction followed. Then again . . . if he found her first, it would come out that I hadn't told her, and Olivia didn't have a history of reacting well to secrets. She also didn't have a history of being able to resist Holden. I would tell her when the time was right, I decided.

I arrived at Olivia's early with breakfast, after plotting and planning our stakeout so she would be hidden, have an easy escape, and the least amount of exposure to jinn. She answered the door sleepily, eyes a little puffy.

"What are you doing here?" she asked in the midst of a yawn.

"I brought breakfast." I waved the coffee under her nose.

"You're my hero."

"We've been assigned a mission. I thought I'd fill you in on it, but not until after a breakfast date."

She laughed hoarsely. "I've created a monster." She took the sack I held in my hand and rifled through it. She emerged with a blueberry scone and snatched the cup of coffee I was tempting her with. She sat at her table with one leg folded underneath her and the other one swinging above the floor. I grabbed a muffin from the bag and joined her.

"How was your day yesterday?" she asked not looking at me.

"Oh, fine. And yours?"

She smiled, but didn't answer. Instead she inspected her scone and blew on her coffee.

"What? Did something happen?" Holden couldn't have found her this fast, could he?

"No, nothing happened. I just have a lot on my mind."

She was hiding something, I could tell. She was different somehow. Our conversation from two nights ago flooded back to me. "You were thinking about what we discussed?"

Her brow furrowed for a moment. "Yes."

"And . . ."

"And I think you're right. I should give you a chance." She took my hand, shoving all thoughts of anything relating to Holden to the back of my mind.

I squeezed her hand, warmth filling me. She had actually agreed to try! There was no way I could tell her about Holden, not now.

"I wish we could just spend today together, no mission. You know, spend time really getting to know one another as people."

I smiled, not exactly sure what she was talking about. There wasn't a "me" separate from my job. It was slightly concerning that she felt she was someone different than who she was everyday with me. "We have forever. Before too long we'll know everything there is to know about one another."

She frowned. "I hope not. Knowing everything about someone isn't all it's cracked up to be." She broke her scone in half, but sat it on the table as if she could no longer stand the sight of it. When she looked back up, she had a smiled stretched across her face. "And if that is the case, you'll be bored in no time."

"I doubt that." I returned her smile gently. She was definitely acting weird.

"What's this mission that brought you here at the crack of dawn?"

"It's top secret. I know you have been asking about this for weeks, and honestly I was forbidden to tell you anything. And even still this has to stay between the two of us, it cannot become public knowledge." Her face was a mixture of impatience and irritation, but she agreed before I continued. "There's a traitor among the guardians. Someone is leaking information to the jinn about what our missions are and where we'll be—and the jinn have been capturing and killing us."

Olivia inhaled sharply. "And what has been done about it? Why are we just now looking into this?"

I took a sip of coffee, trying to find the right words. "I don't know what has been done. All I know is they didn't want any guardians to know about it so I kept their secret."

"Why do they want our help now?"

"Ezra, a high elder, has received information about where this traitor will next be meeting the jinn. We are to sneak in and find out who is the traitor, then report back directly. It might be our only chance to find out, so failure is not an option."

"Who would do something like this?"

"I don't know. Ezra believes it is someone of very high ranking, so be on your guard. It is a very dangerous mission. I told him you were too new for it, but he insisted that your unique powers might be our best hope at accomplishing this task."

"You told him I shouldn't be allowed to go?" She tilted her head to the side in a decidedly annoyed expression.

"Olivia, you are doing wonderfully, but you hardly have a full grasp of your abilities." Now her eyebrows arched. "It doesn't matter what I think anyway. He insisted you are to help."

"Quintus, there's one little point that I'm going to have to make abundantly clear to you: Don't do anything for my own good. I've had enough of that. I don't want to be kept in the dark or away from assignments because you think they're dangerous. I'm my own person, and I will make my own decisions."

I swallowed wondering if she knew and that was why she was acting so strange. "Of course, and as I said it is a moot point because Ezra insisted."

"Now, is that the only thing you need to tell me?"

I startled and peered at her closely. Could she tell I was keeping something back? Her face softened, so I thought not. . . And I chickened out. I couldn't do it. She was already irritated about the mission. I didn't want to make it worse by stoking the fire.

"That's it."

"Fine. So what are we going to do?"

"I have the address of the meeting place. We need to get over there and stake the facility out."

"When will the meeting take place?"

"I have no idea."

We arrived at a warehouse in an exceedingly rough part of Chicago and made ourselves untraceable to the human eye, so we wouldn't invite unwanted attention. The building appeared to be deserted. Positioning ourselves on a rooftop of a neighboring building, we had a perfect view of the comings and goings from the structure. It was tedious work. Most of the day went by without anything happening at all. Occasionally a jinni would patrol by, and Olivia would jot down the time and a description. Mostly though, she sat with her back against the wall, her arms folded over her chest, and her mind a thousand miles away.

"So why didn't you tell me about the supernatural hangouts?" Olivia asked nonchalantly, but I could hear irritation highlighting her words.

"What are you talking about?"

"You know, the bars, clubs, restaurants where all the people in the Abyss hang out. There are more than just guardian coffee houses. Places I could make non-human friends."

She thought I'd intentionally held out on her, but the truth was that it hadn't occurred to me to tell her. I enjoyed our time together so much, I didn't think about the fact that she didn't know anyone else. I forgot the socialization part of her training. My feelings for Olivia were seriously getting in the way of my job. I should ask that someone else be assigned to her, but even the thought of it made me cringe. "You haven't been in Chicago very long."

She gave me the most dubious expression I've ever seen. "Look, I don't care why you did it, but you really need to stop keeping things from me. No more partial information. Tell me whatever you need to tell me and don't worry about my reaction. I can't stand it any longer."

Guilt ate at me. I needed to tell her. The longer I waited to tell her about Holden, the angrier she would get, but she was giving us a chance. . . . If I put him back into the equation, would she still be willing? I took her hand, loving that I could do that now. "I'm sorry. You're right. In the future, I'll make a stronger effort to be more forthcoming."

She frowned. "That's a very political answer. I don't want you to *try*. Don't you understand? I need to be able to trust that you aren't keeping things from me."

"You can trust me."

"I hope so."

"So how did you find out about the Abyss locations?"

"I made a friend yesterday, and she took me there."

"That's wonderful. Who's the friend?"

"Femi. She's a—"

"Bounty hunter." She was known for being wild and impetuous, but she was exceptional at what she did. It made perfect sense that Olivia would find her of all people. Trouble was attracted to Olivia like no one else. "I know her by reputation."

Olivia refolded her arms in front of her chest.

"What?" I asked.

"Just what have you heard?"

"She is a good bounty hunter. She can be difficult and doesn't like taking orders, but she gets the job done."

"And you don't have a problem with her being a Sekhmet?"

"Why would I?"

"She said most guardians don't like her kind."

I shrugged. I normally liked to avoid Abyss politics. "They are an honorable race with their own ideas and opinions. I do not have a problem with them."

Olivia smiled. "Good."

"Where did you ladies go yesterday?"

"Oh, too many places to keep track of," Olivia said, her cheeks coloring. Her eyes flickered back to the street. "It's starting to pick up down there."

I looked through the pink light of the setting sun. She was right. Jinn were swarming the warehouse. It was looking more and more doubtful that anyone was coming tonight. No guardian would walk into a warehouse filled with jinn. But we needed to stay in case I was wrong.

"You don't think he is coming do you?"

"No."

"There's a jinni night club not too far from here. I could go ask some questions."

"No."

"Quintus."

I cut her off. "Did you not hear the part about jinn *killing* guardians? I'm not sending you in to die and if that pisses you off, then you will just have to be mad at me."

"They won't recognize me. I can fully repress my nature."

"We don't know that. We only think it. You can't go in on a theory."

"I know it," she said quietly.

"How could you possibly?"

"Femi and I went there last night. I didn't realize what it was until we were inside. A jinni danced with me and never knew what I was."

I didn't know if I was angry or relieved. "You've been giving me trouble about keeping secrets from you, while you've been keeping them from me?"

Olivia's jaw clenched. "First off, this wasn't a secret. It just happened and I'm telling you about it. Second, my secrets have nothing to do with *you*. Your secrets, however, are in regard to me."

Well, she wasn't incorrect, but I was still irritated. She went to a jinn club. "Were you looking for Holden?"

She raised her chin. "No. Femi took me there." She spoke her words carefully, as if weighing each of them.

"You could have left."

"I could have, but I can't keep running away. I have to figure out a way to live with my past. It isn't your concern."

"I am concerned for you."

She shut her eyes and turned her face from me. "Don't think this is something more than what it is, Quintus. I said I'll give us a chance, but everything has to be taken slow. I need space."

"And if he comes back?"

"We can't be together. I know that."

"But do you want to be?" I didn't know why I kept asking questions that I didn't want to know the answers to, but they kept coming out of my mouth.

Olivia sighed and didn't respond. That was answer enough.

TWENTY SIX

Quintus kept me on that stupid roof top until well after midnight, before he finally gave up on anyone showing. We went back to our respective apartments, and I was relieved to be alone. The more I thought about dating Quintus, the more it seemed like a bad idea. He was nice, but we worked so closely together, it could only lead to trouble. Plus, no matter how much I wanted things to be different, they weren't. I didn't have possession of my heart. Even the shattered bits belonged to one man. I was brushing my teeth when I heard Holden say my name.

How did he always know when my defenses were down? I quickly shut him off and climbed into bed. My eyes were shut, and I prepared myself to drift into my horrible nightmare, when something else happened altogether. I felt Holden cover me like silk. He was thinking about our last night together. My heart swelled. I remembered his touch, his strength, and all of the beautiful reassurances he gave to me as I fell asleep in his arms. We were the only two people who mattered in the all of the world at that moment. We were one, soul mates.

I accepted his gift and gave my own in return, not letting my brain remind me that nothing came of any of those bitter sweet words. They were empty promises from a hollow man. I didn't know what his angle was, but I wanted what he gave me. It was better than smelling his shirt. I felt him all around me, saturating my senses. For just a moment or two, I could pretend everything wasn't different—that we still had a future.

"*I'm sorry,*" he said. The sound of his voice brought tears to my eyes.

"*Wait,*" I nearly begged, but it was too late. He broke the connection. "Damn you, Holden." I once again cried myself to sleep, though no dreams of my death haunted me.

Morning came too quickly. I was late meeting Quintus on the roof. He wore an annoyed, tired expression when I appeared, but didn't say anything.

"Did you stay all night?" I asked, seeing he was still wearing the same clothes.

"I told you—we only have one shot at this."

"Then why did you send me home? I would've stayed."

"You looked exhausted. Still do."

"Hmmm. I'm going to try to take that in a nice way."

"You know what I mean." His forehead creased and the corners of his mouth turned down.

My conscience finally got the better of me, and I let him off the hook. "Look, why don't you go home, sleep for a couple hours, then get some coffee and come back. I can take this watch. It's stupid for us to do this together when nothing's happening."

"I'm not leaving you," he said as if that were end of that, but I wasn't ready to back down.

"Quintus, don't be dumb. No one knows we're up here. If anyone finds me, I'll transport back to my apartment. Honestly, what could happen to me here? They can't even sneak up on me. I'll be perfectly safe, and I don't need you to help me note the one or two jinn I might see this morning. You know as well as I do that jinn hate sunlight."

"Holden didn't seem to have a problem with it."

I sighed at the sound of his name. "*Holden* seems to be the exception to most things."

Quintus looked at me levelly, his eyes narrowing. "Don't believe that, Firefly, not for a moment. Holden is every bit as, if not more, dangerous than the rest of them."

I held off all the defensive comments I wanted to make. Holden might be dangerous to Quintus, but after last night, I was certain he wasn't dangerous to me. No matter how it had ended, the emotions he'd sent during the night were real, and he still held on to them. Everything between us wasn't a lie, but I couldn't let myself think about that. "That isn't the point. The point is, yes, he went in the sun, but that isn't their general practice and you know it. Now stop being a pain in the ass and get out of here, so I don't feel like I have to hang out with you all night. I do have a life you know."

"You have plans?" Quintus seemed amazed by this revelation.

"Femi and I are going out."

Quintus started to say something a few times, but stopped himself each time. He sighed and rubbed his head. "You're right. I need sleep. If anything happens, transport to my apartment rather than yours."

"Fine." I didn't care. I just wanted him to leave. I wanted to think about last night and figure out what, if anything, changed the way I felt.

Quintus squeezed my shoulder and thankfully vanished into a ball of brilliance. I looked out over the quiet morning and the sleeping warehouses. I wanted to talk to Holden. My brain nervously fidgeted and sputtered at the notion. My heart beat wildly in anticipation. I couldn't talk to him until I knew what I wanted, how to handle things with him. I couldn't—or rather, I wouldn't—follow him anywhere. Not anymore. My life had changed, as I was sure his had. We couldn't fit into each other's lives anymore. Even if he really loved me then, did it matter now? It didn't change any of the things he had done. Love or not, his actions spoke the loudest. Holden didn't choose me. Talking to him would be pointless.

I looked back over the ledge, disappointed but resolved. Things had to remain as they were. I had a job to do that mostly entailed undoing the things he did. We were destined to be at odds. Our one chance had slipped through the cracks. I would keep our happy memories locked safely within me, knowing I could never add to them. I was grateful Holden reminded me that we had them. I even felt fairly confident that if I saw him, I could keep it together. I wouldn't smother him in kisses or beat him to a pulp. I'd remain calm and indifferent.

The morning was slow and tedious, even worse than I predicted. No jinn showed up at all. I briefly considered going down to the warehouse and taking my own look around while no one was there, but I knew if anything went wrong Quintus would murder me. So I stuck to my post. However, sitting around and waiting wasn't natural for me. I felt like we should be doing something. People were missing. They were hurt. Why were we lurking in the shadows waiting for something to happen? Perhaps Femi and I would have to make another excursion to Xavier tonight. If I want jinni intelligence, what better place was there to find it than among them? Of course Quintus couldn't know. He would refuse and ruin everything. If he insisted on protecting me, then he was forcing me to keep my plans from him. I had to take care of myself eventually; now was as good a time to start as any.

I pulled out my phone and texted Femi.

-Xavier tonight?

-Prolly a bad idea

-Need to go there. Tell you more later.

-K but UR crazy. See u l8r

I was tucking my phone into my pocket when Quintus appeared, looking much more rested. I smiled. "Did you sleep well?"

"I did. How have things been here?"

"Boring. Absolutely no one has been by yet."

He nodded, hunkering down next to me. "Sorry I was being difficult earlier. You were right. I needed rest."

"No need to apologize. You've suffered through many of my fits of rage. We're good."

Quintus face creased with those dimples you could lose yourself in and brushed a piece of hair from my face. "But I want you to feel like you can talk to me, that I won't judge you or hold anything you say against you."

"Guardians aren't any different than people. You can say you won't do those things, but it's our nature to—and that's okay. I know you're only trying to steer me towards what you think is best, but you have to understand I'm going to do what I think is best."

I had only met one person in my life who listened without judgment and never once threw anything I told him back at me. I thought it was because he was unique, but in reality there was probably nothing I could ever tell him that would have been as bad as what he was hiding from me.

"Just so long as you understand that I do what I do because I want you to be safe and happy."

"Absolutely." I smiled back at him, and he leaned forwards as if to kiss me. I panicked and tried to move away, but my back was against the low brick wall. My ungraceful failed attempt at moving did not go unnoticed. Quintus chuckled softly and kissed my check, which was already starting to burn with embarrassment.

I started to try to explain, but he held up his hand to stop me. "You don't have to say anything, Firefly. You're not ready yet. I understand."

If I was being honest, I would tell him that in all likelihood I would never be ready to move on with him or anyone else, but I wasn't honest—with him or with myself. I wasn't giving up on moving on yet. I would find a way. If Holden could do it, so could I.

We spent the rest of the afternoon watching the empty warehouse remain empty. As the sun began to set, Quintus broke our silence.

"You should go. It's been dead all day."

"It could pick up tonight, and I'm not meeting Femi for a couple hours. I can hang around." I suddenly felt guilty about leaving and withholding my plans.

"Seriously, go. I can handle it here."

"Well, don't do anything brave unless you tell me about it first," I said with a smile. I gave him a little wave, then appeared back in my apartment.

Having a bit of time on my hands, I changed and went for a run to clear my mind for later. I needed to be sharp and focused. I knew where I was going this time, so I'd be ready for them. They didn't know I was anything other than a human, so I couldn't let on that I thought any different of them.

I paid attention to store windows as I ran past them, watching for the most tempting dress I could find. Not necessarily revealing, just something that would draw a jinni's eye. I wished I knew what had attracted Holden to me. Why had I of all people drawn his eye? Then the jinni the other night. . . . Why me? Maybe it didn't matter what I wore. Maybe it was just me. The expression "like a moth to flame" came to mind. What was more tempting to evil than innocence?

I found the perfect dress before I made it back to my apartment. Excited, I went home and immediately created it before the image faded from my mind. It was a stark white linen sundress that hit me just above the knee with an embroidered hem and a princess neckline. I showered and dried my hair, letting it fall in natural glossy waves around my shoulders. My skin looked sun-kissed and dewy from the combination of sitting on the rooftop all day and my run this evening. I applied a little pink lip gloss and some mascara as my finishing touches. I looked like a virgin sacrifice.

Femi arrived at my apartment right on time, a large Chicago pizza in hand. She looked me up and down. "Tonight's not about fun, is it?" she asked.

"What? You don't like my dress?"

"You look like a preacher's daughter at the gates of hell."

I smiled and plopped a piece of pizza on my plate. "I think the jinn will appreciate it."

"You'll have to beat them off with a stick."

"That's what I'm hoping."

"Look, Olivia, you seem fun, and I don't have many non-hunter friends, but I don't want to look for trouble on my nights off—"

I interrupted before she talked herself into leaving. "We're not looking for trouble." I needed Femi on board with my plan, or I'd be in over my head. "We're looking for information."

"Same thing," Femi grumbled, but let me continue.

"This is all top secret, and I'm not supposed to tell anyone about the mission, but I need you to back me up tonight. Jinn are allegedly killing guardians. At least four have disappeared and our elders believe there's a traitor among us. We got a tip about where the jinn would be meeting this traitor, but not when."

She pursed her lips but didn't comment.

"Quintus and I have staked out the location the last two days, but nothing's happened. I don't want to sit and wait while who knows how many other guardians are being killed. I want to do something more proactive."

Femi tilted her head to one side then the other. "Why would the jinn break the treaty? It doesn't make sense, unless they're making some big move or power play. They have nothing to gain." She traced her thumb across her lower lip, seemingly lost in thought. "I'll help you, but just so it's understood, I'm not taking your side. I'm helping you because if the jinn do have something up their sleeve, it could affect the entire Abyss. It's better to know about something like this before it hits."

I clasped my hands in front of me, excited that my plan was going to work. "I don't care why you help, just so long as you do!"

"Just out of curiosity, why do you want my help and not another guardian's? Don't you people like to keep your business internal?"

"I don't really know any other guardians, and I can't trust they aren't the traitor. Also, no other guardians can look as human as me."

"You think I look human?" she asked doubtfully.

"I think you're not a recognized enemy of the jinn, and you look tough. You made that jinni the other night stop in his tracks. You'll make them think twice about messing with me, which is just what I need while I'm playing the wide-eyed human."

"Well hell, this might be fun. You should have told me you wanted me to look like a badass tonight. I would've worn my shit-kicker boots."

I laughed. "Femi, you so don't need the boots." She was wearing tight black leather pants and a top that was closer to a bikini top than a shirt. It wrapped around her in a twisted design showing off the tight, corded muscles of her flat bronze stomach and the tattoo of a tiger rising up from her lower back.

Femi grinned and took a large bite of pizza. She reached down to her ankle and produced a small, shiny silver knife with a wavy blade. "Find somewhere to keep this, in case I get occupied. It won't kill a jinni, but if you aim for their throat, it will slow them down enough to get away."

My mind flashed back to the hotel room, and the jinni who attacked me before I died. I should have had this then. Had it not been for Holden—

"Hey, you okay?"

"Yeah. Sorry. Memories."

"You'll be fine. If your jinni shows up, point him out, and I'll take care of him."

I shook my head. "Stay away from him. He's dangerous."

"So am I," Femi said dryly.

"You don't know Holden."

Femi's hand froze half way to her mouth. She looked over at me, her pupils shifting and contracting vertically. "Did you say *Holden*?"

Argh—I couldn't believe I'd blurted it out like that. "Yes, that's his name. Holden Smith."

"You dated *Holden Smith*." She looked at me with a new appreciation. "The freaking North American commander?"

"What? No, that's not him. Holden, well, I don't really know what he did because he kept it from me, but he couldn't have been commanding anyone. He only ever spoke to me. Holden was more solitary."

"Yeah, that's him all right. He's the new commander. He sort of came out of nowhere. But I've heard stories. Vicious. He's not someone you want on your bad side, but from the way

I hear it he doesn't have a good side. He doesn't like jinn or humans." She wiped her hands on a napkin and leaned back in her chair, eyes still shifting in a cat-like manner. "Are you sure about tonight?"

"I'm positive. Holden doesn't know where I am. We'll be fine."

She looked doubtful. "Olivia, if he wants to find you, he will. He's a jinni. Finding something that's desired is his specialty."

"He doesn't want to find me. But all the same, if he does show up tonight, it's best if you let me handle it. No matter what happens, walk away, forget you ever met me."

Her eyes widened and her brows pulled together. "Have you lost your mind?"

"I'm serious. He won't hurt me, but he will hurt you or anyone else who stands in the way of what he wants."

"And what does he want?"

"It's hard to say. I thought I knew once, but now I'm not sure."

"Well, let's just hope he doesn't show." She grimaced and I laughed at her.

"Holden is the least of our concerns. We need to worry about whoever's killing guardians."

"You're sure it isn't him?"

"Positive. He wanted me to become a guardian from the start. He knows I'm back. If he wanted to kill me, he would've already made his move. I'm 100% sure, especially after last night."

"Wait, wait, wait. What happened last night?"

I told her about our little encounter, and she slapped the kitchen table. "Holy crap, I have to meet this guy. And your other one too," she said with a wink, knowing full well how uncomfortable talking about Quintus in that manner made me.

"You can meet Quintus if you want, but let's hope you never have to meet Holden. When the two of us are together, people in my life start dying."

"Yet you love him."

"I don't know how I feel."

"That's bullshit. They're both standing in front of you right now, asking you to come with them. Who do you choose?"

"It isn't that easy."

"Of course it is."

"I have obligations."

"No obligations, just feelings. Which one do you choose?"

"I don't want to play this game."

Femi smiled knowingly. "That's what I thought. Just because you don't like the answer doesn't change what it would be. You like the guardian, but you love the jinni. You're totally screwed."

"Gee thanks."

"I call 'em like I see 'em. Whether or not he's mixed up in all of this, eventually you're going to have to see him again."

"I'll deal with that when I have to."

She shrugged. "So what's the plan for tonight?"

"I don't really have one. I thought we'd just go to the club, and I'd hone in on the most powerful seeming jinni and see what he knows."

"You're just going to ask him?"

I hadn't really thought it through any further than that. People always told me things. But hearing her skepticism made me doubt myself. Why would a jinni brag to a human about killing guardians? "I don't know how I will get him to talk?"

"How far are you willing to go with his?"

"What do you mean?"

"There are two ways we can do this. The peaceful way or the bloody way. The peaceful way equals you romancing the jinni. A lot is said in the bedroom, and you'd find out a lot without anyone ever knowing what you were doing or that you were watching. It wouldn't be the first time you were with a jinni either so you would be . . . prepared."

I stared at her. I couldn't imagine anything more distasteful. "What's the bloody way?"

"Act really flirty and easy with the jinn, but not too easy or he won't be interested, and get him to take you to the owner's office for privacy—where I'll be waiting. I'll temporarily dispatch the jinni, and we can search the office."

"First, what if the owner is there? Second, how do you know the owner has anything to do with what's going on? And third, how do you know where the office is?"

Femi smiled. "Glad to see you're paying attention. First, owners of these types of establishments are rarely in their offices, and if he or she is, then the jinni won't take you up there. You need to be aware that nothing may come from tonight. We're figuring out the lay of the land and seeing how we can get what we want in the future. I'd be amazed if it did work out for us." She took another bite of pizza, but it didn't stop her from continuing to talk. "Second, Xavier has become a jinn hotspot. Where there are a lot of jinn, there's trouble. That's why I took you there. I needed someone to help me blend in, so I could get inside and check out their operations. You assisted on my own recon mission."

"You used me?" I didn't know whether I was angry or impressed at how well she maneuvered me.

"Yeah, I did. Sorry about that. Third, I didn't see any offices on the main level, but there was a staircase in the back of the club that no one was using. I assume the offices are upstairs—owners usually like to be on the top."

"Femi, you're sort of amazing."

"It's my job. So which one do you want to go with?"

My mind spun. The last time I ran off on one of my hair brained schemes, everything systematically fell apart. Was I ready to do this again? Maybe the stake out was for the best. Maybe I just needed to be patient and wait for answers to come to me. I couldn't get involved with a jinni again. I'd been down that road with Holden, and it didn't work out well. Also, if the jinni in the club was any indication, I wouldn't be able to stand being near one for long enough to gather any intelligence. The second option was much more appealing, but dangerously dependent on everything going according to plan.

"Or we don't have to do this at all," she said sensing my hesitation.

"No, I need to do this. I'm weighing my options," I said weakly.

"Why do *you* have to do this?"

"Because no one else can or will do it."

"Then what's it going to be?"

"Looks like I'm taking door number two."

TWENTY SEVEN

Impatient thumping pulsed through the apartment jarring me out of sleep. Tonight of all nights I needed to sleep. Why was someone trying to stop that? I flung open the door with murder on my mind. Juliet stood in the doorway wearing a trench coat, and I doubted anything else. Either this chick had serious self-esteem issues, or she was undoubtedly behind the guardian killing fiasco. Why else would she constantly be trying to ensnare me? It wasn't like we were friendly or even cordial. Did she really think she could blind me with lust? Greed was more Juliet's strength, but maybe she hadn't figured that out yet.

"What?" I asked not bothering to pretend that seeing her was anything other than annoying.

She pushed past me, untying her coat and letting it drop to the floor. She looked back over her shoulder. "I thought we would finish what we started," she said with a coy smile.

I weighed my options without shutting the apartment door. I could kick her out and ruin the farce I was building. I could have sex with her and perhaps gather more information, but now that my anger with Liv had mostly subsided that idea felt wrong on a level I wasn't even aware I possessed. So which was worse, committing an unforgiveable act against her or failing to obtain the means to save her?

The sound of my door closing filled the apartment as I followed Juliet into the bedroom. Liv wasn't coming back to me. Hurting her, while undesirable, was less concerning than her dying again. If this was what it took, so be it. My mind fell into a blissfully empty state, void of any thought or emotion, during our escapades. She served the only purpose I needed her to serve. Afterwards, I showered to wash the scent of her from me and to give her the opportunity to leave. When I came back into the room, however, she was still lounging across my bed,

"I haven't slept in a couple days." I glanced from her to the door. She arched her back and stretched her arms above her head.

"Mmm, that's not what I have in mind. I was thinking more along the lines of all night."

"Sorry to disappoint," I said coldly, tossing her jacket to her. She ignored her trench coat and stood up. Rubbing her body against me in one long caress, her fingers scraped against the round scar on my back just below my left shoulder blade.

"Is this how you died?"

"Yes."

"What did you make your deal for?"

"Revenge."

"Who deserved such an act of devotion?"

"It's not important. How about you? How did the demon talk you into making the deal?" Last time she had refused to tell me, which piqued my curiosity. I legitimately wanted to know. The information might be pertinent later down the line.

"To keep from becoming schizophrenic."

I vaguely remembered Olivia saying something about Juliet's mother having been institutionalized, but it was a unique angle for a dealmaker. "He knew right away what was happening to me. I never had to tell him anything. I had to hide the signs from Olivia—I didn't want to worry her. Not that she would have noticed." She laughed bitterly.

"I didn't want to die, but I didn't want to be crazy either. As months went by, I felt my life slipping further away. Control was harder to come by. When he made me the offer, I knew it was the escape I'd been hoping for. It couldn't have come at a better time."

That actually made sense. It explained a lot about her behavior. Her death would have stopped the disease in its tracks, but it wouldn't have reversed anything that was already there. Being a jinn, thus ungoverned by rules or any moral fiber, would allow whatever insanity she already had to thrive. Eventually it would still take over, though I'm sure the demon didn't explain that. It also explained why she accepted her fate and took so well to being a jinni. She knew she wasn't missing out on the grand normal life most of us jinn wanted as soon as we realized we could no longer have it. Juliet had managed to use the system to her advantage.

However, I remained unmoved. She had turned Olivia into a villain in her mind. Crazy or not, it pissed me off. I didn't want her here, nor was I interested in her continued attempts at seducing me.

"Hangings always leave an ugly scar," I remarked, running my fingers across her neck. She covered her throat with one hand and stepped back from me with flushed cheeks. Good old Juliet, always worried about how she looks in other people's eyes. I handed her the coat one more time. "I'll see you tomorrow. "

"You're a bastard."

I nodded. I never pretended to be any else. She could have no expectations to the contrary.

I walked her to the door to make sure she actually left. Something caught her eye in the living room. "Olivia had a camera bag just like that." She pointed towards Olivia's tan satchel sitting next to the couch in the living room. I forgot to put it away after I spoke with Marge.

I looked back, pretending like I didn't know what I would find. "Oh, the last girl that was here left that. A student, completely perfect, not a mark on her."

"Isn't that photo on your mantle from Olivia's show?"

"Yes. Quite a good investment—the value skyrocketed after the murder. She was a wonderful photographer, wasn't she?" Christ, I should have thought ahead. Juliet could have stopped by here countless times. Leaving so much of Olivia in my apartment was stupid. "Bye." I pushed her out the door and locked it.

I grabbed the camera bag, made sure everything was back where it belonged, then put it back in its spot in my closet. One little corner acted as a shrine to her. My black shirt she last wore hung in my closet never washed. While I knew I couldn't, part of me still believed I could smell her on it. Her camera, the bag, and the single photograph of us, which I had developed from her camera, were there. I'd burned everything else when I came back home that day and tried to purge her from my life.

I smelled the shirt and the emotions I fought so hard against snuck back in. I would never be rid of her. Not completely anyway. Olivia was part of me. It was undeniable. Perhaps that was why she didn't want me to know she was back, because I had stolen a piece of who she was and wouldn't relinquish it. Maybe she was worried I would take more, take everything. "Olivia." I said aloud, holding my breath for a response.

I felt a surge of panic, but it dissipated quickly. It made me smile. A real smile that started deep in my chest and spread until it reached my lips. She was always near. Even if I couldn't see her, she was right here. Those little surges of panic, hurt, anger all meant she felt what I was feeling too. She would never be rid of me either. I wanted Liv to be happy, but I liked the fact that I was literally on her mind.

"Liv," I tried again, but received no response.

I changed the sheets on my bed, mulling over what was different between the times she heard me versus those she did not. Every time I felt her in my mind, strong waves of emotion washed over me. When she responded to me, those feelings built up to the point of needing release. If I focused what I felt, maybe she couldn't keep me out. I suddenly had a very real phone right into Olivia's mind. Tempting, very tempting. A little test wouldn't hurt any anyone. I lay in my bed and thought of the last time we were together. I relived taking off her clothes piece by piece, the softness of her skin, the vibrancy of her eyes, and the blend of our emotions and sensations as we came together.

I let the gentle, protective feelings I had for her fill me completely before I shoved them all towards the little light shining brightly in my mind. A moment later, Olivia filled my senses. I could smell her, taste her, nearly feel her on my skin. She didn't snap the connection closed right away like she normally did. This time it lingered. I was careful not to converse, worried that the sound of my voice in her mind would make her break the connection, and it felt too good to let it go. I continued letting those feelings flow from me to her, and she began to return them with her own, but underneath her happy, content memories of that morning, I felt something new. Grief, sorrow, pain lay underneath the surface. I was hurting her doing this.

"I'm sorry," I said aloud and broke the connection. I didn't want to hurt her. I closed my eyes and worked on steadying my racing heart. I couldn't do that again. If I did, I would find her no matter how determined I was to give her space and let her take her second chance. She was back and I didn't have to feel guilty anymore. No matter how it played out, I got what I wanted. She wasn't dead. She just wasn't with me. I would make sure she got to have this new life. Olivia was a drug that I couldn't leave alone. A taste would always lead to a binge which would undoubtedly lead to regret. I would focus on saving her now and spend the rest of my existence battling not to partake in any more of her goodness.

I had to find out who Juliet was working with—and get her phone from her—but I wasn't sleeping with her again. I could beat it out of her, perhaps—not subtle but effective. Or I would have to get her to let her guard down. I chewed on that thought until sleep finally found me. It was the best I'd slept in four years. I awoke the next morning with a plan and a new outlook on my existence. I texted Juliet to say something had come up and that Baker and I had to go to St. Louis. If she had any problems, she'd better think of a way to fix them without my help. Next I called Baker and told him to stop following her.

If she didn't believe I was in the city, there was no reason for her to sneak around. She wouldn't watch her back, and she'd screw up. I followed her from her apartment to an office building downtown. I watched as she entered and waited several minutes before I went to see what was housed in the building. It looked like a normal office building. Several floors belonged to an insurance company. There was a magazine, an advertising agency, a law firm and several other businesses. The only company I didn't recognize was on the top floor and went by ADA Inc. I googled the company while she was in the building, and it definitely appeared to be shady. It took me several moments to see what I should have noticed right in front of me. It practically shouted the connection. How had I missed it? Danica was always so vain. ADA Inc. was no more than Danica rearranged.

Now it was only a matter of finding out what exactly they were up to with their scheme. I arranged to rally with Baker, and decided to return later to check her office. If it was anything like the last office, it would take me the better part of the night just to find her desk, but I would get to the bottom of everything before the night was through.

TWENTY EIGHT

I watched Olivia disappear into her lovely white light. Everything was suddenly complicated again. I had gone how many hundreds of years with no problems and in the mere four years I had known her it was one fiasco after another. Not the least of which were my very inconvenient feelings for her that continued to grow even as she shied away from me. The only thing I knew for certain was that I wanted to keep her safe, and right now every obstacle imaginable stood in the way of that.

Not only did Olivia all but refuse to do anything I wanted her to do, acting as if she were invincible, but Ezra was completely on her side. Neither of them would listen to reason. It must have been an elder trait. I was able to sleep for a few hours when I left her earlier, but Ezra's call yanked me from peaceful slumber. Minutes later I stood in his office, waiting to see what new impossible task he was going to assign me. I think I liked it better when the elders mostly ignored me.

"Hello, Quintus. How is your progress?"

"Fine. We're set up and have maintained a 24-hour watch on the warehouse. There has been jinn activity, but no sign of the traitor."

"Good, good. I have heard of no more disappearances."

"That's wonderful."

"Perhaps. I believe they are building towards something. We need to stay vigilant and invisible. Discovering their plan is the priority at this juncture. I believe you mentioned Olivia has the unique talent of repressing her light?"

"Yes." Where was Ezra going with this?

"Would she be willing to go amongst the jinn as a spy?"

"No," I said immediately.

Ezra nodded, frowning. "I understand it would be distasteful for her, but it would be an invaluable service to our cause."

"You can't ask her to do that. She hasn't even finished her training. She'll be killed."

Ezra furrowed his brows. "You know as well as I do, Quintus, the life she has chosen is not her own. She exists to serve the will of the elders. If we wish her to sacrifice herself to save many, then that is what she will do. It is best she hasn't finished her training. It will make it easier to maintain her cover and if she is caught, she will be able to tell them less."

"But she is one of you."

"Yes, and she was sent here out of her time. It must have been for some purpose. Perhaps that purpose is to save us all."

"So you have decided? Are the rest of the elders in agreement?" I couldn't believe what I was hearing. Never in all of my time as a guardian had anyone been asked to sacrifice their life. If this was how it was going to be, perhaps it was time for my retirement.

Ezra patted my hand. "I have no reason to believe she will be detected. In all likelihood, she will return home unscathed and save us from a drawn out war with the jinn."

I had so many thoughts it was hard to speak. This was a horrible idea. "How do you expect her to be accepted amongst them? She can make herself appear human, but she can't make herself a jinni."

Ezra shrugged me off. "Many jinn take human girlfriends. Ideally, we would like her with someone of importance—not just any jinn. If she could use a lesser jinni to work her way towards the North American Commander, that would be best."

It was amazing that my head didn't explode and my eyes didn't pop out, or at the very least my heart didn't stop beating. Did Ezra really say what I thought he said? He wanted Olivia to pretend to be Holden's girlfriend? There was no way. It wouldn't be pretend. Once he had his claws in her again, she wouldn't come back to us. She would stay. Not to mention there would be no undercover. Holden knew exactly what she was.

"What if she doesn't want to come back once she's there?"

Ezra frowned. "You know full well what it feels like to be around a jinni. No self-respecting guardian would choose them over us. I'm not at all concerned about her switching sides. Do you have a particular reason for this fear?"

"No, just covering all the possible outcomes." My brain was screaming for me to explain to Ezra why this was monumentally wrong, but my heart wouldn't allow my mouth to speak. I couldn't tell him. He would take her away from me.

"I would hardly call that a possible outcome. Anymore concerns?"

Oh God, so many. If he only knew. "You no longer want to try to stop this? You don't want to keep the stake out going and catch the traitor? Wouldn't that be better and more valuable than sending a fledgling into a pack of hyenas?"

Ezra sighed. "I understand your concern, but you have yet to produce results. If the tip I received doesn't pan out, I would prefer to have another plan in action. If the stake out does produce results, then she will not have to continue on her mission."

"When do you want her to go in?"

"As soon as possible. Time is of the essence. You understand the necessity, don't you, Quintus?"

"Honestly, no. I cannot understand demanding this sort of sacrifice from anyone."

"I do not wish to send her into harm's way either. But I am asking no more of her than I would of anyone else with her abilities. Olivia was given these remarkable gifts—and given to us—for a reason. We must use them to secure our position."

I couldn't argue with him anymore, so I nodded.

"Excellent," he said. "I'll leave it up to you on when and how you present the new mission to her."

And here I thought it couldn't get any worse. "Me? You aren't giving her the mission?"

"The less she knows about us the better."

I stared at him, disgust seeping from my pores. He wasn't even going to tell her, and he was protecting himself. Had Ezra always planned to use her in this matter? Was this why he didn't want me to tell her about our meetings? Why he wanted the weekly reports? I couldn't stand to look at him any longer.

"Are we done?" I asked, my calm voice sounding foreign to my ears.

"Yes—let me know when she goes in."

I went back to my apartment to calm down before I returned to the warehouse. But when I got back to the rooftop, I had no words to tell her what they wanted her to do. I saw her earnest face and wanted to cradle it, not convince her to go back to him. I couldn't accept that outcome. There had to be another way, so I said nothing. I would make results happen tonight. Giving her to the jinn was a last resort, a last straw. I wouldn't remain a guardian if that was where we headed.

I watched her all afternoon, wanting to know what she was thinking and feeling. Wanting her to tell me she wanted me, not the jinni. He didn't deserve her. He had done nothing right since she died. He didn't change. He didn't try to be a better person. Holden became worse, more infamous for his brutality and calculating, kill-first approach to life. Yet now he was the jinn commander, and he got to have the girl he should have never had a chance with. How was any of this fair? How was it fair she loved him after all he did? How was it fair he haunted her even when she was with me? How was it fair that despite everything I wanted her more than ever?

Olivia seemed as lost in her thoughts as I was. We barely spoke all afternoon. When it came time for her to leave I wanted to draw her to me and kiss her, but I knew she would shy away and get that far off look in her eyes. I watched her go, hoping I would find a way to prevent her future.

The jinn traffic was steadily increasing. Something was going down tonight and a little flutter of hope began in my stomach. Maybe Olivia wouldn't have to know what they wanted her to do. New round after new round of jinn arrived. I had never seen so many collected to one area. I watched and took notes, looking for familiar faces. One in particular stood out to me. I knew I recognized her face, but couldn't quite place where I had seen her. Every jinn that arrived stopped to talk with her before she pointed them this way or that. She definitely appeared to be the one in charge, or at least the person organizing whatever this was. She was a pretty blonde jinni in a turtle neck. She seemed very organized and efficient, and so familiar. Where had I seen her before? I knew she hadn't been there in the past couple days. I would have remembered—but I had seen her before.

I watched as jinn carried in crates, boxes, and paint. I needed to see inside the warehouse. They were doing something, but Ezra had been very clear: I was not to interact. They continued as they were well past sunset. Jinn came and went, but no one else. It occurred to me that we'd been operating under a false assumption. We were waiting for the traitor to walk into the warehouse. If the traitor was a guardian, however, he wouldn't walk in from the outside. He would appear inside. I had us watching out here the whole time, while they could have had countless meetings right under my nose.

I needed to see Ezra. I transported to his office. Ezra looked up from his desk, surprised by my sudden appearance.

"I did not summon you, Quintus. I'm very busy."

"There has been movement at the warehouse. They're doing something big. I've never seen so many jinn in one area. You wanted me to keep you informed. I think we need to look inside. Make our move."

"Did you see the traitor?"

"Well, no. I was thinking about that. A guardian wouldn't walk through the door. He'd transport in. We need to see what is going on in there."

"Quintus, what is this really about?"

"I thought we were stopping them."

"We cannot barge into jinn territory without evidence. You know that. If you see the traitor, then we can deal with that guardian on an individual basis. To barge into their warehouse would be an open act of conflict."

"Who cares about conflict? For crying out loud, they're killing guardians. Is that not an act of conflict? Open your damn eyes! We're the only ones playing by the rules. We have to make a stand or they will destroy us."

"This is about Olivia, isn't it? You've become attached?" He folded his hands in front him and gave me a disapproving look.

"This is about them waging war on us, while we sit idly by!"

"Quintus, bring me evidence, and we will move. Until then my hands are tied. Now if you don't mind," he looked at me pointedly, "I am very busy."

"You are a spineless, cowardly bureaucrat who doesn't see what's happening right before your eyes-"

"That will be enough, Quintus. I strongly suggest you leave now and consider whether or not you wish to remain a guardian. We will speak more later. Goodbye."

"I'll get what you need, but I won't forget this." I left enraged, and transported back to the warehouse.

No sooner did I get there, then I felt Holden's request to speak with me. Rage filled me. I had nothing to converse with him about. He would never get Olivia, and he wouldn't get away with his plot either. I ignored his prayer and moved forward. If Ezra wanted evidence, I'd give him all the evidence he could swallow.

TWENTY NINE

Xavier was crowded, hot, and filled with beautiful people. Attracting a jinni in this mess might not be as easy as I hoped. Femi and I were ushered in, past the ever growing line outside. Once we walked through the doors, she nodded to me and disappeared into the sea bodies. I stood back for a moment and took a deep breath, gearing myself up. I could do it. I could be flirty and seductive. It wasn't completely impossible. Jinn liked me. I nodded to my own absurd thought. Jinn didn't like anyone.

I smoothed my pristine dress and fluffed my hair before pushing into the mosh pit of a room. I sashayed my way up to the bar and waited for my turn to order. The cute jinni bartender finally made it down to my end of the bar with a crooked grin.

"What can I get you?" he asked, his blue eyes twinkling despite the lack of light in the club.

I started to answer when a drunk barreled into me, shoving me against the bar. I glanced back in annoyance. The man behind me regained his balance, but didn't remove his hands.

"Did it hurt?" he asked.

"Oh my God, don't finish that line." I pointed to my face. "See this face? So not interested." I removed his hand from my waist and turned back to the bartender, who was watching the interaction looking rather amused. It felt amazing to finally say the things I thought. I'd never done it before. Had I called Ron on his bullshit that night Juliet and I were out, I'd have saved myself the headache of listening to him talk. There was something to be said to honesty. Who knew?

I gave the bartender my own smile. "Enjoying yourself?"

"Oh, immensely. What can I get you? On the house for dealing so well with that."

"Rum and coke."

He nodded and began preparing the drink, scanning the bar. When he topped it with a lime, he took the drink in the opposite direction from where I was standing, then bent in close and said something to the guy at the other end of the bar. The man abruptly left his stool and disappeared into the crowd. The bartender looked back at me and beckoned. I pushed my way to the seat he stood in front of and climbed up.

"Thank you. You didn't have to do that. It was very nice of you."

"I had ulterior motives."

"Oh, really?" I asked leaning closer. This game was turning out to be a lot more fun than I thought it would be. I briefly wondered what Femi was doing, and if she was enjoying herself as much as I was.

"If you didn't have a seat, you might not have stayed at the bar, and I wanted to talk to you."

"Did I do something wrong?" I ask wide-eyed and innocent.

He laughed, totally buying it. "Besides coming to a bar like this, not at all. How'd you end up here?"

"Oh, I met a new friend today while I was out on a walk. She told me I just had to come here with her tonight, but she seems to have disappeared. I can't find her anywhere. But it looks like fun, maybe a little crowded, but fun. I bet you love working at a place like this."

"It has its perks," he said, letting his eyes roam up and down me in one long sensual stare. "Has anyone else told you, you're absolutely stunning?"

I look up at him through my eyelashes. "No."

His hand reached out and trailed lightly down my arm. "Well, you are." That hollow empty feeling once again washed over me with his touch. I didn't let myself pull away, though I wanted to. Something about a jinni's touch just felt wrong.

People all along the bar were trying to get his attention, but he continued to gaze at me. As he poured his energy over me, I knew I was supposed to be enamored and unable to see all of the people staring at us, so I forced my attention to remain on him. Someone pushed up behind me and leaned over the counter, pushing his glass at the bartender. The bartender rolled his eyes and looked at the man.

"What?"

The pushy man stammered as if he didn't know what to say. I giggled, breaking the tension in the air. "It seems I have distracted you from your job."

He grinned and filled drink orders, glancing back as he went. I waited patiently for him to come back to me, having no doubt he'd be back. While he was at the other end of the bar, another jinni found his way over to my seat. Apparently, I didn't need to worry about finding jinn. They were finding me just fine. This one was less cute and more rugged. Mmm, this bar really did have something for everyone . . . .

"Would you like to dance?" Mr. Ruggedly Handsome asked and caressed my thigh. Before I could respond, the bartender was back, looking none too pleased.

"She's fine where she is, Jacob," he growled.

"I don't know, Will. She looks bored to me."

"Why don't we let her decide?" Will said, laying a hand on my arm. I felt them both pouring energy to me, and I wanted to throw up. I felt dirty and vile. Neither of them was even remotely attractive anymore. They both watched me expectantly as if I was supposed to do something other than just keep breathing. Oh right, I had to choose between disgusting and vile. I focused on who felt stronger, and they seemed about even. So I went with the bartender because he seemed a little more sweet and gentle than the other. I looked at him as if he was the only other person in the room, and he gave a dismissive wave to Jacob.

"She doesn't seem bored to me. Leave before the boss finds out you're causing problems."

"He isn't here tonight."

"He'll be back, and you know how he feels about violence in the club. You know what he'll do to you." Jacob scowled and walked away. Will continued rubbing his hand up and down my arm.

"Your boss sounds scary."

Will laughed. "You don't know the half of it. But he really isn't so bad as long as you play by his rules. He's actually pretty smart. Best thing that could've happened for us really."

"Us?" I asked innocently.

Will cleared his throat. "The club, of course."

Damn, lost him. I brushed my hand down his cheek, lingering at the edge of his mouth. "Do you have a break soon?"

He pressed his inhuman lips against mine. I forced myself to respond and stay relaxed. When he showed no sign of coming up for air anytime soon, I nipped at his lip. He pulled back slightly, his eyes darkened with lust. I moistened my lips with the tip of my tongue. "I could arrange a break," he said, tracing my mouth with his thumb.

"Do," I purred taking his thumb into my mouth for a moment.

Will stood up abruptly and waved to someone to come closer. A female jinni came over, and Will said something to her then came around the bar pulling me into his arms. "Let's get out of here," he said.

"I can't leave my friend," I told him with wide eyes. "Isn't there somewhere we could go here? You said your boss is gone. Maybe he has an office." I pressed against him suggestively.

"We really shouldn't."

"Why would it be naughty?"

His eyes darkened again. "Very. I bet you're never naughty."

"You'd be surprised," I said over my shoulder as I began walking in the wrong direction. Will pulled my hand.

"This way."

He led me to the stairs Femi had described. I still hadn't seen her at all. Nervous butterflies did the polka in my stomach. Will seemed nice for a jinni, but I wasn't prepared to take this any further than I already had. But given my behavior if Femi didn't show up, I was in trouble. I would have to transport out and blow my cover or compromise my morals. As she had warned me, he took me all the way upstairs and pulled out his keys, opening the door at the top.

The office was large and very clean. I didn't have time to get a good look before he pulled me to him, his mouth leaving a wet trail from my jaw down my neck. His hands loosened to run down my back, and I had a chance to escape. I twirled out of his arms and put the couch between the two of us. Will looked at me with one thing in his eyes.

I shook my finger at him with a teasing smile. "I thought you said it was naughty to be here. Perhaps, you should be punished."

"Oh, you can punish me as much as you like, angel," he said, licking his lips.

I smiled and continued moving him in a circle, praying Femi would show up. Will started to take a step towards me when a hand curled around his neck and sliced his throat in one fluid motion. Blood gushed from the wound, and my stomach heaved. Will's body crumpled to the floor, and Femi stood behind him, blood dripping from her knife as she surveyed the room.

"That doesn't look very temporary, Femi!" My hands were shaking, and I felt like I might throw up. I liked Will. I didn't want her to kill him.

Femi slid her arms under his shoulders and dragged him towards a closet I hadn't even noticed. "This is temporary. We need enough time to do your search. He'll heal."

She went to the sink and searched the cabinets and drawers.

"What are you doing?"

"Looking for towels. Are you going to stand there all day, or are you going to do what you came here to do?" she asked, making an irritated gesture at the desk behind me.

She was right. I had to get a grip. I went around the desk and sat in the soft, supple leather chair. I picked up the first couple sheets of paper I saw and glanced at them. They seemed club-related, not what I was looking for. I was about to move on, when my brain finally started working again and pieces came together. I took a second look at the document in my hand. I knew that hand writing. It wasn't possible.

Suddenly it was hard to breathe. I sat the papers back where I found them, steadying myself on the desk. I looked around the room for what felt like the first time. How had I missed it? The room was immaculate, border-lining on meticulous. All dim lighting and warm accents. I didn't recognize anything in particular, but it was all his style. It reminded me very much of Holden's apartment. Forcing myself to stand, I let my hand linger on his chair. I inhaled deeply and faint traces of his aftershave tickled my throat. This was Holden's office. He'd been this close to me all along. I could have run into him countless times. My heart thumped so loudly in my chest, it was all I could hear. Part of me wanted to run and the other part wanted to have a seat on those soft couches and wait for him to come back.

He filled my mind. It was impossible to tell if I had made the connection or if he had. I kept my mind blank, hoping he wouldn't notice me before I could find the will to break away.

"*We need to talk.*" Though his voice came to me quietly, I could feel anger and agitation. I must have been the one who connected. He probably thought I was spying on him. The last thing I needed was Holden to berate me.

"*No,*" I said, forcing myself to close him off. "Femi, we have to leave." I grabbed her arm as I walked towards the door. There was nothing to find here. I was wrong. This club had nothing to do with anything. I shouldn't be here at all.

I didn't let her relock the door. We had to keep moving. What if he knew I was here? I had broken our unspoken truce. I invaded his territory. What would his next move be?

"Olivia! Are you listening? Did you find what you came for? What happened?" Femi kept throwing questions at me as we walked downstairs and out the back door. I ignored her until I felt the cool night air embrace me.

"Olivia!" Femi stopped, tearing her wrist from my clutch.

I looked back at her. "It's his club. He owns it."

Femi looked blank for a moment, then her head tilted back in understanding. "So he's killing your people?"

"I don't think so. I didn't make it too far in the search, but I don't think there's anything except for trouble in there." I rubbed my forehead, trying to clear my mind from the waves of panic. "I shouldn't have brought you here. You need to leave. I have to tell Quintus that Holden is here. I can't stay in Chicago. I'll have to relocate." Thoughts spewed from my mouth as soon as they entered my mind.

"Wait, wait, slow down. What about the people dying?"

"I don't know."

"You're just going to run away?"

"You don't understand. I can't resist him. He has a hold over me I can't explain. I'm not ready to see him yet. I'm not strong enough."

"That's bullshit. You can resist anything you want to resist. You can face him, and you have to. People are dying; you can't just run away because you're scared."

She was right. I was panicking. I couldn't abandon the other guardians, even though I didn't know them or feel any connection to them. I couldn't leave them to be tortured and killed; I knew exactly what that was like. I nodded and took a couple deep breaths. "You're right, but I still have to see Quintus."

"I'm coming with you."

"It's faster if you don't. Go back to my apartment, I'll get Quintus, and we'll regroup there and come up with a plan."

"Okay. Where are you meeting him? Just in case."

"I appreciate your concern, but we'll probably make it to my apartment before you do."

"If you don't, I'd like a place to start looking."

I rattled off the address and started to leave, but she grabbed me and gave me a tight squeeze and firm pat on the back. "You be careful."

I smiled. "You too."

An instant later I was standing on the roof across from the warehouse, but there was no Quintus. Surely, he wouldn't have gone home. I looked around. There were a few jinn sitting outside of the warehouse and a couple more who seemed to be continuously circling the perimeter. Quintus wouldn't have left. Maybe he'd moved closer. I snuck through the building to get back to ground level, worried that transporting would draw attention to me in the darkness. I circled around looking for any indication of his presence, but came up with nothing.

I zipped over to his apartment in Rome, when I was far enough away from the warehouse that they wouldn't see my light, but it didn't look like he had been back.

He wouldn't have moved into the building, would he? I went back to where I'd transported from and started creeping towards the warehouse. If he was inside, I should let him be. If I went in and got caught, would it force Quintus to give up his position? But on the other hand, if something had happened to him, I might be able to help him. I chewed on my lip and watching the jinn outside of the door who were talking intently.

Quintus might not even be inside. I moved closer, needing to hear what they were saying before I decided.

"I don't like it," the more serious of the two said.

"Stop bitching. Danica's better than the new guy with a stick up his ass."

"But why hasn't she killed him? Why are we keeping this one alive? It's one thing to capture and pass them off. It's another thing to store them. If we're caught, it's our asses being deported not hers."

"We haven't gotten caught yet."

"I don't like it."

"He might have information. Just think how many more guardians we can catch with him on the hook."

"I don't know. That bitch is crazy. Did you see the look on her face? She's not thinking straight, then she up and leaves to meet with the commander. What the fuck? It doesn't feel right."

"Can I get you a purse to go with that skirt you're wearing?"

"You'll see, man. This is all going south."

"Whatever, princess. Why don't you go get us some beer?"

The complaining jinni stood up and walked away, still mumbling. I wasn't sure what they were talking about. I knew the commander was Holden, and obviously they weren't fans. I had no idea who Danica or the crazy person were—or even if they were two separate people. As for their prisoner, whether or not it was Quintus was questionable. They definitely had someone though, and regardless of who or what it was, I couldn't leave him to their mercy. I had to do something and right now.

I pulled the knife Femi had given me from beneath my skirt, chanting in my mind, "It won't kill him, it won't kill him."

I transported to one side of the warehouse and made a noise, then transported behind the jinni as he got up to take a look at the disturbance. I used the knife just as I saw Femi do it. The feeling of it easily slicing through the soft flesh and tendons made me ill, but I finished the cut, knowing full well he would kill me if I didn't. I slipped inside, not dwelling over what I had just done. I would find their prisoner and get us the hell out of there.

The rows of doors threw a wrench in my plans. This wasn't going to go as smoothly as I hoped. I started for the first door and knocked gently. After waiting a few seconds and hearing no reply, I moved on to the next one. I knew this would likely draw attention eventually, but it wasn't quite as bad as yelling out, "Who needs help?" into the darkness.

Finally I knocked on the fourth door and heard rustling. I tried to transport in, but couldn't. Oh, this was bad. I turned to leave, so I could find help, and ran straight into the chest of the complaining jinni. He grabbed my shoulders, his brows furrowing. "What are you?"

"Human," I said immediately, hoping he would buy it.

"No way did a human get the jump on Otis. Plus I saw your little light trick. What are you?" His fingers dug into my arms as he shook me.

"I'm a guardian," I told him, trying to focus enough energy to burn him, but a voice broke my concentration.

"Olivia?" A muffled voice came from behind the door.

A sinister smiled spread over the jinni's face as he looked at me. "Two for the price of one." He dragged me by the arm to a room on the other side of the warehouse and tossed me inside. "She'll be pleased."

A lock snapped into place with a sickening thud.

THIRTY

Baker wanted in on the plan to take Danica and Juliet down in one swoop, but there was a problem with that. Now that Liv was involved, I couldn't have him or anyone else near this. I needed to keep her as far away from my world as I could and Baker wasn't stupid. He'd recognize who she was to me right away. So I gave him a different task, one that required a serious amount of faith on my part that I could trust him.

"You want me to do what?"

"There's a woman in St. Louis. I don't want you to worry her or panic her in any way; just get her somewhere safe in case things go wrong tonight."

He shook his head. "Everything's going down and you want to me hide some dame?"

"Yes. She doesn't know anything about this world, and we're going to keep it that way."

"And what are you going to do?"

"End this all tonight."

"By yourself?"

"I work best alone."

"I think I'd be more useful here. I can move the dame in the morning."

I shook my head. "There are too many balls in the air. If they start to fall, she'll be in danger, and I don't want her killed. I need to know she's with someone who can protect her, someone I trust. Right now, that's only you."

"Who is she?" He wiggled his little finger at me with an arched eyebrow.

I sighed. "Her mother."

A small smile creased his square face. "You're always full of surprises." Baker stood up and morphed into me. I stared at him for a second. He was good. "She trusts you, right?"

Hell, he even sounded like me. Baker was better than any shifter I had ever seen, and I had the sneaking suspicion he hadn't told me everything about what he was. "Yes."

"Good, then this will work."

"Baker." I caught his arm. "If she gets hurt or you double cross me, I will spend the rest of my life hunting you down and spreading the pieces over the globe."

He gave me a curt nod. "I won't let anything happen to her. You have my word, but I expect a detailed story about the mystery woman you go to such lengths to protect when I get back."

"Why do you care?"

"I am a connoisseur of human nature."

"I'm not human."

"You're more human than you think, Holden." And with that he walked out in my body to pick up Marge. I headed back to the ADA Inc. office building just before closing and hid on the floor beneath Danica's. It was a boring, mindless wait in the air duct while I listened to the stragglers leave, then to the janitors come through and finally the watchman.

When I was fairly certain I would be alone for a while, I lowered myself to the floor with a soft thud. I scanned the dark room for any signs of life. I didn't want to have to kill anyone, but I also couldn't be bothered with police at the moment, so I would do what I had to do.

I weaved my way around the random groupings of half cubicle walls towards the door of the stairwell. The office didn't have alarms on the doors and the security cameras were the only obstacle I had to avoid. So far so good. I made my way up the final flight of stairs two at a time and came to Danica's new office. The door was locked.

I pulled out my tools and set to work. In moments the sound of the bolt clicking echoed in my ears, and as easy as that I had access to her office. She had nothing in the lines of security except that one flimsy lock. Chances were she had nothing worth stealing, but also jinn didn't like to involve mortals if they had the option to handle it themselves. Undoubtedly she had her own security cameras and would come after me in her own time, if I didn't get to her first. I looked up at the security camera, paused so she could get a good view, and waved. My fight with Danica was going to end very, very soon. This was my territory now, and she was done being a pain in my ass. Thankfully this office wasn't quite the pit the last one was. I made my way to her desk, took a seat, and began sifting through papers she had strewn all about. The woman had absolutely no organizational skills whatsoever.

After what felt like hours, I produced something worth my time, but I wasn't quite sure what it meant. She'd recently purchased property near the club—some old warehouse, probably the one Baker mentioned. She also had bids from several contractors and iron workers, but the most concerning item I found was notes of names, dates, times, and places. If I had to place bets, my money said it was info on the missing guardians. How had Danica managed to get her filthy hands on these details?

The last two names on the list stood out: Quintus and Olivia. Next to Quintus's name was today's date and the time was about 20 minutes from now. There was nothing next to Olivia's.

Shit.

This complicated my plans. I wanted to take care of the problem before Olivia was involved. If they already had her—I shook off the thought. Grabbing the papers, I headed out. It wasn't hard to sneak out of the building. I managed to do so with very little effort or moments of concern. Once outside, I jogged down the street to a church and picked the lock without hesitation. Sinking into a pew, I clasped my hands together.

"Quintus, you son of a bitch. If you can hear me, I have information for you." I waited and he didn't appear. "Quintus. Are you out there? I need to talk to you." Still nothing. I didn't even know if prayer could still work for me. Had enough of my soul perished that the guardian couldn't hear my prayer? I waited around for about fifteen minutes, but when he didn't come, I couldn't risk it any longer. What if Olivia had been with him? If they knew where he would be, chances are they knew where she was too.

I left the church, not needing prayer to reach Olivia. My adrenaline was running too high. It was hard to trudge up the emotion necessary to speak with Liv. I gathered what I could, though it mostly consisted of anger, worry, and impatience. Her image came to mind easily, softening the edges of what I'd collected. I pushed out towards her and felt the connection almost immediately. It wasn't as strong as before, but it was there. It was enough.

"We need to talk."

"No," she said back abruptly, ending the connection.

God damn it! If she wasn't the most stubborn, frustrating woman in the world! I wanted to hit something, strangle someone, anything. But I kept walking. Glancing at my watch, I didn't have time to help Quintus. Whatever they had planned for him, the wheels were in motion. I didn't even know if I wanted to help Quintus. He was an asshole, but the idea that Liv might be with him tore at me. If they killed him, she'd be next, no doubt in my mind. I had to do something. Running to the address on the paper halfcocked and blind wouldn't help anyone. There was only one person left who could tell me anything. One way or another, Juliet was coming clean tonight.

I made a beeline for the club, leaving a trail of agitation as I went. I needed to pull it back in, but I couldn't. I'd just got Liv back and already she was about to be killed again. I'd never met anyone who could find trouble as quickly or effortlessly as she could.

"God damn it, Olivia," I growled, hoping she could hear me. If I ever saw her again, I would shake her until she showed the capability of rational thought.

The club was still in full swing and a rhythmic thumping vibrated through my body when I entered the building. I nodded to one of the employees, indicating for him to follow me, then took the steps two at a time up to my office, the young jinni at my heels. I pulled out my keys, but the door was unlocked. I didn't mention it to the jinni behind me, but I didn't open the door either. I turned back to him.

"Where's Juliet?"

"Who?"

Shit, I didn't have time for this. "Julie. Where is she?"

He shrugged. "Haven't seen her all night."

And things just kept getting worse. "Find her for me. I want to see her now."

"Okay," he said, but didn't move.

"What are you waiting for? Go!"

He jogged back the way we'd come. Hopefully he was able to keep the thought in his head long enough to accomplish the task. I looked back at my door. Who was in my office?

I pulled the gun from my jacket and pushed open the door. My office looked nearly as it had before. A few of the papers on my desk were shifted slightly and my chair was rolled back a few inches. However, the real giveaway was the smell. I inhaled deeply. It was her. Olivia had been here. It was undeniable. Clean, sweet, with a hint of vanilla. What was she doing here?

My first thought was she had found me. She had come to see me! Joy sent my heart soaring. My next thought was how could she have come into a jinn club, regardless of whether or not she wanted to see me? She could have contacted me anytime, and she knew it. Why would she come here? The only reasonable explanation was she didn't know this was my office. That son of a bitch Quintus hadn't told her. She was investigating in the most Olivia like manner—all heart, no head—following some trail that led her here, to me.

I opened my laptop, logged onto my security system, and pulled up the video for my office. Fast forwarding through most of the evening, I finally saw my door handle twitch not even an hour before I arrived. Will, one of the better bartenders, walked in, pulling a girl in behind him. All my anxiety melted into a seething pile of rage, as I did a double take of the girl on the screen.

Will wrapped his arms around Olivia's waist and nuzzled her neck—then she coyly danced away from him. She put the couch between the two of them, waggling her finger at him with a come-and-get-me smile on her face. I couldn't even think through my fury at seeing him touch her. I nearly stopped the video to kill Will, but I kept watching. I needed to see this. I had to know.

She looked like a gift from heaven. Pure and innocent with a streak of wild. That white dress, those slender shoulders, the curve of her neck . . . she was . . . *bait.* Understanding thundered down over me. She wanted in the office, so she roped herself a key with a jinni attached. Maybe the bartender could die fast. Olivia continued her seductive teasing, letting him get close enough to touch her before darting away again. When his back was to the door, another girl came through and in one fluid, graceful motion slit his throat. Olivia's eyes went wide and all traces of humor melted from her face. She said something to the other girl who merely shrugged and dragged the body to my coat closet.

I paused the video and walked over to the closet. Sure enough, my bartender was folded on the floor, well on his way to making a full recovery. Had I not just watched him paw at Olivia, and had he not had the potential to be a problem for her later, I might have let him live. He was a good bartender. Instead, I pulled a saw from the shelf of the closet and finished the job, removing his head. Jinn could come back from most any injury, but I didn't know of anything that could survive decapitation. I tossed the head on the floor and shut the door. After washing my hands quickly at the sink, I went back to my computer to finish the video.

The girl, who definitely wasn't a guardian, pointed to the desk and said something to Olivia. Olivia walked over to the desk and sat in my chair. The other girl began cleaning up blood from the floor. Olivia picked up a few of my papers. She looked at the first one, then leaned in closer and looked again. She set the pages back down and looked around the office slowly, like she was memorizing everything she saw. Her mouth fell slightly open, and she pressed two hands flat against my desk. Then she stood up and ran a hand over the back of my chair. Her shoulders and chest rose as if she were taking a deep breath. The other girl's mouth moved, but Olivia didn't respond. Her face was an impenetrable mask as she went back to her partner and pulled her by the arm out the door.

I wish I could say seeing her made me want to let it go, made it possible for me to walk away from all of this, but it didn't. All it did was resolve me towards seeing her in person. She was just here. We were in the same city. How could I resist such a temptation? She was within my grasp so long as I could find her in time. I glanced at my watch. Where the hell was Juliet? I went back down to the club. It was a pit of sweaty flesh and deafening music. I found the jinni I'd sent after Juliet and inquired after her whereabouts. He said she wasn't there, but he'd called her and she was on her way. I told him to send her up when she arrived, then went back upstairs, unable to concentrate among the hordes of people. I paced around the room when sitting still failed me—God knew what happening to her out there.

I forced myself to settle down. If Juliet came in while I was acting like this, she would immediately be on edge. With several deep breaths and all of my concentration, I refocused my energy and walls. I picked up the last thing Olivia touched on my desk and held it as if I were reading it, rather than imaging her hands on the paper. After what felt like hours, my office door opened and Juliet strolled in with a wide smile.

"Holden, I thought you weren't coming in tonight."

"Oh, I'm not," I said, glancing up at her and giving her a small smile. "I'm here for you."

She strutted around the desk and lay a hand on my chest. "I'm flattered."

I took her wrist and twisted it to the point of breaking. "Don't be."

"Hol … Holden," she sputtered.

"Don't bother begging. It won't help. It's time you tell me about your little side projects with Danica."

"I don't— I swear—" I cracked her wrist, and she cried out in pain. Minor injuries might not kill, but they still hurt like hell.

"The thing about being *here* is no one will hear you scream. Have you heard that music downstairs? Positively deafening. I suggest you start talking because you have a lot more bones to break, and I have all night."

"What do you think I'm doing?" she asked in a high pitched voice lined with fear. It was a good show, but not one I was falling for.

"Tell me about the warehouse, Juliet."

"You … you know about that?"

I twisted harder. Tears streamed down her cheeks.

"Fine, fine. I have a side project, which is none of your business."

I yanked her arm out of its socket. Her knees gave out, her face went red and her eyes bulged, but I caught her before she hit the floor. "Unacceptable," I breathed into her ear.

"I've been working with Danica."

"Tell me things I don't know. How long? Why? What's your plan?"

She didn't say anything. I tightened my arm around her waist taking hold of her other arm. Juliet tried to pull away from me. "No, don't, please," she begged.

"Answer the question, Juliet. I can do this all night." I twisted her arm back accenting my point.

"Since the beginning. I was supposed to keep you distracted, occupied. But I was unnecessary. You distracted yourself better than I could distract you. You've hardly shown any interest in me."

"Why, to what purpose?"

"So you wouldn't stop us."

"What exactly are you doing?"

"It's not a big deal. She has a guardian in her pocket. He arranges for us to be able to capture guardians, and we sell them to demons for a little sport."

"You've been doing *what*?"

"What's the harm? There's good money in it, and there's no rule against killing guardians. Besides, technically we aren't killing them, the demons are."

"Could you really be this stupid? There's no Abyss law, but do you honestly expect the guardians to sit idly by and let you capture and kill them? Do you really think there won't be repercussions? We've had a treaty with the guardians since the beginning. We leave them alone, and they leave us alone. It has worked for thousands upon thousands of years and your little bit of "sport" could undo everything. We're talking *war.*"

"They're weak," she snarled.

"You're an idiot. Are you listening to yourself? You're following Danica. I can't remember the last time she had a good idea. I thought you were smarter than that. War isn't good for business. If we get caught up in battles, how will we continue to recruit? Without souls, the demons have no interest in us. They'll abandon us up here and the guardians will eventually kill us all. They may seem passive, but have you ever encountered an angel?"

She didn't respond.

"I didn't think so. Think natural disaster, hand of God, plague—we don't want to poke that bear. Really, Juliet, *Danica?*"

"She's the only one who cared enough to help me after I changed. If it weren't for her, I would've failed. She took the time to teach me things, to explain this world to me. I owe her my life. I owe you nothing."

"Danica's using you."

"And you're not."

245

"I absolutely am, but I've never expected loyalty from you. Just obedience. This cannot continue. I will kill you if need be—you understand?" She nodded sullenly. "I mean it—it stops now. Do you have anyone captured at the moment?"

"Yes, we have one waiting to be picked up tonight."

"Only one?"

"Yes, for now. We were supposed to have another, but plans changed last minute."

"Does Malphas know?"

"No. He's management ... he's no fun. Just like you."

"I should call Malphas. You both deserve to be sent to hell for this. Why would you jeopardize everything you have for a little guardian killing? You can't possibly need the money."

For the first time real fear penetrated the crazy in her eyes. "Holden, no! Don't do that, please. *Please.* I'm sorry. I'll make it up to you. Whatever you want, just give me a second chance. I was blinded by my loyalty for Danica. You're right, I knew better. Don't send me to hell. I'll do better, I'll be smarter."

"Why did you do it?"

"I told you for Danica."

"Okay, then why did she do it? What's her angle?"

"I don't know. You have to ask her. I can take you to her."

"Where is she?"

Juliet rattled off an address. I knew I should kill her, or, at the very least, involve Malphas, but what she knew about my past was dangerous to me. They only had one guardian right now, Quintus. If I could end this racket tonight, then Liv would be safe.

I couldn't trust Juliet, but I didn't want her dead, not yet. I let go of her arm and she began to relax. I snapped her neck before she could say anything else. "Stay," I commanded, letting her body crumple to the floor.

I left without calling Malphas. I'd kill Danica and release their prisoner before deciding what I needed to do with Juliet. It would take her a while to heal, so I had time. I couldn't have her plotting against me, trying to trip me up with every step.

There had to be a way to spin all of this so it worked to my advantage and eliminated my enemies.

And how would I fit Liv into everything? I had no idea. All I could do was take one step at a time. Make no rash decisions. I left my office, locking the door behind me.

****

I went back to my apartment before seeing Danica. I needed supplies. My mind was still and quiet, ready for what I had to do. I put on my bulletproof vest and leather jacket, then filled it with knives and spare clips. This wasn't the first fight I had been in, nor was it the first war. Danica had no idea what she had called down upon herself.

The address Juliet gave me was in Gary, IN. I drove with the traffic on the way there, not wanting to draw any police attention while I was armed to this extent. The house was large, old and looked like it had seen its better days thirty years ago. Lights were on inside, otherwise I would have never believed anyone lived there. I sat in my car and watched the house for movement, as I spun the silencer onto my gun. I looked at the saw in my passenger seat. I'd have to come back for it later.

I walked up to the porch, gun drawn, without slowing or hesitating even slightly. My foot met the door, cracking the frame and sending the feeble lock flying. I didn't bother with witty one-liners or any words at all. If they were in this house, they were going to die. Firing off six shots, I put a single bullet in the head of each jinni in the room before they could even draw their weapons. Movement and footsteps rumbled above me. I slowly walked to the stairs and waited to pick them off one by one.

After the first couple fell, the others thought better of the stair route and retreated back up, firing shots at me over their shoulders. I abandoned my post at the bottom of the stairs. I wouldn't waste bullets on pointless shooting back and forth. They would come for me without that nonsense. I loaded a new clip in the gun and pulled out my other gun as well. With my back to the brick wall, I patiently waited for them. They came at me in all directions. A couple I shot through the window, a couple as they came down the stairs, and a couple as they came through the garage door—but there were too many. When the bullets in my spare gun ran out, I tossed it to the side and replaced it with a knife. Jinn continued filing towards me. I started choosing my shots, only shooting those who had guns and leaving the others. Bullets whizzed past me, some connecting, but nothing that I couldn't handle.

Something attacked behind the group to the left hand side of me and drew their attention away. I couldn't see what it was, but I was grateful for the distraction. Blood and bullets sprayed the room, painting the walls red. I sank my knife to the hilt in someone's chest and twisting the blade, then shot two more jinn. They were finally starting to thin out. I took another three with my knives, then moved back to work on the left side.

The mystery assailant seemed to be doing fine. Bodies kept falling. I snapped a few necks and finally recognized the other jinn slayer—the girl from my security video. My shoulder burned with every movement as I started to feel some of my injuries—including what felt like a massive gunshot wound—so I let her kill the last jinn standing—well, except for me. When his body hit the floor, she looked up at me. I twirled my knife in my good hand, waiting for her to make her decision. Was she with me or against me?

She narrowed her eyes. "I take it you're Holden."

I nodded. "And you are?"

"Looking for Olivia."

"Last I saw her, she was with you." Something other than cold detachment inched back into my chest.

"She went to find her partner and never came back to meet me."

"They have Quintus."

"I figured as much. They probably have her too."

My stomach plummeted. I turned and ran up the steps, ignoring the bodies and the pain in my leg. I followed the foul stench to Danica's room.

She had a gun and fired it wildly, but each shot went wide, slamming harmlessly into the walls above and beside me. I hurled two knives. One caught her wrist, making her drop the gun. The other buried itself in her heart. I pushed her against the wall and applied upwards pressure on the knife.

"Where are the guardians?" I snarled.

"What's the matter, Holden? Can't keep control of your region?"

"I don't have time for this. Where are they?"

Olivia's friend's voice came from behind me. "I know where they are."

I glanced back at her, and she nodded. I pulled the knife up as far as I could, lifting Danica from the floor before I threw her across the room. "Something you could have told me sooner."

She lifted an eyebrow. "Olivia might trust you, but I wasn't convinced you didn't have her until now."

"Where is she?"

"I'll show you."

"No, tell me. I'll get her, and you make sure they all stay dead."

"I don't take orders from you."

"And I don't work with people I don't know. If you knew where Liv was, why are you here rather than saving her?"

"As I said, I thought you might have picked her up. When we split she was pretty worked up about you—and then she failed to meet me. I found where you live and followed you here, hoping I'd find Olivia. Instead you started this bloodbath. I figured you're more useful to me alive than dead, if we have the same goals."

I took a deep breath and willed myself not to stab her. "Look, these jinn need to stay dead or they'll come after us. I cannot dispatch them and save her. Time is of the essence. You clean up here, and I'll get her. If I fail, then you know where we are, and you can alert whoever in the hell a guardian would alert. They're a lot more likely to talk to whatever you are, than to me."

"Where do you want to meet?"

"You choose."

"Olivia's apartment, one hour."

"Fine." She gave me the address of a warehouse and told me what she knew. I gave her my saw before driving back to the city, no longer caring about cops. Outside the warehouse, I peeled off my blood soaked shirt. My shoulders still hurt, but were healing. I noticed another bullet wound in my side that was all but healed. I was going to be sore tomorrow, if I lived through tonight. I pulled on a black t-shirt and a leather jacket that were in my trunk, then once more, reloaded with knives.

The warehouse looked deserted. I walked towards the door, waiting for a trap. Two strapping jinn stepped out, blocking my way inside.

"What the fuck do you want, pretty boy?"

"Do you know who I am?" It was worth a shot.

"Dead," the one on the right answered, coming towards me with a slow right hook. Side stepping him, I grabbed his arm and stomped the side of his knee, dropping him. The other jinni came at me and soon he too was on the ground.

"Let me introduce myself. I'm the North American Jinn Commander—Holden Smith," I said cheerfully as I crushed the second one's throat with my boot and tugged the first one's arm until it cracked. "Danica's dead, my condolences. If you'd like to join her, please keep pissing me off."

Neither of them said anything which I took as a good sign. "Where are the guardians?"

"Inside," one of them said.

"Is the girl still alive?"

"How'd you know about her?" the one trapped under my boot asked, causing me to stomp down.

"You don't have the right to ask questions. What about you? You got questions?" I asked the other one. He shook his head. "Is the girl alive?"

"Yes, I put her in a cell."

"Unharmed?"

"We haven't touched her."

"Good. You seem smarter than your friend. Tell me exactly where she is, and I'm going to let you go. You're going to get the hell out of my region. If I see you again, you die. Understand?"

He nodded, said she was in the third room on the left, and I let him scamper off. I needed someone to spread the word that Danica was dead and I had complete control of *my* region.

I stepped over the other jinni, who was still unconscious on the ground, and opened the door. Looking around the best I could before stepping inside, I realized I'd forgotten to find out if anyone else was there. I pulled keys off the jinni's body and walked in, knife in hand, ready for the assault.

Two came from the right; they each dropped to the ground with a soft thud. I was moving cautiously toward the door the jinni had told me held Olivia, when she popped into my mind.

"Holden . . . I need help."

"On my—." I heard the shot before I felt it, then everything went dark.

Liz Schulte

THIRTY ONE

Stupid, stupid, stupid, I admonished myself.

I had transported into the warehouse, determined to get the evidence I needed with the intention of transporting immediately out, but they had some sort of symbols all over the inside of the building that prevented guardians from releasing their form. I had underestimated the jinn and now they had me locked in a cell with even more symbols on the walls, ceiling, and floor.

I listened for signs of other guardians. Perhaps they weren't dead; perhaps the jinn had another plan for us. The thought gave me hope. Ezra knew where I was. . . . How long before he sent the cavalry? I wasn't just another soldier. Surely he wouldn't leave me here. I was here on his mission after all. I nodded to myself. They were coming and this would all end tonight. If the jinn wanted war, war they would get.

I sat calmly against the wall and waited to be released. The night replayed in my mind. It still disgusted me that the elders would willingly sacrifice Olivia, but if anything good came from my foolhardiness, she would no longer have to go back to Holden which eased my mind. Ezra would be forced to come here and stop the jinn, and Olivia wouldn't know anything happened until I told her about it after the fact. Everything was going to work out okay.

The cell door clicked and the blonde jinni strutted through the door, as I stood up. She tilted her head and smiled at me. "My, you are a handsome one."

"You have no idea what you're doing."

Her laughter filled the room like bells ringing. "Don't I?"

I shook my head. She really did seem familiar, but I couldn't place where I had seen her.

"Well, everything seems to be going according to plan." She checked her clipboard. "Yep, everything is in order, and you will fetch me a pretty penny, handsome." She hooked her finger under my chin and that simple touch made my skin crawl. "But I might keep you around for a couple days. I could use a new toy."

I gave her my own smile.

"Oh, dimples to boot. Tempting, very tempting."

"Do you have any idea who I am?"

She glanced at her clipboard. "Quintus. Head of training and recruits. *Impressive*." She flipped the page, and my heart sank. "You're an old one too. I'm surprised you were so easy to capture. Not quite at the top of your game anymore, are you?"

How was this possible? How could she know so much about me? About all of us? My mind spun with uncertainty. Nothing made sense.

"It says here you have a partner though. Olivia." The pretty smile and the sparkle in her eyes gave way to a waxy, blank expression. "I used to know someone named Olivia."

It dawned on me who she was. This was Olivia's friend, the one who died. What was going on? What were the odds of all of this being a coincidence? What did Holden have up his sleeve? How did he set all of this up? Better yet *why*? "You shouldn't have taken me. The elders will not look the other way."

"Oh, I'm counting on that, but I have one more to get to complete my set," she said, crossing her fingers.

"You want to start a war?"

"That's what I was hired to do."

There was something much larger at work here than I anticipated. Someone needed to warn the council, someone needed to stop this—and I was stuck talking to this psychotic

Barbie. "I want to speak with your commander, Holden Smith," I told her with a steady voice and firm eye contact.

She puffed out her lower lip at me. "That's unfortunate. He's out of town, and you'll be dead before he gets back. But out of curiosity, just exactly how do you know Holden?"

"We've crossed paths." I didn't want to tell her anymore than I had to. She didn't seem to be aware of Olivia being alive, and if that was Holden's way of protecting her from this, then I would play along until I figured out exactly what was happening.

She pulled a small handgun from her purse and pointed it at my chest. "How do you know Holden?" she repeated, all flirty, friendliness gone, her buttery voice now hard and strained with something like fear. She had no fear of the elders or war, but she was scared of Holden.

"Who do you think sent me here to check on you?" I asked, hoping to confuse her loyalty enough that I could catch her off guard.

The gun wavered slightly, and she glanced over her shoulder. "Holden doesn't know about this. He couldn't. . . ." she mumbled to herself, and I dove at her, the full wattage of my light filling the tiny room to a blinding degree.

I struggled to get the gun away from her, but she was smaller and more nimble. She evaded my grasp and pressed the gun directly into my chest, as I continued to try to blind her with the light.

"I'm going to have to insist you stop at once, or I'll shoot you," she said in a composed voice.

"Bullets won't kill me."

"No, but they hurt like a son of a bitch," she said and fired off two into my shoulder.

The pain was excruciating. Liquid fire spread down my arm and back. Those were not ordinary bullets. "Who are you?" I asked, nearly doubled over with pain.

She walked up to me and lifted my face with her hand. "The last person you'll ever see." She held the gun to my head, and her phone went off in her purse. "Hold that thought," she said, then answered her phone.

"What?" she said into her mobile. "He's here? I thought he was out of town." She turned her back to me. "Tell him I'll be right there."

"Damn it!" she yelled at the ceiling, then marched for the door of my cell and slammed it closed behind her. "Don't do anything with him. I have more questions for him. I'll be back."

"You can't leave us here with a guardian," another jinni protested.

"I don't have a choice. Holden's here." I heard another door slammed and everything went quiet.

What kind of mess had Ezra sent us into? I was beginning to have serious doubts that Holden was behind any of this. Something much larger seemed to be happening, and I suspected Olivia was the last piece of the puzzle Juliet needed. She was in danger, and I had no way to warn her. I hoped Holden would get to her before she came looking for me. Who would hire Juliet to start a war between the guardians and the jinn? Who would gain from that? Why was this all focused around Olivia again? Why was she sent to be an elder when the elders didn't even know she was coming? Something terribly odd was happening and our world was beginning to crumble around her.

My shoulder healed while I mulled over the various pieces of the puzzle that didn't seem to fit together. The sound of a soft knock and Olivia's voice just outside of my cell door tore me from my thoughts, but before I could offer any sort of warning, they had her too.

We were in serious trouble. The elders were our only hope, and I wasn't sure they knew enough about what was happening to stop any of it.

THIRTY TWO

Damn it, damn it, damn it. Now what are we going to do? Think, Liv, think!

I surprisingly didn't feel panicked. Yes, I was captured by people who were killing guardians, and Quintus was captured as well, but I remained calm. I just needed to think. I could get out of this; I'd made it out of worse. I studied the room. There was no window. The walls appeared to be solid iron and were carved with odd symbols. *Probably to keep us inside.* Why hadn't we been killed? Why were they saving us?

I tried the door handle for the hell of it. I didn't expect it to magically open or anything, but it had to be done. I knocked on every inch of the wall, looking for weak spots, but the room was solid. I was going to have to talk my way out.

"Hello! Is anyone out there?" I yelled at the door.

Silence was the only reply. Dead silence. I sat in the corner of the room and stared at the door. If only I could will it open. I hated being trapped. I sighed. My second chance at life wasn't going so well. Had I known it was going to be this short, I would have thumbed my nose at the rules and called my mom. Hell, for that matter, why did I stay away from Holden? So what if I was mad at him? It didn't seem to matter much anymore. There was no reason to go through missing him. I imagined how different my year could have been had I gone to Holden immediately, ignoring the fact that it would have damned him. Sure we would have been hunted, and he had likely changed in the years it took me to come back, but I preferred to think our time would have been like it was when I stayed with him in St. Louis, minus the mourning and the secrets. It would have been perfect. We could have been happy for just a little while longer. Didn't I deserve that? How was any of this fair?

I looked up at the ceiling. "How is any of this fair? You let me taste happiness, then take it away. You send me back with all of these rules that make me miserable, only to kill me again! Seriously, God. Seriously."

Arghhhh! Think Liv, think!

My mind went back to Holden again, my heart squeezing, the air in my chest evaporating. I just wanted to talk to him one more time. *I wonder.* I couldn't transport, but my connection with Holden wasn't like that. So far it was different and stronger than anything else. Maybe this prison wasn't designed to prevent something they probably didn't even know about. Focusing my mind on that portion of my head he permanently occupied, I probed gently.

At first nothing happened. I didn't feel the connection click into place. I pushed harder, desperation feeding me. Faster than a snap of my fingers, Holden filled me.

"Holden." My heart fluttered. Why did he have this effect on me? "I need help."

"On my—" Three shots gun shots rang through the warehouse. The sound startled me back into my own mind, cutting Holden off.

Shit!

I paced around my cell, heart thumping as I unsuccessfully tried to reconnect with Holden. I couldn't even find him in my mind. *The anxiety must be blocking me. I need to calm down and just breathe,* I tried to coach myself, but my mind kept wandering back to the gun shot. Who did they shoot? Was it Quintus? Was I next? Did bullets even kill us?

My door slammed open, and I flinched back against the wall. Two jinn I'd never seen before stood in the doorway, a body flung over the bigger one's shoulder.

"Who are you?" the smaller one demanded.

I stared at the body. It wasn't Quintus. The pants and shoes were different. *Thank you, Lord!*

"It doesn't matter. Throw him in. She can deal with this when she gets back."

"But the girl is human."

"She's dead either way."

The big guy shrugged and threw the body down unceremoniously, then they slammed the door shut again. My eyes fell to the person bleeding all over the floor, and my knees buckled.

"No," I said in barely a whisper. Crawling over, I pulled his head onto my lap. I pressed my hands over the clustered wounds leading directly into his heart. Blood pumped through my fingers. He wasn't breathing. As I felt his last heart beat, the blood slowed over my hand.

"Holden. Holden stay with me," I said to his lifeless form. Blood still seeped through my fingers. "No, you can't do this, damn it. Holden, Holden come back," I pleaded with his waxy body, but it remained still.

His expression looked so peaceful, nothing like he ever looked in real life, not even when he was sleeping. I let my trembling hands fall from his wound and wiped them on my dress. Nearly his entire shirt was drenched in the gooey, red substance that filled my nose with a coppery scent. I ran my hand across his sharp cheek bone and pressed my forehead against his.

"Jinn heal. Please heal. Please heal," I whispered. "Don't you leave me."

Our connection was stronger than death, I knew from experience. It was stronger than my death, but I couldn't find him in my mind. There was nothing there, like he never even existed. I tried to do what he did. I thought of the night we were together when our connection solidified. I pressed my head against his, as if the nearness would make a difference, and sent him my memories. Anything to entice him back to me.

"Dear God, please don't let him die. He may not have been the best man, but there is goodness in here. I can see it, and if I can see it, I know you can too. He doesn't deserve to die. He deserves a chance at happiness, please. I don't know what qualifies as a mortal wound for a jinni, but please don't let this be one. Please," I begged.

I sat with him on top of me until my legs fell asleep from his weight, and I had to walk around. Once they felt normal again, I resumed my position of holding him. Still no sign of life. Every time I looked at him, I cried—and I couldn't stop looking at him. It had been so long. I never thought I would see Holden look fragile, but as he lay in my lap, lifeless and pale, he looked oh so human.

I pressed my lips to his cold mouth, wishing I could breathe life back into him. I straightened my back, resigned to the idea he might not return. I had to prepare myself for the possibility. Holden might finally get to rest, and I had to go on, as he had gone on without me.

The feel of his fingers running through my hair was a wonderful hallucination, and I had the urge to lean into it, but when the sensation intensified, I realized it wasn't just in my head. My eyes popped open to meet those hazel pools staring at me as if I were a ghost.

That was when I knew I couldn't do this again, and my heart broke. I couldn't watch him die again, which was the only thing our being together would ever lead to. He could live as a jinni, but he couldn't live with me. I had to really let him go and not just in well meaning words that never fully took root. It wasn't Holden and I being together that killed the people I loved—it was being around me that killed people.

THIRTY THREE

I woke to water dripping on my face. I found myself cradled on Olivia's lap, tears streaming from her perfect eyes. Love and sadness swirled around in my mind making me dizzy.

Was I dead?

I reached up to touch her again, making sure this wasn't a marvelous dream. My thumb trailed after a tear rolling down her cheek. I didn't have to move to see she was covered in blood. The grogginess was replaced with a flush of panic. What had they done to her? I sat up quickly, triggering pain that I ignored. I grabbed her shoulders. "Are you okay? Are you hurt?"

She looked startled, her wide eyes still swimming in tears. Emotion showed openly on her face and cut through the air. Such sadness, such pain. If they hurt her—

"You're alive," was all she said, as if she couldn't believe it.

She reached towards my face, but stopped before she touched me. Letting her hand fall loosely back to her side, she continued to stare at me.

It took a moment to recall what happened, but then I remembered everything: my conversation with Juliet, killing Danica, Olivia's hunter friend, and finally walking into the warehouse and hearing Liv just before the gunshots. I looked down at my chest. Three bullets wounds centered on my heart—I must have been in here a while.

"Olivia, what happened?" I felt the weight of my question on many levels, and from her reaction, so did she.

Her soft emotions dissipated, leaving only my years of confusion and hurt to fill the room. My thoughts were still foggy and I was a little woozy from blood loss, so I didn't have the barriers under control. Seeing her caused unspeakable elation as well as a twist of the knife she held firmly in my shredded heart. All I wanted and all that caused me pain sat in front of me in a bloody white dress.

"Where do you want me to start?" she asked, with a wariness she'd never had before, and I knew exactly what her tone meant, because I felt the same, like it was only a matter of time before we hurt each other.

"Let's just start with tonight."

"We'd been watching the warehouse because of the guardians who'd been disappearing. I was tired of pointless stakeouts that lead to nothing, so I came up with a plan."

Dear God, I knew exactly what type of plans Olivia came up with when left to her own devices.

"I told Quintus I was going out with my new friend, Femi, which wasn't a lie—I was going out with her. I met her a few days ago and she took me to this new club, Xavier—I think you know it." She frowned at me, but continued, "I figured if we wanted information about jinn business, who better to ask than a jinni? So I talked her into taking me back there tonight, so I could snoop. She's a bounty hunter, so I wasn't totally unprotected. Anyway, when I got there, I convinced a young jinni to take me to the manager's office." She grimaced slightly. "Femi cut his throat, but swore he would heal. And I started looking for anything that would tell me about the guardians. That was when I realized it was your office. Then you popped into my head all angry, and I figured somehow you knew, so I got Femi and we left. I came here to look for Quintus. I needed to tell him you were in Chicago, but he was gone from his post and not at his apartment, so I snuck in here to look for him."

That rat bastard never told her. She didn't know. He left her totally unprepared. What if I had wanted to kill her? He basically put her in my lap and left her blindfolded. I'll kill him.

"They caught me and threw me in here. I can't transport out. A couple hours later I heard gunfire, then you were tossed in with me. Bleeding—not breathing. I thought . . . Well, you looked," she let out a ragged breath, "*dead*."

Part of me wasn't sorry she thought I was dead. The agony was a feeling I knew well. I looked around the room carved with ancient runes. If I were to make a guess, they were to keep guardians in their place. We were in trouble. "Where's Quintus?"

"In one of the rooms on the other side."

The new dominate feeling in my mind was fear, and I was positive it wasn't mine. Our connection was stronger than ever. Her walls were thin and barely contained her thoughts. Nonsensical fragments slipped through and frantically rushed my mind. "And the blood?" I prompted.

"Yours," she whispered.

I didn't know what to say. There was so much I'd planned and dreamed of saying if I was ever able to see her again, but now looking at her, bright-eyed and bloody, in front of me, I didn't have the heart to do it. Anger and love battled inside of me. For every inclination I had in one direction, there was an equally strong urge in the other. I drank in the sight of her, but wanted to look away in the next breath. I never believed I would see her again. Even coming here to save her, part of me believed she would be dead.

Olivia shifted uncomfortably beneath my gaze. Her bloody hands fidgeted, her dress clung to her. She had never looked more beautiful. It took everything I had not to grab her and stake my claim once again. "You look …"

She glanced down at herself and made a face. A moment later she was shrouded in sparkling moonlight, which drew me to it like gravity. When the light faded she wore fresh, blood free jeans and a t-shirt and looked much more like my Olivia. As tempting as she was in the white dress, this was how I pictured her in my mind, casual and effortless. My shift in thoughts seemed to bring color back to her cheeks, and she snapped her mind closed, leaving me empty—but not for long. The void was quickly filled with bitterness.

"Neat trick," I said quietly, my throat feeling like it would close.

She nodded, but didn't say anything. I couldn't quite place what I saw in her eyes. It definitely wasn't happiness and not quite fear.

"Are you sure you're okay?" I asked, barely containing the steady stream of indignation rolling through my mind about her actions since she came back.

"I'm fine."

"You don't seem fine."

Olivia shrugged.

Our connection may not have changed, but Olivia had. *My* Olivia was vibrant and filled with understated passion. She would have yelled or thrown herself into my arms by now. This Olivia was reserved and withdrawn. I felt like if I yelled at her, like I wanted to, she would pass out. I got up and paced around the room. I didn't care which Olivia was here with me, I'd save her if I could. There had to be a way to escape. She watched me search the tiny room to no avail, keeping a wide gap between the two of us. When I was satisfied that there was absolutely no way out, I had nothing left to distract me from the feelings boiling just underneath the surface. I might never see her again. I had to know the truth, no matter what it was.

"Why didn't you tell me you were back?" It came out harder than I intended, as anger gnawed at my insides.

Her face went through a range of emotions. First sadness, then resolve, then irritation. Finally she settled on her own apparent rage. Her eyes sparked with lightning.

"What makes you think you deserved to know I was back?" Her voice was clipped and soft.

What did they do, brainwash these people? "You too? Christ, Olivia, I'm a jinni, not Satan." The room managed to go from calm to volatile in a less than a second, just like old times.

"Like that ever made the least bit of difference to me, Holden!"

"Then what did? Please enlighten me. Why did I not *deserve* to know? Please explain, because I think I *deserved* to know, especially since I'm the only one who sacrificed a God damned thing in all of this." All my pain morphed into something ugly and infinitely dangerous.

"You were there. You know exactly what you did." She rolled her eyes. "You were never the person I thought you were. You let me believe in you. Do you remember what he did to me, Holden? How could you stand by and let that happen? How could you smile and laugh with him, while he tore pieces from my soul?" She ran her hands through her hair. "I'm not the girl I used to be. I see things much more clearly now, and I have you to thank for that. I believe I can trace it back to the moment you put a bullet in my brain." She stepped towards me, fists clenched at her sides.

"Or maybe you did love me just a little. At least you put me out of my misery." Her eyes continued flashing like a thunderstorm was raging on inside of her. This was my Olivia. This creature filled with passion and emotion, with a temper like a fuse and a heart like butter.

Her resentment only fueled my own. That energy and intensity took over, making me want to simultaneously shake and kiss her. Olivia was back.

"The only thing I could do was watch and play along. Had I made a move before I did, he'd have dealt with me and you would have been alone. He used me against you, and *you* folded. You just gave up. I told you not to go, but you wouldn't listen. You never listen. You forced me into that position. You do not get to be mad about the outcome."

She laughed bitterly. "Well, I'm glad *you* made it through unscathed."

"Unscathed, unscathed? Is that what you call this?" I poked my own chest forgetting the bullet wounds until physical pain shot through me. I ignored it, too consumed with anger to think of anything else. "I'm sorry, I've obviously been operating under a misapprehension. I thought you understood me better than that. Let me spell it out for you. Death would have been preferable to what I've been living with. I would have gladly accepted hell over these last four years of my life. You felt what it was like for me to be dead for what, an hour? I lived with four years of it."

"Then why did you do it? Why did you wait so long? If you wanted to go to hell, you could have made your move at any time. Why watch him do that to me?"

"I couldn't abandon you. I naively thought my staying would keep you from doing something monumentally ignorant. I had hoped we would make it out. But apparently my staying only assured your stupidity. You weren't supposed to give in. That wasn't part of the plan—*your* plan. You should never have let him use me as leverage."

"The only reason you were leverage was because when push came to shove, there was only one choice I was ever going to make. I knew it, Quintus knew it, and I thought you knew it too. It didn't matter if a demon or an angel stood in front of me. I would have always chosen you over any of the rest of it. But you couldn't do the same for me."

I laughed, knowing it would send her into a rage. Part of me loved watching her angry and yelling at me. Anything was better than the wide, blank eyes she'd had moments ago. Her hands tightened until her knuckles turned white. "That's what you think?" I scoffed. "You've been hiding from me for four years, and that's the best you could come up with? That I didn't *love* you? You could read my fucking mind. How do you think I faked that or anything with you? Did I never once get the benefit of a doubt?"

She threw her arms to her sides like the martyr she had turned herself into. "What was there to doubt? I offered you everything. Everything! And you cast it away as if it were nothing. I was stupid and naïve. I believed in you. I believed in us. I believed we would find a way. But you stole that from me, Holden. Now I can never have it again."

"I wanted it too, just not like that."

"Oh really? Funny because you made it impossible. So what was it? You weren't ready to settle down? Got the jitters at the idea of spending an eternity with me? I wasn't pretty enough? Funny enough? Interesting enough? What? Where did I come up short in all of this?"

"Olivia," I said patiently, trying to keep my temper, though her anger made it increasing impossible. I always underestimated how much her feelings affected my own. "I had no choice."

"That's because it wasn't your choice, Holden. It was mine."

"You made the wrong decision."

"Obviously." That one word spoke volumes. She didn't just mean nearly deciding to be a jinni. She meant me. I was the wrong choice. I stung like she slapped me. "You loved me so much and were so honorable at the end. I must have changed you deeply. What exactly *have* you been doing with your life? Please tell me all of the wonderful things you've done while I was gone. What did you do to make me want to come back to you?"

"It's not like that. You have no idea."

"Well, as you said, *enlighten me.*"

"Any humanity I had left died with you." I sighed, not wanting to see the disappointment on her face when I told her all I had done since she left. How I had earned my new post—"Is this really the only thing that's been bothering you?"

Her eyes narrowed and her mouth set in a firm line. "I think this is plenty to deal with at the moment."

"You accused me of knowing what I did that night. Well, let me elaborate on exactly what I did. I remember everything that happened. I have been haunted by each and every one of your screams. Your pain washed over me that night and scorched my memory each and every day. I catalogued every bone break, every bruise, every fucking finger he laid on you. Don't think it hasn't played over and over again in my mind. I have yet to pass a day without remembering it, without feeling it always in the back of my head. Standing idly by while he hurt you without letting my feelings show . . . you have no idea what that did to me. Hell, Olivia, I can't even sleep anymore. That was the hardest, most painful thing I ever had to do, and I did it for you. No one else."

"Oh, well, I'm sorry it was such an inconvenience for you." Her sarcasm dripped from each word she spit from her mouth. "I mean, *poor you*. You had to watch all the horrors befall me. How could you stand such a thing? It was so much easier to actually experience it firsthand."

"Yes, I guess 'inconvenient' is one way to put it. Tell me, Livi, were you always this sanctimonious or does it just come with the job?"

Olivia eyes widened. I couldn't decide if she was about to blow her lid again or start laughing. She seemed to be struggling with some sort of mental battle. The lightning drained from her eyes, leaving only a lively twinkle. She covered her mouth with her hand to block a smile. Thank God she knew somewhere in that mass of anger that she was being ridiculous.

She shook her head and took a deep breath. *"I've missed you."* Her voice rang loud and clear inside my mind, while her eyes liquefied once again. The intimacy was almost too much to bear with all the exposed nerves. I couldn't return it.

"You've been blocking me for the past year?" The tension may have melted from the cell, but situation hadn't changed. The bruised feelings were still the same and new wounds were opened wide.

"Not quite a year. How do you know how long I've been back?"

"Don't avoid the question. You've been *purposefully* blocking me?"

She nodded. "It was a matter of survival."

"I would never hurt you."

She lifted an eyebrow.

"Well, except for the shooting you thing—you know what I mean."

Olivia shook her head, her eyes closing. "It takes an amazing amount of energy and focus to block you out. I never realized how hard it must be for you to keep everything you feel so neatly tucked away all of the time. I couldn't do it. There were times . . ." She sighed. "It was for the best."

Her actions were a knee in the balls. I tried not to dwell on them, as in all likelihood we would both be dead very soon, and I might as well enjoy the time I had with her, not focus on resentment and anger. As she would say, *I neatly tucked those feelings away somewhere deep inside.*

"I wish you hadn't done that." I may have decided not to be bitter, but I wasn't letting her off the hook. She needed to understand.

"Let my walls down or put them up?" she asked, watching me.

Now that was a good question. Had she not put them up, I would've known right away, but what would that have done? The situation would have been the same. We couldn't be together, but I would have known she was safe. I would have stopped beating myself up over her. However, I also would have obsessed and never accomplished what I accomplished when I thought I had nothing to live for.

And if she'd kept the walls up permanently, I would be clueless right now. "I wanted to know you were back, but if you didn't intend to speak with me or listen to me, I wish you'd done a better job with your walls instead of torturing me."

Her head tilted, but she didn't respond. I couldn't read her face, so I tried probing her mind. "Stop," she said firmly.

"You're the one who said you missed me." I took a step towards her.

She sighed. "I do . . . I did."

"You have all the control over that—and you have had this entire time. When I knew you were back, I could have come to you, but I didn't. I gave you space. I could have pushed into your mind like I did that night, but I felt your pain at my being there. I don't want to hurt you, but I want you to let me in. Make us whole again." I could hide my anger from her. I could forgive anything she had done to me if she would just say she was still mine. If these were our last moments together, I wanted to be with her as we were.

"Holden, this conversation hasn't changed anything. Nothing is resolved. My feelings haven't changed. We can't be together. If we're suddenly released and could go our separate ways, I wouldn't do anything different."

What was she saying? Her part of our conversation replayed in my mind. "You said you *didn't* care that I was a jinni. Do you care now?"

Her eyes met mine. They were direct and expressive. Her pain and loss came at me in tidal waves I recognized well. "Before, I had the benefit of not truly understanding what that meant," she whispered.

"And now you understand?" My voice matched hers. I wouldn't have believed she could have caused me any more pain than I already felt. Part of me wanted to stop her from saying the words I knew she was going to say, but I needed to hear them.

"I have seen the effects with my own eyes," she said, her voice barely audible. "I've fought to help those whose lives had been touched by jinn. I have met other jinn and been repulsed by them, and what they are. Let's just say, I understand what Quintus warned me against." She seemed far away from me, as if she was no longer seeing me.

How could she think of me as anything but a monster? That was exactly what I was. We all were. I nodded to her slowly, understanding what she was not saying. It dropped to the bottom of my stomach in a thick knot. I repulsed her now.

I had evaded her question about what I had been doing. Now seemed like as good a time as any to get all of the disappointment out of the way. "I'm the new North American Commander, at least I was. I may not be for much longer."

She bowed her head, perhaps to shield me from her disappointment. Quintus had told me to honor her life by being a better person, but I failed. Honestly, I didn't really try. I was more worried about numbing myself than about making improvements.

"North American Commander, impressive. Do I even want to know how you got that promotion?"

"Probably not." The air between us was thick, but it wasn't angry. It was much worse than that. It was filled with resignation. "Let's just say I didn't handle your death well. I had a lot of pent up anger, and it made me all the better at my work." I glossed over the details, because I didn't want to get into it. I wanted to hear about her; hear about the one thing in my life I managed to do right, every dying man's wish. "How is it you're a guardian, yet you have no light?"

"I repress it." She gave me a half shrug and looked at her feet. "I don't think I'm a very good guardian, but I'm trying."

"Well, aren't you just full of walls and repressed emotion these days?" I teased, trying to get her to look back at me. "Why do you repress the light?"

Her gaze stayed locked on my shoes. "So I don't draw attention to myself. I feel more comfortable that way."

"No one else is here. I think the secret's out for those in the room."

"It makes you uncomfortable, and despite what you may believe from my actions, I don't want to see you suffer."

Was I her new Christopher? She had told me once she didn't want her ex-boyfriend to suffer. All she wanted was for him to be happy—and not in her life. Was I the same way to her now? "I want to see it."

She bit her lip, then nodded. Slowly a white light began pouring forth from her. Her light didn't pain me or burn my eyes like Quintus's. It made me tingle as if every one of my nerves were sparking with sensation. It was warm and accepting, just like Olivia had been. Perhaps as she still was with other people. I moved closer to her, enchanted by the wonderful diamond like glow. My hand reached out to touch the soft halo. It was so beautiful. I would have given anything to be a part of it. I took another step, wanting to be fully immersed in it. The light retracted away from me as I moved closer.

"What's happening?"

"Your freckles are starting to show. If I remember correctly that means I'm burning you." She gently ran a finger over the bridge of my nose, closing her eyes against her own pain.

"I miss you too," I whispered, my lips nearly touching hers. I heard her breath catch in her throat and a tear slipped from her eyelid. I leaned the rest of the way in to kiss her and was met with her cheek.

"I can't do this, Holden." She put a hand on my chest, her breath shallow, tears freely falling. "I love you. I'll probably always love you, but I can't be with you. There's no way we can . . . be together. You see, I need to learn to let you go, as you have me. You found a way to move on in your world, and I don't blame you for that. I'm happy for you. You seem to be doing well. I have to do the same in mine. Each day it feels as if my heart is being shoved through a meat grinder, but—" she swallowed hard, fighting for composure. "But I have to have faith it will get better, that I can live without you."

She so candidly described the last few years of my life without her. She thought I had moved on, but nothing was further from the truth. She sounded so wretched I didn't want to tell her that there was no hope of moving on without me. If anyone could do it, maybe it was Olivia. Perhaps I could give her up if I was assured of her happiness. "Olivia—"

"You have no idea how hard this is for me. I smell your shirt just to feel closer to you, and I think about you all of the time. You still consume me, but I need find Olivia in this tangled mess of a person I've become. If I were to kiss you now, then deny myself ever having that luxury again, I may never make it back."

"What shirt of mine could you possibly have?"

She smiled. "I created it from memory. The black button down one I wore…" Her voice trailed off as her cheeks colored.

I chuckled, slipping my arms around her despite everything she had just said. "I know *exactly* how you feel. I have that same shirt hanging in my closet. It's the only thing I have left that still smells like you. I also have your camera. I was saving it in case you came back."

"Are you trying to make this harder?" She lay her hands on my cheeks. "You have to stop being so wonderful to only me."

"Maybe a little." I pulled her closer. "You're the only one I care about, the only person I'll ever care about. It doesn't matter what you are or how opposed it is to what I am. Truth be told, Liv, we probably aren't going to make it out of this. I admit nothing about our past has changed, but it doesn't really matter when our futures are this short."

Olivia wrapped her arms around me, burying her head in my chest. I felt her opening back up. Slowly she lit up my mind, burning away all the pain of the last four years. I once again felt whole.

"I'm glad we got to have this," she said, her head still pressed into me.

Cradling her face, I tilted her head towards me. "Me too." I leaned in to complete the bond when the door opened. Juliet strolled in, all drama and entrance.

"Well, isn't this cozy," she said in a saccharine voice.

Olivia looked up and her face glowed. Happiness and surprise filled my mind, and her hope surrounded me. I sent out a warning to her, but it was overshadowed by her joy at seeing her best friend. She pulled away and went to embrace Juliet before I could stop her.

"Jules!" she exclaimed as Juliet hit her across the face with the back of her hand, sending her stumbling back. I stepped between them, knocking Juliet back with my fist.

"If you touch her again, you'll lose the arm."

Her eyes narrowed, but she kept a safe distance from me. "I'm glad to see the two of you getting along so well. I was worried you wouldn't. You obviously remember your dear sweet Holden, Livi? But do you remember how you ignored me to chase after him like a fool? I bet you didn't know he was a jinni. And you a guardian, how delicious. How scandalous."

Olivia looked at her blankly, a hand pressed to her bruised cheek. Juliet frowned at the lack of reaction. "Perhaps you do know." Juliet looked back and forth between the two of us, then started laughing. "He's a pretty good fuck though, once you get past the icy exterior. You never shared that tidbit with me, Livi. Then again, you never were a kiss and tell sort of girl. I bet he rocked your world. He definitely shook mine for hours." She watched Olivia intently.

Olivia didn't have a good poker face. She narrowed her eyes at me, betrayal splattered all over her. .

"Who was better, Holden? Me or her? I don't really have to ask though, do I? Just look at her, all pent up and repressed. I do feel sorry for you, what a boring target she must have made. Did you have to listen to her drone on and on for hours about her stupid, insignificant life and her brain-numbing *art*?"

Olivia gasped and shook her head in denial.

Juliet's smiled broadened. "Yep, if it weren't for me, Olivia would have had no life to speak of. Come on, you're a connoisseur of women, which one of us was more to your tastes?"

"Her, always her."

Olivia stared at me darkly, once again completely closed from me.

"Oh this, this is glorious." Juliet laughed, clasping her hands together. "The two of you are in love, aren't you? I mean Holden could just be a whore—how many women is it you've slept with since Olivia died?"

I chose to ignore her question; Olivia's eyes continued to bore into me.

"But this makes more sense. You were trying to fill a void. I've been looking for a weakness in you, Holden. Something you were not perfect at, something I could exploit and here it was right in front of me all the time. And now I don't even have to exploit you." She flipped her hair back with sheer glee. "I can have the demon outside come in and send you straight back to Hell and finally be rid of you for good. Then I'll watch him tear Olivia apart. Who knew today would be such a wonderful day? You took care of Danica for me, and now I can kill my two most annoying birds with one stone named Gaius. The region and revenge will be mine."

Juliet stuck her head out of the cell door. "Gaius! I have something for you." A large sluggish looking demon came in the room. Olivia still stood behind me frozen. "Gaius, if you send this jinni back to Hell, you can have this guardian for free."

Gaius eyed Olivia. "Pretty. What did he do?"

"Fraternized with guardians. He's a traitor to his race." Gaius looked at me with dead eyes then back to Olivia.

"Do we have a deal?" Juliet asked, her back to me.

I grabbed Juliet from behind, snapping her neck for the second time that day. The demon charged faster than I would have believed he could move. I knew it was hopeless in this small of a space, but if I had even a slight chance of freeing us, I would try it. I dodged his first attempts to grab me, smashing his knee with the sole of my boot.

Olivia tossed me a knife, and I slashed the demon on his next near grab, but the room was too small and his reach too long. He caught me. The room began going dark, as I plunged the blade in his chest. I heard Olivia shout before everything turned white.

THIRTY FOUR

I knelt in my cell, praying over and over again that the elders were on their way. They should hear my prayers. I knew of no symbols that could block a prayer and yet no one came. Maybe it was too dangerous, maybe we were an acceptable loss. I didn't like to think like that, but if it came down to the safety of the whole then I understood. I tried to relay the information I had, so they would be better prepared. How I hoped they were hearing me.

Three shots echoed through the building and my stomach sank. Had they shot Olivia? Were they hurting her now? How did they plan on killing us? Worry and uselessness blanketed me. Silence surrounded and tortured me. Why wasn't I more careful? Why did I come in here? Because of me, we were both going to die.

I heard raised voices of a man and a woman, but I couldn't understand what they were saying. I focused on the muffled sounds, but they were too far away to make out anything.

I stalked around the cell, frustrated, and tried praying again.

"Ezra, if you can hear me, I have hope that you are coming to rescue us, but I understand if you do not. You told me to pull back, and I disobeyed a direct order. I did not want to send Olivia among the jinn and thought I could stop it, but I only managed to get both of us caught." I rubbed a spot just above my eyebrow trying to decide what to say next.

"I know it's a little late for confessions, but I have made so many mistakes with regard to Olivia. She saw me before her

277

time, I let her fall in love with a jinni, I told her about her choice and death. And her training—well, it hasn't gone as smoothly as it should have either. I think I liked her too much. I was never sure what I was feeling, but I loved being around her. The life and energy surrounding her was intoxicating. She doesn't deserve this fate. Even if you leave me here, please save her. I think she will be the best thing to ever happen to our people."

A woman yelled something that sounded like "Gaius," then there was loud shuffling, followed by more muffled talking.

"I know you weren't sure about her, but Olivia being sent to us is a blessing. I have been a loyal and faithful follower my entire life. I have never asked for anything, but please save her. Please save her." I kept echoing the last word in my mind, hoping the repetition would make it so, as I slumped against a wall and let myself slide to the floor. A white glow under my door caught my eye. I watched as it continued to grow and spread, seeping into my cell through the cracks until it filled the room. It was like Olivia's glow. The elders were here. They'd come. They'd answered my prayer!

I stood up excitedly, but no one appeared. The light grew brighter and brighter until I couldn't even see the door. Though I had no idea what was happening, I basked in the glory that we were not left for dead. I heard screams and choked cries from outside the door. They were definitely here. It was only a matter of time now.

A few minutes later, the light began to recede. I beat on my door and yelled, "I'm here."

There was no response, no rustle, no noise whatsoever. It was like the whole world had disappeared, and I was left alone locked in a cell. I continued yelling into the silence, hoping someone, anyone would hear me. Finally I heard movement outside my door and an unfamiliar voice.

"Who are you?" a woman's voice came from the other side.

"Quintus. Who are you?"

"Where is everyone? What happened here?"

"I don't know. Who are you? Are you a jinni?"

"No. I'm a friend. Is Olivia here?"

"She was—I don't know anymore. Are you a guardian?"

"No. Just a second. Let me find some keys."

I waited, heart pounding with both worry and hope. After what felt like hours, the sound of the key in the lock made me step back from the door. I had no idea what to expect. The door opened to reveal a catlike woman with golden skin. Holding a gun trained on my head, she looked me up and down with strange, honey-colored, vertically contracting eyes.

"You must be Femi," I said when I remembered the name of the new friend Olivia had mentioned.

She nodded and lowered the gun. "Where's Olivia?"

"I don't know. They captured her when she came to look for me. I haven't seen her since."

"What about Holden?"

I frowned. "I haven't seen him. Is he behind this?"

"No. He came to look for Liv."

I shook my head, but the gun shots came to mind. He could have rescued her and taken her away. Maybe she was already safe while I was worried about it. "I'm sorry, I really don't know anything. I've been in this cell. I heard a man and woman arguing, and there was a temporary bright light—since then nothing."

"The light . . . Was that your people?"

"If it was, why did they leave me? Have you checked the cells?"

She shook her head and turned to walk out of the cell, keys in hand. I followed closely behind. Bodies of jinn littered the floor of the warehouse. I looked at Femi and wondered what on earth she had done to them.

She glanced back at me. "They were like this when I got here."

I systematically opened each door down the line while Femi stood guard. Every room came up empty, so we moved to the other side. As we moved down the row and passed the only room standing open, I saw Olivia lying motionless and lightless on the floor inside. Her hand rested on Holden's similarly still form, while the blonde jinni was crumpled with a twisted neck a few feet away from them.

"Found them." I swallowed hard and looked back at Femi.

She raised an eyebrow and peered around me into the room. "What happened?"

"I have no idea."

"Wait—is she glowing?" Femi leaned into the cell.

I looked closer and she was right. Olivia did have a small, yet steady, halo around her. She was alive. "Check the rest of the warehouse; I will try to help her.

THIRTY FIVE

"Olivia, wake up. Olivia." Someone was shaking me from somewhere far away. My head rattled with each shake. I tried to worm my way out of the grasp, but it was too strong. "Olivia, open your eyes," the voice commanded.

I obeyed and discovered Quintus leaning over me, worry creasing his face. I sat up and the room wobbled. It felt like the worst hangover I ever had.

"Ugh." I pressed my hands to my skull to try to push back the throbbing energy.

"What's happened?" I was so very confused. Looking around the room, Juliet lay dead on the floor, the demon had turned to dust, and Holden sat against the wall with a dazed expression.

"Olivia, focus. Try to remember, okay?" Quintus was agitated and jittery. I'd never seen him like this. His eyes darted around the room, like it was the first sign of the apocalypse. Femi appeared in the door way. Quintus raised an eyebrow, and she nodded.

"Are they dead?" I asked.

"Whatever that was, definitely is." He pointed to the ash. "I imagine the jinn will all heal in time, so you need to be quick. Tell me what happened."

It was beginning to come back to me. I remembered the demon lunging towards Holden. I remembered all my intentions melting away and one thought taking over. I had to stop it. I ignored Quintus's urging to tell him what happened and crawled to Holden, my legs not feeling strong enough to walk.

"Holden?"

He stared at me for too long, not talking, not blinking, just staring and touching his own face as if it was foreign to him. "I'm okay," he said, amazement thick in his voice. "I feel … different." Holden's emotions were making me dizzy. I had to close my mind to him once again, so I could work through the fog that hovered in my own head.

"What happened?" Quintus repeated, obviously not sharing the hazy dream like trance Holden and I had fallen into.

"I don't . . . I don't know. A demon grabbed Holden, and I threw myself at them. After that, I don't remember anything."

Quintus looked at Holden then back at me. He pressed against the wall and slid slowly down until he was on the ground with his elbows against his knees.

"Quintus?"

He looked up, his eyes gleaming. "This is bad, Firefly."

Quintus's reaction scared me. What exactly was so bad? I'd saved Holden; I couldn't let them have him. "What is?"

"What do *you* remember?" Quintus asked Holden, ignoring me.

"Olivia screamed and threw her arms around me when the demon touched me. Next thing I knew, I was covered in light and all I could hear was white noise."

Quintus looked back at me for confirmation.

"I told you . . . I don't remember anything after jumping towards Holden until you woke me up."

Quintus became paler and paler, the more we tried to explain what we remembered. His mouth pursed into an unnatural frown. Femi stood uneasily in the doorway, checking over her shoulder every few seconds. "How did you do it?" Quintus whispered.

"I don't know what I did."

"You disrupted the natural order. The repercussions—I don't even know." He laughed in a way I had never heard

Quintus laugh, defeated, bitter even. "It's bad, really bad. We have to leave, now."

"I don't understand what I did."

Holden looked just as perplexed as I felt, but there was something different about him, something I couldn't quite place.

"Olivia, you, for lack of a better word, *stole* Holden's soul. You reached into purgatory and yanked him out. By all rights, his soul belonged to Hell. It wasn't yours to take. Now his soul has been returned to his body. No one will be happy about this on either side."

"I think he's saying a major shit storm is about to rain down," Femi piped up. "So we need to get the hell out of here."

"What are we going to do?" I looked back and forth between them.

"First thing we need to do is get out of here before the jinn start waking up," Femi said from the doorway.

"Seconded," Holden said, looking more together. He stood up, pulling me with him because he wouldn't relinquish my hand. "Better yet, we should kill the jinn. It will buy us more time."

Quintus also stood up and gave Holden a threatening look as if to say, *You've done enough.* "We aren't killing anyone." Quintus said.

"I'm with Holden," Femi said. "It's smarter to kill them than to leave them to pursue us."

"We aren't killing anyone," Quintus repeated. "Hasn't enough blood been shed? We need to leave and come up with a plan. There's no time for killing sprees."

Everyone looked at me as if I should cast my vote. I didn't know what to do. Holden and Femi's logic made sense to me, but I felt Quintus's desire for peace. "Let's just go," I said.

Quintus smiled and pulled my hand away from Holden, dragging me out of the door behind him. Holden casually followed behind us, but I could feel jealousy and anger radiating from his mind at the mere sight of Quintus touching me. Femi pulled up the back, gun still in hand, eyes darting around the room. I removed my hand from Quintus's, not knowing what else to do. We maneuvered our way through the fallen bodies of the jinn toward the warehouse's door. "How did you get out?" I asked Quintus.

"I got him," Femi said. "When Holden didn't meet me like he promised, I came here. But everyone was like this. I found Quintus beating on his door and the two of you out cold."

"So this is you not taking sides, Femi?" I tried to muster up a smile.

"Yeah, I've never been good at neutral," she said with her own grin.

"So I did all of this?" I asked, surveying the bodies.

"I think so," Quintus said. "Why did you come here?"

"To save you."

"You weren't supposed to do that."

"Maybe she wouldn't have, had you told her everything," Holden said snidely. I chose to ignore my irritation at the notion that they'd both kept things from me. We'd hash that out later; I was too tired now.

Quintus glared at him. "Well, had you not started this fiasco, she wouldn't have been in danger to begin with. Who was your informant, Holden?"

"I didn't have an informant, *Quintus.* I knew nothing about this before you told me about it, and you damn well know it. I came here looking for Liv."

"The two of you were together the whole time?" Quintus looked at me. Jealousy looked foreign in his eyes, but it was unmistakably there, while Holden smiled devilishly at him. I stood dumbly in the center.

Quintus tried to dismiss him. "Thanks for your help, Holden, but you are free to leave now. You've caused enough trouble."

"I think we should stay together," I countered. "Until we know what's going on, we shouldn't make any rash decisions."

"Don't worry, Liv, I'm not going *anywhere.*" Holden stared directly at Quintus, practically daring him to challenge.

I looked at Femi who shrugged. "Hell, I'll stick around for a while."

"Great," I said weakly. As we walked out of the warehouse, I surveyed our motley crew: Holden, the jinni with so much blood on his hands they may have been permanently stained, Femi, the bounty hunter who wasn't supposed to take sides, Quintus, the lighthouse on a rocky shore, and me, the guardian who messed up everything. And thus it ends. And thus it really begins!

The end.

Liz Schulte

ABOUT THE AUTHOR

Many authors claim to have known their calling from a young age. Liz Schulte, however, didn't always want to be an author. In fact, she had no clue. Liz wanted to be a veterinarian, then she wanted to be a lawyer, then she wanted to be a criminal profiler. In a valiant effort to keep from becoming Walter Mitty, Liz put pen to paper and began writing her first novel. It was at that moment she realized this is what she was meant to do. As a scribe she could be all of those things and so much more.

When Liz isn't writing or on social networks she is inflicting movie quotes and trivia on people, reading, traveling, and hanging out with friends and family. Liz is a Midwest girl through and through, though she would be perfectly happy never having to shovel her driveway again. She has a love for all things spooky, supernatural, and snarky. Her favorite authors range from Edgar Allen Poe to Joseph Heller to Jane Austen to Jim Butcher and everything in between.

Come visit Liz online.
Blog- **www.LizSchulte.com**
Facebook- https://www.facebook.com/liz.schulte
Twitter- **http://twitter.com/#!/LizSchulte**

Coming 2012 by Liz Schulte

Consequences

The Guardian Trilogy
Book Three

In the final installment of *the Guardian Trilogy*, hope is born, alliances change, and the fate of a world is held in the hands of two people.

Forced to face the wrath of either Heaven or Hell, Olivia and Holden must choose a side before a war begins and tears their lives apart forever. They always felt an unseen force brought them together, but was it to prevent the end of their world or to ensure it?

Their *Secrets* threatened to destroy them. Their *Choices* lead them to this moment. The *Consequences* cannot be avoided.

Made in the USA
Charleston, SC
14 April 2012